STARHAWK

STORM OVER SATURN

Also by Mack Maloney

STARHAWK

STORM OVER SATURN

MACK MALONEY

SPEAKING VOLUMES, LLC

NAPLES, FLORIDA

2011

STARHAWK: STORM OVER SATURN

ISBN 978-1-61232-139-4

PART ONE

After the Flash

Chapter 1

7205 A.D.

The *KosmoVox* was the second-fastest spaceship in the Galaxy.

It was a strange little craft belonging to the Earth Guard of the Fourth Galactic Empire. Like the Empire's mainline warships, they being the enormous two-mile-long Starcrashers, the *KosmoVox* was wedge-shaped, needle-nosed, and powered by a remarkable star engine known as a prop core. This allowed it to enter the seventh dimension and fly at a velocity known as Supertime. But while prop-core-equipped Starcrashers could travel at two light years a minute—traversing the Milky Way in one took less than a month—the *KosmoVox* could fly at nearly *three* light years a minute. This, even though the diminutive craft was only about one-hundredth the size of a monstrous Starcrasher.

No one knew who had built the *KosmoVox* or why it

could go so fast. By twin sins of neglect and disinterest, much knowledge had been lost in the Fourth Empire over its seven centuries of expansion and dominance, including the secret of what made the prop cores work. The same held true for the *KosmoVox*. It was obviously a very old vessel, with bizarre nacelles and an overextended tail nearly belying its wedge shape. Yet it derived its power from the same source as the Empire's massive warships— the mysterious slab of black rock located in Earth's western desert known as the Big Generator—and could do just about everything they could do. It was just different, and no one had ever bothered to find out why.

An obscure war poem written in the early days of the empire speculated the *KosmoVox* had been built to transport spies around the Galaxy. As the official history of the realm only went back a couple hundred years, there was no way to verify this. But true or not, it was an appropriate backdrop for the *KosmoVox's* mission this night, as the lone person riding back in its passenger compartment was indeed an Imperial spy.

Nothing less than the fate of the Milky Way would soon be in his hands.

The Fourth Galactic Empire was on the verge of collapse. Its two main military arms, the Space Forces and the Solar Guards, had been fighting a brutal war against each other for the past three months. The hostilities had already taken more than one hundred million lives on both sides and destroyed thousands of Empire warships. While battles between the two services had been fought all over the Milky Way, the most significant combat had taken place inside the Two Arm, the second of the Galaxy's nine major arms, and just one over from the swirl that contained Earth itself. No less than seventeen major battles had taken place in the Two Arm, nightmarish clashes involving thousands of Starcrashers blasting away at each other with weapons of almost inconceivable power, this while vast armies of star troopers fought each other, hand-to-hand, across the airless battlefield of space.

Nowhere in the annals of human history had war been fought on such an immense scale.

Why the two services were fighting each other was both a simple and complex question.

The Solar Guards were essentially the military policemen of the Empire. Just 300 years old, their main responsibility was security within the Pluto Cloud, as the boundary of the Earth's Solar System was now called. However, through mostly nefarious means and a knack for holding political sway with the Emperor Himself, the SG had been able to spread its seamy influence throughout the Milky Way. This included eight of the Galaxy's nine major arms, its heavily populated center, and the area known as the Fringe, the outer ring of stars that served as the last frontier of the realm. To most eyes, the Solar Guards were thugs in uniforms, widely known for their heavy-handed tactics. Long on intimidation and indiscriminate use of force, they were roundly despised throughout the Galaxy.

On the other hand, the Space Forces were the Emperor's front-line military troops. With nearly thirty billion soldiers under arms, and millions of spacecraft in their employ, the SF was twice the size of the SG. Their specialty was invading and holding hostile planets. Space Forces troopers were well-trained, highly motivated, and very loyal to the Emperor. And as their roots went back to at least the beginning of the present Empire, its members considered themselves the real professionals of the Imperial armed forces. More often then not, they acted that way.

It was a difference in philosophy that lay at the heart of this internecine conflict. The Fourth Empire encompassed more than 100 billion star systems, 500 billion planets, and trillions of subjects. Three previous empires and several Dark Ages had passed since humans first left Mother Earth more than five thousand years before. During the First Empire just about every planet in the Milky Way, from the rocks to the gas giants, had been discovered, explored, terra-formed, and made part of the realm. But with three successive Imperial falls, billions of those planets became lost again, many not even realizing they were still part of a huge galactic empire. In fact, the inhabitants of some of these planets believed that life itself did not exist beyond their own atmospheres.

The current regime had reclaimed more than 85 percent of the Milky Way during its nearly seven centuries of absolute power. About a thousand additional planets were added every day—and this was where the clash in doctrine between the SF and the SG came in. Steeped in its jackbooted ways, the SG believed the best path to success was to reclaim these lost worlds as quickly as possible, no matter what the means. This included invading unsuspecting planets without prior warning, a hugely traumatic event for the inhabitants of the unlucky worlds. The Space Forces were dedicated to reclaiming every last planet for the Empire as well. But its leaders believed the best way to ac-- complish this was to go after the troublesome worlds first—those millions of Fringe planets inhabited by space pirates, criminals, tax dictators, and other interstellar lowlifes—and bring the more peaceful, law-abiding planets back in gradually.

So the dividing line between the two military branches was how humanely the Empire's expansion should be carried out; simple on the face of it, but complex when the myriad sociological, psychological, and especially political elements were added in. For the SG, it was all about galactic turf; for the SF, it was about respect, both on Mother Earth and throughout the cosmos. No one in the Imperial Court dared favor one service over the other, at least not in the light of day. And characteristically, the Emperor, the Supreme O'Nay, was mute on the subject. Thus, the fuse for this disastrous conflict had been smoldering for years.

Hostilities finally broke out when officers of the SG's elite Rapid Engagement Fleet discovered a Space Forces spy sent to the mid–Two Arm to investigate the mysterious activities of that special operations force. The SF man was captured on a barren and forbidding planet known as Doomsday 212 and summarily executed by the REF. When Space Forces ships rushed to the dying man's aid, they, too, were attacked by the REF. The SF returned fire, and just like that, three centuries of bitterness boiled over. The war was on.

Again, all this happened three months before. Now, after a major defeat during some very bizarre circumstances surrounding a second battle near Doomsday 212, the SG had ordered nearly all of its far flung fleet back to the One Arm, close to one million vessels. Most of these warships took up positions on the edge of the One Arm, along a line straddling the main star road leading to the original Solar

System and Earth itself. When this happened, the Space Forces recalled many of its ships, too. Soon nearly a million SF vessels were also in the area, many positioning themselves opposite the immense SG line, nose to nose with their adversaries. An apocalyptic battle seemed both imminent and inevitable.

But strangely, the two gigantic redeployments resulted not in an immediate engagement but in a standoff, what in the old days would have been called a *phony war.* There were two reasons why. Surely, both sides were battered and tired, in need of regrouping after nearly one hundred days of intense battle. But more disturbing, both sides were suffering from serious, if intermittent, power shortages. In fact, the entire Empire was suffering from a case of cosmic brownout.

This was a result of an event that had become known as the Great Flash. At just about the same time as the mysterious second battle near Doomsday 212 was being fought at a place in space called Zero Point, the entire Galaxy experienced a brief but frightening power outage. The blackout lasted just a few seconds, preceded by a burst of light that was seen Galaxy-wide. But because all power in the Empire was derived from the Big Generator, the outage affected everybody and everything in the Milky Way, from the smallest atomic lightbulb to the prop core aboard the Empire's largest warship.

There was no mystery as to what caused the Great Flash. O'Nay's wife, the Empress of the Galaxy, broke into the desert stronghold where the Big Generator was located and, using a concealed weapon, fired a neuron beam directly into the heart of the big black slab. A piece of the holy rock broke off, and the blackout came a nanosecond later. The damage might have been more extensive had the

Empress's ray gun not derived its power from its target; the gun shut down right away. Still, the Big Generator blinked, and everything went dark.

(What happened to the Empress after the attack was not so clear. Some reports said she was killed by a squad of Imperial eunuchs guarding the Big Generator. Others said the Empress took her own life, possibly by dagger, possibly by poison. She *was* dead however, though this was not widely known throughout the Empire. The eunuch guards who witnessed the incident were widely rumored to have been killed, too, via state-mandated euthanasia.)

The weirdness didn't end when the Galaxy's lights came back on. However slight, the damage to the mysterious power source was apparently the cause of some very strange things that had happened throughout the Empire since the Great Flash. Aftershocks of a sort, or so it was believed. *Blinks* is what people had begun calling them.

A Starcrasher belonging to the Expeditionary and Exploratory Forces, the third of the Empire's three major military arms, was flying in toward Earth after a long voyage up the very wild Five Arm. It was about to literally crash a star—that is, fly right through it, hence the big ships' name—when its prop core inexplicably popped, pushing the vessel back in time a little bit. This was a very dangerous moment, as going through the heart of a star at Supertime speed took precise calculations and expert steering. Momentum alone carried this particular ship through the star's nuclear fires, but there was extensive and baffling damage to the monstrous vessel upon coming out the other side. Besides blowing out nearly every string circuit on board, the ship's aft quarter had transformed itself into what appeared to be the gigantic tail section of an ancient

World War Two airplane known as a B-24. What's more, all of the massive weaponry inside the stricken Starcrasher had turned into salt—yes, *salt*. And for the remainder of the voyage home, the crew found themselves being trailed by strange green ghosts. More blinks: on the Three Arm, an artificial moon suddenly disappeared, only to reappear way over in the Six Arm. On the Nine Arm, a group of schoolchildren suddenly gained the ability to fly—by sprouting wings, at least for a few minutes. On the Four Arm, the entire water supply of a tiny planetoid turned itself into the ancient liquor known as *bourboni*—and then at the first sip, changed back to water again.

Before leaving Earth on this mission, the Imperial spy in the back of the *KosmoVox* had witnessed a blink himself. He'd been sitting inside a very tony café atop Special Number One, the Imperial Family's grand floating city, when suddenly all the lights went out. When they came back on seconds later, they were burning a fiery red, and everyone in the place had become transparent, turning into living, human skeletons. Several terrifying moments went by, then the lights went out again. They were glowing bright yellow when they came back on this time, and all the patrons had become hideous caricatures of themselves, complete with scarred faces, overgrown fingernails, and fanglike teeth. The lights went out a third time, only to come back on in deep orange. Shadows cast by this strange effect made it seem as if the café and everyone in it were engulfed in flames. So many patrons panicked, the air was absolutely sizzling with people transporting themselves out of the place. Seconds later, the spy found himself sitting alone in what had been a very crowded room, his body whole and presentable again. The experience startled him greatly. It was crazy and very strange, but he was even more amazed at how the Big Generator, which controlled absolutely everything in the Galaxy, could create such bizarre events simply by being on the fritz.

The words that came to his mind were prophetic: *God is playing games with us.*

These tales, along with millions of others, were running rampant throughout the Galaxy, which, everyone knew, was actually a surprisingly small neighborhood, prone to gossip and superstition. Some of these events must have had rational explanations, but many did not. Certainly not the incident the spy had witnessed in the posh café. No matter, everyone was blaming anything even remotely weird these days on the aftereffects of the Great Flash. And the blinks seemed to be growing in number by the hour.

No military commander in his right mind would go to war under such conditions, not when every subatomic connector, quick-quark portal, and intradimensional diode within his two-mile-long starship was powered by the suddenly quirky Big Generator. This was the main reason the two major space armies now faced each other along a front that stretched more than 500,000 miles.

It was the conventional belief that the blinks would settle down eventually, though, and everything would return to normal.

Then the terrible war could resume.

It took the *KosmoVox* twice as long as usual to leave the Solar System.

The enigmatic little ship encountered a storm of invisible turbulence just outside the orbit of Mars, a mysterious disturbance not picked up by its battery of flight sensors.

Passing by Jupiter, its compartment was suddenly filled with static, from the depths of which ancient rock 'n roll music could briefly be heard. On approaching Saturn, a strange mirage: so many Solar Guards supply ships were orbiting the great planet, they appeared to make up yet another ring. By contrast, the heavily populated Neptune and its coterie of colorful moons seemed all but abandoned.

More blinks, the spy thought, staring out his porthole in back. *God is still fooling with us . . .*

Very real, however, was the traffic jam of spaceships clogging up the approaches to a Solar Guards border checkpoint known as Saint Michael's Pass.

Thousands of vessels were backed up, trying to get through the enormous, midspace frontier crossing, each one subjected to a long, thorough and, more often than not, very stressful SG scanning. The Solar Guards had declared martial law within the Pluto Cloud weeks before, and this was one result of that decree. No one got in or out of the original Solar System without the SG inspecting every subatom in said person's body and ship.

Only by his special Imperial pass was the spy able to get the *KosmoVox* to the head of this line. And while the Imperial agent was supposed to be above such things, the gruff SG border troops insisted on probing his ship and its passengers not once but twice. Finding nothing, they were harshly sent on their way.

Once in open space, the *Kosmo*'s crew did a last check of their flight systems, then set their controls to the outer part of the One Arm, where the two fleets of SG and SF ships were facing each other. A long-range forward scan of the area confirmed what the spy already knew: that many planets in this part of space had been evacuated long ago. Few Imperial vessels other than those belonging to the SG were permitted to fly within this corridor, and indeed, tens of thousands of SG supply runners could be seen shuttling between the trouble zone and the Pluto Cloud.

As for civilian vessels, none were allowed within a thousand light years of this very crowded piece of space.

They reached the edge of the One Arm less than an hour later.

Even from a great distance, the enormous double line of warships seemed to stretch to infinity. The spy had been in the service of the Empire for nearly two hundred years, still a young man by contemporary standards. (If you were lucky enough to have some of the life-prolonging Holy Blood in your veins, as did many in the very-extended Imperial Family, you could live nearly four times that long these days.) The spy had seen many strange things in those two centuries of undercover work. The aftermath of endless wars. Entire planets vaporized. The stars themselves turned upside down.

But he'd never seen anything like this.

On one side, that being the direction roughly pointing toward Earth, were hundreds of thousands of Space Forces warships, gleaming blue and white. On the other side, facing in the opposite direction, were the similarly numbered SG ships, sinister in their dark gray. They were separated by only a few miles in some places—not the hundreds the spy had envisioned for some reason. In fact, it was almost frightening just how narrow the separation between them was, especially when most of the warships facing each other were Starcrashers, two miles long themselves.

Early on, someone had dubbed this celestial front line the Star Trench. It was a good name.

And it was into the heart of it that the Imperial spy now had to go.

Because the *KosmoVox* belonged to the Earth Guard, neutrals in this fight, it was allowed, however grudgingly, to move through the SG lines and into the Star Trench. The pilots slowed their speedy craft to a crawl and flew the very narrow space separating the two gargantuan forces. The spy had his nose pressed up against the scout ship's bubble canopy now, his huge floppy spy hat curled back, his jaw dropped in astonishment as he eyed the warships on both sides of the Trench, side by side, almost entangled in one another.

He was struck by the same thought as anyone who'd been able to view this bizarre front line: all it would take is one crew member, on one ship, to make a mistake, or go mad, or misinterpret an order and launch a weapon. Cosmic brownout or not, the resulting volleys back and forth would destroy every ship along the Trench and kill the billions of crew serving inside them. One shot . . . and both fleets would be subatomic ash in a matter of minutes, and almost two-thirds of the Empire's warships would be gone. And that would mean the core of the Empire would be vulnerable for a very long time to whatever outlaw horde chose to attack it.

So the potential for disaster up here was nothing less than colossal.

Though he was astounded by his tour of the Star Trench, it was not the reason the spy had come out here.

The real purpose of his trip was a very secret meeting

that had been arranged on a planet nearby. The name of the planet was Toons 20. It was an M-class world about the size of Earth's sacred moon, Luna. Like many bodies inhabiting space between the One and Two Arms, it was mostly rocks, valleys, and mountains. A very desolate place, it had no rivers, no ocean, no seas. It was also empty of its inhabitants; they'd been forcibly evacuated by the Solar Guards weeks ago.

There was a small city located just north of its barren equator called Tiny Toon. A collection of gambling halls and saloons mostly, one boarded-up barroom here was called Bozzy's Botsy. A place once notorious for gunrunning and illegal drug sales, it had a back room that, in the distant past, had been electronically soundproofed by way of a hum beam. This made it impervious to any kind of eavesdropping, either by human ears close by or superstring scanning ones bounced from a very long distance away. The room also had several means of access and exit, in case a quick getaway was in order. Such things were occupational hazards for the people who used to do business here.

Sitting at a table in the middle of this small room now was a man dressed in an indistinct one-piece spacesuit and a skully cap. Short, pudgy, with very dirty hands, he was nervously stirring a large mug of slow-ship wine, the opiate liquor that could be found just about everywhere in the Galaxy. At exactly midnight, there was a bright green flash in the corner of the room. An instant later, the Imperial spy was standing before him.

"I was getting worried," the man at the table said. "I thought you might not show up this time."

The spy threw half his black cape over his shoulder and pulled his huge floppy hat farther over his eyes. An Imperial spy never revealed his face, and that was certainly the case here. The man at the table saw only a shadow under the big hat.

"You never have to worry about me not keeping one of our appointments," the spy told him. "The Empire would fall first."

The man at the table frowned and took a long swig of his drink. "Best not to joke about such things, my friend," he said. "I fear the day of the Empire's decline is finally upon us."

The mild rebuke stiffened the spy. This was not an idle comment made by an ordinary citizen. This man was Jak Dazz, a well-known high commander of the Solar Guards and ten-stripe officer in the SG's elite 101st Space Combat Division. Devious and ill-mannered, Dazz had nevertheless served as a secret informant for the spy for years, exchanging bits of information about the SG in return for money and privileges back on Earth. It was he who requested this latest meeting, their first since the war broke out.

The spy took a seat and waved his hand over the table. A glass of slow-ship wine appeared. The spy rarely imbibed, preferring to get high on star music. But this night, he needed a little extra buzz.

"Considering what's going on up in that Star Trench, you took a big risk coming here," he told the SG officer. "It must be important."

Dazz nodded glumly. "The tension up on that line is unbearable. Everyone's on edge. I've been a military officer for nearly three hundred years. I much prefer battle to *waiting* for battle.

The spy tipped his glass in the SG man's direction. "I agree with you there," he said.

"And I see no way of preventing a catastrophe," Dazz went on dolefully. "Not just up on the Star Trench but elsewhere. We have some fanatical people at the top of the Solar Guards—people who can't be controlled by me or my superiors and frankly not by the Emperor, either. They're highly unpredictable. And some of them, rather unstable."

Again, the spy was taken back. Disparaging anything, in any way, having to do with the Emperor or his armed forces was considered highly verboten in the Fourth Empire. People were given painful brain wipes or even executed for such things, be they high military officers or the lowest of citizens. This was why hum-beamed rooms were so popular around the Galaxy.

"These fanatics will not back down," Dazz went on. "They are bent on carrying this fight through, this stupid war, however it started, by devils I suppose . . ."

The spy almost laughed. If only the SG officer knew just how accurate his last statement might be.

"The Space Forces commanders believe they have the moral high ground," the spy told Dazz.

Dazz just shrugged. "Why? Because one of our commanders attacked one of their ships to begin this whole thing?"

"And that they executed the SF intelligence agent," the spy added. "Revenge ranks very high on the scale of human emotion. Not to mention the perfect motive to go to war."

Dazz drained about half his cup of slow-ship and shrugged again. "I don't deny it happened that way. And I can tell you that many people in our top command are as baffled by that action as I'm sure the SF is. But your friends in the Space Forces are not so innocent. . . ."

The spy sipped his drink. "Please explain."

Dazz smiled darkly. "Do you know *all* the details of what happened out near that godforsaken planet Doomsday 212? I mean, before *and* after the war started?"

The spy shook his head. "I'm not sure anyone does," he replied.

It was a mystery, most of it. First the SG's elite Rapid Engagement Fleet disappeared while hunting for a rebel group who'd vowed to take down the Empire. More than thirty Starcrashers, suddenly gone. Then, just as suddenly, the REF reappeared, just long enough to kill the SF agent on Doomsday 212 and then shoot down two Space Forces warships without warning. This was the action that started the war. Soon afterward, the REF disappeared yet again, only to return a third time. And on this occasion, they began a rampage of terror across the Galaxy the likes of which no one had ever seen. Their warships, which for some reason had turned crimson from the SG's standard gray, streaked around the Empire, relentlessly attacking innocent people and undefended targets, seemingly intent on causing as much human misery as possible.

The enigmatic fleet then reassembled near a point close to Doomsday 212. It was there that ships belonging to the aforementioned rebel fleet, helped by a motley collection of other soldiers of fortune, met and somehow defeated the REF, while, it was widely reported, the SF stood by and did nothing. By some opinion, the SF's inaction amounted to aiding and abetting an enemy of the realm.

"I might be getting ahead of myself," Dazz said, slightly drunk now. "But do you really think those rebels and their shit-kicker friends were enough to defeat the REF on their own? Or do you think they had special help?"

The spy was not so surprised by the question. Many things were still unanswered from that day. "Well, we know Hawk Hunter was there," he replied.

Again, Dazz nodded glumly. Hawk Hunter. Bane of the Solar Guards. The man who led the rebel fleet. The man who'd vowed to topple the Fourth Empire itself. He'd been reported right in the thick of this strange battle. He and his awesome Flying Machine. It was the fastest ship in the Galaxy.

Everyone knew about Hawk Hunter; he was an authentic living legend. He'd been found stranded on a desolate planet at the far edge of the Galaxy nearly three years before. His origins unknown, even to himself, he was brought to Earth shortly afterward, and with his incredibly fast space fighter, he won the illustrious Earth Race. As a result, he was lavished with riches and praise and given a ship's command in the Empire's forces.

Hunter soon went missing, however, part of a scheme fomented by the Emperor's own daughter, the unimaginably beautiful Princess Xara. She'd allowed Hunter to search for the remnants of the people he called the Last Americans. And sure enough, he found this lost civilization living on a planet so far off the star roads, it wasn't even inside the Milky Way.

But the word on the streets around the Empire said Hunter not only located his lost Americans but also found evidence that Earth had been stolen from these Americans and the other original peoples who lived on the mother planet several thousand years before. Indeed, they claimed this sinister aspect of history was woven into the fabric of all four Empires. But was it true? Had Earth been stolen from its original inhabitants? There was no way to tell. Almost nothing of the history of the empires had survived the handful of Dark Ages that separated the realms. In fact, very little was known about the Galaxy prior to the rise of the present Fourth Empire. But many people in the Milky Way were beginning to believe this tale, just on Hunter's charisma alone.

It was Hunter who'd led a previous rebel attack on the Empire, one that nearly reached the One Arm itself, until he and his allies ran up against the REF. That's when Hunter's fleet disappeared, too, only to return just in time to meet the reemerging REF. And that's when the second battle near Doomsday 212 took place.

"And it is no surprise he was on hand," the spy went on. "Hunter seems to be everywhere sometimes. . . ."

The SG officer laughed darkly again. "Well, he *is* a superman, the son of a bitch," he said. "I saw him fight at the Siege of Qez. And before that, I saw him win the Earth Race. Only the stars know what he is planning next. What deep thoughts and machinations are going through his brain. They say he never sleeps. That he is always thinking. Planning. Plotting against us. Dreaming up new ways to take us down. I'm sure at this moment, that mind of his is racing like a string clock, conspiring our demise."

The spy nodded in agreement, but in truth, he was getting impatient. Everyone knew about Hunter's enormous talent for combat and intrigue. But rehashing such things couldn't possibly be the reason that Dazz had risked all to meet him here.

"So?" the spy asked him. "There is something else, I assume—besides this history lesson?"

Dazz sipped his drink again. "I have three things for you

today," he said, getting down to business. "Here is the first:
Where were you during the Great Flash?"

The man in the big floppy hat just stared back at him. It
was an odd question to ask, only because the spy knew
something else that Dazz and most people in the Galaxy
did not: the Great Flash didn't just happen; the Empress's
attack was not a random, spontaneous event, although it
seemed that way. The truth was, it came at a crucial moment during the battle near Doomsday 212, disabling a
number of ships belonging to the rampaging SG Rapid Engagement Fleet, thus swinging the fortunes back to that unlikely collection of weapons dealers and rebels, and
allowing them to somehow defeat the hellish SG special
ops troops. This begged the question: was the Empress in
league with the rebels?

That, no one knew. Not even him.

But because very few people were privy to the exact
timing of the attack on the Big Generator, the spy was certain this couldn't be the rebels' special help that Dazz was
talking about. In reality, many things went right for the in-
surgents that day.

But to the question, where was the spy when the lights
went out?

"I was asleep," he lied to the SG officer.

"So was I," the SG officer lied back.

The spy shrugged. "I hear they are repairing the damage
though," he said. "That it really wasn't so extensive."

Dazz shrugged again. "But it is precisely those repairs
that you and I and the rest of the Empire should be very
concerned about. . . ."

"And why is that?" the spy asked.

The SG officer lowered his voice again. "The Special

Solar Guards have taken over the repair of the Big Generator. This is a closely held secret. But as they are fixing it,
they are trying to change it as well. Alter the way it works."

The spy was shocked to hear this. The Special Solar
Guards were a quasi-secret detachment of the regular SG.
While they were known for their ultrafanaticism in pre-
serving the SG's ill-gotten power, they were actually little
more than superthugs and perverts in uniforms. Why
would these heavy-handed clowns want to fool around
with the Big Generator? The sacred piece of rock was the
lifeblood of everything in the Galaxy. Moreover, no one
was sure where it came from or how it even worked, least
of all the SSG.

"What is their motive for getting involved in such a
thing?" the spy asked him. "That repair should be left to
people who know what they are doing."

"I agree with you," Dazz said. "But the SSG believes,
true or not, that they can tweak the Big Generator in such a
way that it will provide power *only to things they own*. In
other words, they want to be able to control who gets
power and who doesn't. Can you imagine the ramifications
of that? SG Starcrashers flying, SF 'crashers not? SG
weapons working, SF weapons not? Even I know that's
unfair."

The spy collapsed back into his seat. "This is non-
sense!" he cried. "It has to be—"

But Dazz was shaking his head no. "I only wish it
were," he said. "But I got this from a very high source back
on Earth. Besides, why would I come all this way just to
tell you something that wasn't true? No less than death
would be my fate if I were caught talking to you like this."

He sipped his drink again. His cup was almost dry.

"I am not a genius, nor am I a hero," Dazz went on. "I'm just a soldier. I have no idea what the SSG is doing exactly, what gave them the idea to do it—or what might happen should they fail. But certainly it's a dangerous thing they are attempting."

"Very dangerous if they succeed," the spy half moaned.

At that moment, as if taking a cosmic cue, the lights in the room, in the bar, and all across the tiny planet, blinked. Outside, in the wind, the spy and Dazz heard the most frightful chorus of screams rise up. They were so disturbing, the SG man pulled his ray gun from its holster. The noise got louder. In seconds it seemed like an army of the dead was ready to burst through the door.

"Is it any wonder the entire Galaxy is going crazy?" Dazz screamed over the ghostly racket.

But then, just as suddenly, the noise calmed down. The lights came back to full power. And only the wind could be heard outside.

The spy gasped. "That was frightening. . . ."

The SG man nearly drained his drink. "Even more so, these aftershocks—these accursed blinks—are being made worse by the SSG's tinkering. That I know for a fact. The SSG is so crude, most of them, I close my eyes and see them pounding away on that rock with electron hammers and chisels!"

The spy stared into his empty wine cup. Suddenly, he wanted more.

"That's item number one," Dazz said now, wearily. "Here is number two: Along with this Big Generator thing, the SSG has also been up to some very unusual activity on

Saturn. As you know—as *everyone* knows—the regular SG has a lot of its administration centers there. Truth is, it's where you wind up when they don't need you anymore, pushing an electric pen.

"But the SSG has been paying a lot of attention to a certain part of the planet lately. A very dull place called Imperial Records Section 066. It's essentially a huge warehouse with billions of comm bubbles in storage. Only the cosmos knows why it is of sudden interest to them, but the rumor is there might be some kind of new weapon being built down there, one they are planning to use on a very specific target."

"Such as?" the spy asked.

Dazz thought a long moment, choosing his words very carefully. "The SSG may be brutes, but they aren't completely stupid," he began again. "They know something very unusual happened out near Doomsday 212 during that second battle. That the irregular forces that beat up the REF were not so irregular. Again, they are convinced Hunter and his rebels had some very special help."

The spy just stared back at the informant. "Go on," he said.

"The SSG also knows Hunter's rebels and their allies have started their own little star system out there around Doomsday 212," Dazz said. "They know they're still a threat, despite what's going on up in the Star Trench. So, once the SSG gets control of the Big Generator, their first order of business is to attack Doomsday 212—and I mean even *before* the war resumes with the Space Forces. And if this *is* a new weapon down in Warehouse 066, it's going to be used against Doomsday 212 and whoever is out there. The problem is, my sources tell me, this weapon may be *so* powerful, it will affect not just Doomsday 212 but anyone within a thousand light-years of ground zero. That's a lot of innocent people, especially with all the war refugees wandering around the Two Arm these days."

The spy slumped back into his chair. "So much bad news," he moaned. "I'm not sure I can take any more."

"Well, you must," the officer told him. "For here is item number three: I've heard a lot of rumors that the SSG also has something else—something very secret, hidden away on Earth—that they are also hoping to use very soon. Not a weapon exactly. Though what it is, no one is sure. The SSG is calling it the *magilla* in their confidential bubble reports. That's a code word, I think. It might not be connected to the Big Generator repair or the 066 warehouse, not directly, anyway. But whatever it is, this magilla is something they've recently acquired, from persons or methods unknown. And they are being very smug about it, always a bad sign."

Dazz finally licked the last few drops from his empty cup. He was fairly drunk now but still wanted more. "So there you are," he said. "The Big Generator repair, the mystery in Warehouse 066, and the magilla."

The spy groaned. "They used to call this a triple whammy," he said. "Bad news times three . . ."

The SG officer got up to leave. "Call them whatever you like," he said. "Because now I pass these burdens on to you. I must get back before I am missed. Just promise me you will use this information wisely. Obviously, the attempt to manipulate the Big Generator is the most immediate concern, but the other items have the potential to be just as disturbing, simply by the amount of chatter I'm picking up on them. All three things are highly secret. And if anyone ever finds out I gave them to you, I'll have no other choice but to fall on my sword. So please, be very careful who you share them with."

The spy reached into his pocket and numbly came out with a bag containing thirty pieces of aluminum-silver. It was the standard payment for Dazz's information.

But the SG officer surprised the spy by pushing the bag back across the table.

"No thanks," he said, putting his skully cap back on. "With all that's happening around us, taking your money this time just doesn't seem right."

He started for the door, but the spy, startled that Dazz had refused his payment, had one last question for him.

"Why did you choose to do this in the first place?" he asked him. "Be my source, I mean? I checked your dossier way back when we first started. You've been a loyal SG officer for nearly three centuries. Yet many things you've told me over the years ultimately wind up hurting your own cause."

Dazz just shrugged.

"Not all of us in the SG are bad, my friend," he replied, adding sadly, "just most of us are. . . ."

Chapter 2

Somewhere on Doomsday 212
Mid-Two Arm

Point Zero?

Zero Point?

Hawk Hunter, alleged superman, woke up in Purgatory, spitting these words out like broken teeth.

At least he _thought_ it was Purgatory. He'd had a glimpse of Hell before, and this was not quite it. But it was damn close.

It was hot here. Very hot. And he was perpetually drenched in sweat. Lying on his back, sharp rocks sticking like knives into his spine, a strange red fog surrounded him. He thought he could see flames crackling somewhere beyond. In his ears were the sounds of people crying. In his nose, some very nasty smells. Burned metal. Burned flesh. Burning souls . . .

Zero Point?

Point Zero?

God damn, where the hell am I?

He raised himself up on one elbow and tried to get his bearings. He was atop a very steep plateau. It rose above a high, cratered plain that, in turn, topped off the flattened peak of a dark, hideously twisted mountain. Volcano-type ash was falling all around him. Streams of smoke and fire were rising up from below. The crying got louder. All this craziness—hearing it, smelling it, tasting it! He wiped his eyes and thought, *This isn't where I went to sleep . . .*

Point Zero . . .

Zero Point . . .

He collapsed back down to the hard ground and tried to shut his eyes again. But they refused to close. There was something else he had to see. Even though it was daybreak, billions of stars in grand formations were passing overhead. He could almost reach out and touch them, they seemed so near.

This might be the closest I'll ever get to the stars again, he thought.

Zero Point . . .

Point Zero . . .

Why these two words . . . and not two others?

He couldn't remember the exact moment he went mad. Maybe it was during the battle against the ghostly ships of the Solar Guards' REF, blasting them as they flew out of a rip in space that led directly to Hell. The *real* Hell. Or when he found himself tumbling out of control and falling among those same SG Starcrashers, like them, his Flying

Machine's power systems failing because of the Great Flash. Or maybe he cracked his head when he ejected from his stricken vessel, opening his brains and allowing the insanity to seep in. Or maybe it was when he saw his beloved craft going down in flames, lost in the smoke and fog of battle.

Or maybe . . . maybe it was after he hit the ground that fateful day, nearly smothering in his parachute, when he lay dazed and injured, and of all the things running through his mind, realizing just one thing: that he would never see Xara again, the love of this, his very crazy life. How beautiful was she? Well, how does one describe the indescribable? What words can possibly be used? As soft as the glow from a neutron star? As warm as the colors of a rainbow nebula? As light as the kiss of Venusian rain upon the face? Or the touch of a hand on a dark night? Sweet. Gentle. Erotic. Intelligent. Big eyes, big smile. She was cosmically gorgeous. At least that's how Hunter remembered her now.

He'd played in the fields of Heaven with her no less. The *real* Heaven, for it existed as surely as Hell did. It was the place where nothing ever went wrong. Where departed souls were happy for eternity. Where love, and peace, and harmony and all that good stuff ruled, and the sky shimmered like jewels. It was also the place Hunter had managed to escape to—only to leave to take on the evil empire once again. And Xara? She had no choice but to stay behind, stranded forever in Paradise, while he went off to fight his impossible war and be the only thing he really knew how to be: a hero. And while he did that almost too well, life for him, without her, had become insanely lonely.

If madness had set in then at that dark moment, knowing he could never be with her in this life again, his condition was surely not helped when he realized all his brave and loyal friends had been so suddenly lost as well. Erx and Berx, the two spacemen who'd first brought him to Earth. Calandrx, the famous warrior-poet. Steve Gordon, courageous CIA agent from Planet America. The Great Klaaz, a man renowned by nearly a quarter of the Galaxy for his heroism. Zarex Red, celestial explorer and freedom fighter. All gone . . . fallen in battle.

And Pater Tomm, the monk who was as fierce in battle as he was in prayer. He was gone, too. Along with Erx and Berx, Hunter probably missed the holy man most. Tomm had guided Hunter on his journey to the Home Planets, the prison camp in the sky inhabited by the long-lost descendants of Earth. It was for these people—the Last Americans—that Hunter had vowed to topple the Fourth Empire and return the Galaxy to its rightful owners. Indeed, a fleet of ships from the Home Planets had fought in the initial assault on the Empire. Then a second fleet from this lost star system magically appeared during the Battle at Zero Point just in time to help defeat the rampaging REF.

But even this great victory could not replace losing both his love *and* all his friends.

Point Zero?

Zero Point?

Lolita Island? Is that a clue?

When he looked down at his hands these days, he saw the hands of a madman, bloody and gnarled. His clothes were tattered, his flight boots creased and dirty. The X-Forces cape, once worn so proudly, was now ripped and full of holes after being dragged behind him for so long. His hair, nearly down to his shoulders, was spiked from neglect and abuse; his face was bearded and burned. No longer was he the deep-space hero with the star-idol looks. Just the opposite. Were there any string mirrors around, he would have probably scared himself.

Zero Point?

Point Zero?

Oh God, what do they mean?

Since finding himself stuck in the seventy-third century, he'd acquired a habit of obsessing on whatever strange item bubbled up from his past life. Now it was these two words, spoken two different ways. As inconsequential as they might have seemed, he believed any memory, any reminiscence, any flash of recognition might provide him another clue to his past. And if he was able to figure them out, another little piece of his memory might come back.

But this? This was tough . . .

Point Zero . . . Zero Point . . .

Target Point Zero?

Wait! Maybe it was trying to decipher these two words that had driven him insane. Maybe it was *that* simple.

But insane he was. . . .

There was no doubt about that.

This planet, Doomsday 212, was once a little bit of Hell itself.

A former ringed gas giant, it had been first terra-formed thousands of years before by the original Ancient Engineers. Made ailing by centuries of neglect and royally cursed by all the terrible things that had happened here, it had been Hunter's mysterious allies from the Seven Arm who'd puffed it again right after the Battle at Zero Point.

The problem was, large parts of the planet did not take to this new terra-forming. Vast stretches of land north of the equator had resisted the fantastic technology that could make a dead planet come alive again. Why? No one knew. Sometimes the presence of an ancient pyramid could affect the terra-forming process. The mysterious, billion-year-old monuments could be found all over the Galaxy, and they were fanatically avoided by just about everyone, so steeped in bad luck they were supposed to be. Perhaps one was buried on the planet somewhere. Or maybe something even stranger was at work here.

Whatever the reason, while two-thirds of Doomsday 212 now flowed with grass and trees and streams and held fresh, clean air above the surface, the remaining third was still haunted ground. Grotesque rock formations, perilous ledges and cliffs, bottomless ravines, mile-high mountains shooting off at nearly impossible angles. Any rivers that ran here now were thick with bloodred hydraulic fluids or even real blood.

And Hunter had been adrift in this nightmarish landscape for what seemed to be an eternity. Not talking to anyone, not seeing another human being. Not knowing what else was happening in the Galaxy.

He was beginning to feel at home.

Lost as he might have seemed, though, this was no idle wandering, this trek he'd undertaken through these forbidding lands. This was a search mission he was on. He'd lost Xara. He'd lost his friends. He'd lost his mind. He only had one thing left that he hadn't lost completely: his Flying Machine.

What good was he without it? The Flying Machine was as weirdly wonderful as he used to be. Designed from a dream and faster than anyone could comprehend, at cruising speed it could go two light years a second. It had taken him to places that existed only in the wildest of imaginations. It had vanquished many a foe, saved many a friend. If losing Xara and his compadres had torn out his heart, then losing his aircraft had ripped out his soul.

So he was out here, searching for that one last thing that might restore just a bit of what he once had. True, he'd seen it go down, seen it fall into the clouds of war as surely as he'd fallen into those of despair. But he never saw it crash, never heard the impact. So where was it now? Still burning at the bottom of a crater someplace? Scattered in microscopic fragments over a stretch of this phantasmic horizon?

He had to find out. For even if he was able to recover just a tiny piece of it, something to always carry in his pocket along with his battered American flag and the faded, well-worn picture of Dominique, the stunning beauty in his other life, then maybe the rest of his days could be saved from complete madness.

But searching for it was like searching for a loved one's body. You want to go on looking forever, but always in fear of what you might find.

Sleep came fitfully in this place, these miles of cosmic badlands that after so many days seemed vaguely familiar to him now. And frequently, where he lay down to rest here was not the place he woke up, another symptom, he supposed, of his mental drift.

Fully awake now, he crawled to the edge of the plateau and looked out over the precipice, expecting to see another stretch of ravaged land. But wait—something was different. The landscape below him was idyllic. Fields and valleys with gentle rivers curving through them. Small gatherings of trees, long grass swaying in the gentle breeze. A girl below, familiar in her cosmic beauty, was waving up at him . . . calling to him . . .

But then he blinked—and when he opened his eyes again, the girl and the trees and the fields were gone, and the landscape below had returned to something from a very bad dream. Hunter felt his stomach turn inside out. His head began to spin. *Not again,* he thought.

He'd been seeing visions like this for weeks now. The day before, he'd imagined a barrage of old-fashioned nuclear missiles crashing down on top of him, only to see them hit the ground like raindrops and disappear into tiny puddles. The day before that, a strange aircraft with a propeller and stubby wings and red ball insignias on its fuselage and tail dove out of the rising sun and tried shooting at him, only to have its bullets turn into flower blossoms the moment they touched his skin. And the day before that, he imagined he was trudging through deep snow, firing his gun at a huge moving structure that might have been an ancient radar station—on wheels. And the day before that, he thought he saw a huge battleship floating on what should have been a gently flowing stream. On and on, so many, he couldn't remember them all. Some lasting a mere second or two, others going on for hours. The common thread? Each hallucination began with a flash and ended with a blink.

Madness. What else could it be?

He looked back down into the valley now. Fires roaring out of control. Cracks in the surface spewing unimaginable vapors. Gigantic rocks shooting up like monster's teeth, saw blade sharp and black as a night without stars. Badlands, indeed. So much so, a sane man would have turned back long ago.

But staring into this particularly horrid part of 212's netherworld, Hunter knew it was where he had to go.

He found wreckage two hours later.

It was halfway across the killing plain, still smoking, surrounded by blue flames exploding up into violent flares, blinding his bloodshot eyes even from a mile away. The smell was awful. Burnt subatomics, scorched superglass, white-hot electron steel—but another smell, too. Again, burned flesh . . . And it was this stink that told Hunter this was not the holy grail he was seeking. This, and the fact the wreckage stretched on for nearly a half mile.

Not his cherished, lost Flying Machine, these were the remains of an Empire starship, one that had been driven by a prop core. It was dispersed, in pieces, around a huge crater. This was where the nuclear singularity had gone off, once the prop core died its quick, nasty death.

After much climbing and trudging through the smoky muck, he finally reached the largest piece of the wreck: the hind end of what had once been a Space Forces cargo ship. It towered over him. Hunter took out his quadtrol, the know-it-all device carried by just about everyone in the Galaxy. He asked it a simple question: what ship was this? The answer came back right away: *JunoVox*. Hunter knew the name; it was one of the first vessels shot down in the opening minutes of the war between the SF and the SG, the mighty conflict that had started here, above this hellish place.

"Fucking great . . ." he mumbled as he felt a little more mind juice run out of him. This was the thirty-third wreck he'd come upon in his quixotic search. Just his luck that Doomsday 212 had been a graveyard for crashed space-ships in the centuries past. There were wrecks everywhere.

In sheer frustration, he took out his ray gun and began firing at the carcass. Pieces of fuselage and pipes and su-perstrings and electron steel suddenly went flying in all di-rections. His barrage created more flame, more smoke, more stink, but it unleashed something else as well.

Humanlike forms suddenly began rising from the wreck. They were wearing SF uniforms. Some were whole, others were skeletons. Hunter watched in dumb astonish-ment as they ascended into the filthy air. They were laugh-ing at him, emitting the most outlandish shrieks. Crying for him to join them. It all coalesced into a weird chorus of screams and ethereal song.

Hunter began firing at them as well, but his rays were going right through their transparent bodies. This only made them howl at a more frightening volume. One mo-ment, he felt like his eardrums were going to burst. In the next, it seemed like his entire head was going to explode. Louder . . . and louder . . . and *louder* . . .

Then came another flash of light. It caused him to blink. When he opened his eyes again, the spirits were gone.

He took a deep breath and tried to compose himself, but only rotten air entered his lungs. How much more of this could he take? He put his ray gun back into his holster and stumbled on his way.

These weren't the first ghosts he'd shot at since coming down here.

Beyond the wreck of the *JunoVox*, the terrain grew hilly again, then dipped into a gigantic ravine.

Hunter descended into the narrow valley almost without thinking, one foot in front of the other, a living ghost of sorts, trudging the haunted badlands. The vapors pouring out of the landscape down here were more putrid than the grounds above. The thick fog covered what was left of the sky overhead, nearly turning day into night.

He forged on, finding fields of wreckage every few miles, all of them from ships crashed here long ago. He passed more than a few ancient skeletons as well, preserved by all the formaldehyde-like gases hissing up around him. Always with death smiles on their faces, their fingers crooked in his direction, they were bidding him to sit and talk a while.

Back in his hero days, Hunter had displayed an amazing talent, in combat and out. It was a kind of natural long-range scanner—or *radar*, back in his previous life—that allowed him to sense flying machines heading in his direction long before they arrived. This feeling would come over him in the form of an electrical jolt running through his body, making the hair on the back of his head stand at attention. This sixth sense was always with him and had never let him down in the past. It was as normal a part of his makeup as breathing.

But not this time.

This time all he saw was a shadow. It came over him at first like a huge cloud, blotting out all that was left of the murky sunlight. He turned, slowly, and discovered an enormous starship hovering above him. No warning. No noise. No electrical jolt to the back of his head. Suddenly, it was just there.

Another vision, he was sure . . .

It was not shaped like a wedge as all Empire starships were. It didn't have a needle nose or a large ass end, and its canopy was not a bubble top, with a little city inside full of people meant to steer it. Nor was its fuselage white or blue or gray.

Rather it was gold. Pure gold, gleaming and brilliant even now, in the darkest of hours. And the ship was sleek, with flowing lines and sails that looked built for nothing less than to catch superneutrinos from the stars. It had wings and a large deck, and golden strings glistening from front to back. And it appeared that when it flew, even in space, men could still stand out on that deck and look over its sides and see where they were going and know where they'd been.

Hunter had been seeing weird things for weeks. This was one of the weirdest.

The ship slowly lowered itself and was soon right in front of him, huge and glittering, its underside not ten feet above the ground. Hunter reached out and touched its golden hull. It felt real, but of course, that was no proof.

The ship had three tall star masts. Two men were stationed in the tallest. One of them called down to him.

"Major Hunter, you are needed desperately . . . Can you come?"

Hunter froze in place. Again, he'd seen many strange things in his time in Purgatory. The gases, the flashes, the ghosts, and the wrecks. They'd all conspired to make him imagine things that weren't really there. On closer inspection, these people and this ship did resemble those belonging to his allies from the Seven Arm, the same group who'd tried to repuff this planet.

But were they real?

Or not?

He took out his ray gun and began to aim it. But in the next moment he decided that would do no good. Even if these were ghosts and they wanted him to go with them, how could that be any worse than what he was doing now?

So finally he just raised his hands over his head and called up to them, "Take me. If you must . . ."

The next thing he knew, Hunter was standing before a pale blue picket fence with red and pink roses growing all over it. Beyond the gate was a small cottage that looked like it was right off a greeting card from twenty-first-century Earth. Painted bright white with yellow trim, the cottage was highly picturesque, quaint almost. It, too, had flowers growing all around it; many climbing on trellises, others spilling out onto the well manicured lawn. Behind the house, two faint orbital rings gave the sky a soft glow forty degrees above the horizon. This haze radiated across the grass and the trees and the flowers. It all looked, well . . . *heavenly.*

Hunter picked up some dirt from near the fence and rolled it through his fingers. He sniffed it, then tasted it. It seemed real, just as everything around him seemed real. The ground, the air, the fauna were the exact opposite from where he'd just come. All indications were that then he was back in the repuffed part of Doomsday 212.

But he would have to be careful here.

He'd been fooled by these strange visions before.

Vision or not, he recognized this odd house. As unlikely as it seemed, the cottage served as the military field headquarters for Hunter's allies from the Seven Arm, the ultrapowerful Star Legion that, in whispers only, was also known as the long-lost Army of the Third Empire.

This cottage was a very secret place, as by ancient agreements, the Third Empire was not supposed to venture out of its enclave in the distant seventh swirl. As, too, the golden ship he'd encountered out in the badlands. (That type of ship was called a *galleonis* by some, for its resemblance to the ancient wooden ocean-sailing ships of Earth. Its proper name, however, was a StarLiner.) Until recently, its kind had not been seen in this part of the Galaxy in more than 1,000 years.

Not knowing what else to do, Hunter opened the gate, went up the path, and through the cottage's front door. There were no guards. The interior of the house was unusual, to say the least. Paint-by-number pictures hung above doorways, teakettle patterns adorned the walls. Narrow hallways. Low ceilings. Thick rugs on top of heavily varnished floors. And everywhere, furniture exclusively by Sears Roebuck. He knew these unlikely things made the powerful Star Legion members feel comfortable, simply because they reminded them of their real home, way out on the Seven Arm, so far away.

He walked into the main room of the tiny house. It, too, featured homey wallpaper, knickknacks, vases of fresh flowers. An impressive grandfather clock was ticking away in one corner. On one open windowsill sat a Westinghouse AM radio, turned on, but with its volume very low. In another corner was a Quasar TV that appeared older than the Galaxy itself. It was switched on, too, but its picture showed nothing but a test pattern.

At the center of the room was a large wooden table. A dozen men were sitting around it. They jumped to their feet when Hunter entered the room. Horribly ragged, his skin dirty, his mind still firing blanks, he felt foolish when they saluted him. He weakly returned the gesture, knowing they were horrified by his ghastly appearance.

He recognized these men, too. Six were commanders from the United Planets Forces, the military arm of the Home Planets, that being the extragalactic star system where Hunter had found the Last Americans and the other descendants of the dispossessed peoples of Earth. They were wearing the sand-and-red camouflage uniforms of the UPF; each had an American flag patch on his left shoulder. They'd traveled here from the Home Planets, their squadron of war ships arriving at the height of the Battle at Zero Point and helping to turn the tide against the devils of the rampaging REF—this, even as their predecessors, the 40,000 men of the First UPF fleet, had crossed over from Heaven at the climax of that same battle, and like Hunter's close friends, gave their souls in the titanic struggle that followed.

The other six men at the table were wearing the shiny gold uniform of the Star Legion. Like those he'd just encountered on the golden ship, they were large individuals with flowing hair and winged helmets. Each wore a slew of medals on a red sash across his chest and had a ceremonial sword at his side. Each man also had a slightly burned face, the telltale sign of long voyages in their magnificent golden starships.

Despite his schizo condition, Hunter was glad to see them. When he first arrived in the seventy-third century, with little more than the clothes on his back, he was quick to notice that he was different from everyone else. It wasn't clear just why at first. He looked the same, talked the same, walked the same. He was just *different*.

This was strange because the modern seventy-third century human was, no argument, well-built, well-fed, and well-groomed. Handsomeness and beauty were the norm these days. But modern humans were also highly self-absorbed, highly pampered by the thousands of exotic conveniences of the day, and while educated, few seemed to be particularly brilliant. They were also pathological gossipmongers, extremely superstitious, and, almost to the last, obsessed with somehow getting a few drops of the Holy Blood in their veins so that they, like the Emporer O'Nay and The Specials back on Earth, could live up to eight or nine centuries, instead of just two or three.

It wasn't like that for the Star Legionnaires or for the inhabitants of the Home Planets, for that matter. They were more like Hunter—or better put, *he* was more like *them*. They thought in the same ways. They were curious. They questioned things. They questioned authority. While it was customary in the Galaxy for men to refer to each other as Brother, Hunter really did feel like these people were his brothers. In the past, upon meeting any one of them, he was always struck by the sensation that he'd known them all his life. And they felt the same way about him. They were people of the same blood.

The question was, would they really show up—this vivid, this real—in one of his manic visions?

There was an empty seat at the end of the dining table. Several of the men motioned Hunter toward it, but he hesitated. He'd worn his fingers raw pinching himself by now, trying to convince his mind and body that this was all real, and that just like seeing the girl earlier that day, and the many other visions he'd experienced, it wasn't all going to go away with another blink of the eyes.

The lead commander of the Star Legion was a man named Erikk. He was a huge, powerful individual, built along the same lines as Hunter's departed friend, Zarex Red. Erikk motioned to Hunter again.

"Hawk, please, sit with us," he said. "We have some very important things to discuss."

Hunter finally relented. Vision or not, he was exhausted. He collapsed into the empty seat.

Erikk spoke: "My friend, we would not have come out to get you unless it was extremely momentous. We know the search for your Flying Machine is important to you. But something has come up. Something rather frightening. I'll try to explain this situation as best as I can to you. But truthfully, I have trouble believing it myself."

The Legionnaire started talking about something being wrong with the Big Generator. Hunter heard mentions of the Empress, she being the wife of O'Nay and Xara's mother, and how she tried to damage the omnipotent power source and how that had created the Great Flash and how some really bad elements within the Solar Guards—they being the SSG—were trying to repair it in such a way that they would be able to have control over who got its awesome power and who didn't. Erikk talked nonstop for about ten minutes. Through it all, Hunter pretended to listen, pretended to be interested. But the story was so crazy and his condition so deteriorated, that with every word he was more convinced that this was indeed another grand illusion, and it would end, just as surely as all the others out in the badlands had ended, and he would be back, lying on the ground, sweating and nearly on fire.

He had to admit, though, that not all of it sounded insane. A few of these words made sense, especially about Xara's mother and her attempt to damage the big black rock, and her paying the price for such an act with her life. The Empress had indeed passed on. Hunter knew this because he'd been told on good authority—that being a *real* ghost—that she was now in Heaven with Xara. And he was also familiar with the episode Erikk was calling the Great Flash. It was the reason all the REF Starcrashers fell at a crucial time in the Zero Point battle—and was the reason his own beloved spacecraft went down as well.

But it was the part about repairing the Big Generator that was confusing him. Those particular words were going in one ear and out the other. Especially the ones about how the radicals of the SSG were trying to alter the Big Generator, to put them in a position to control the massive, all-reaching, awesome, power-producing device. Could that be possible?

Erikk ended the first part of his speech with a particularly ominous sentence: "The Special Solar Guards will either succeed in being able to control the Big Generator's power, or they will break it for good."

Delirious or not, Hunter felt a shudder go through him.

If the Big Generator went out for good, all means of power across the Galaxy would be gone. The blood of life for trillions of people would be no more. Cold homes. Cold bodies. No food. No warmth. No nothing. The Galaxy would go dark. God would be dead. And the Great Flash would be a blip on the screen compared to the Great Blackout. Such a thing would likely end most if not all life in the Milky Way.

Erikk took a breath and soldiered on: "By our count, the SG has close to two million Starcrashers, and probably just as many smaller but no less lethal ships. If the SSG was somehow able to control the Big Generator, then only SG ships would be able to fly in Supertime. Only the SG would be able to fire the big weapons. The Space Forces would be impotent. The rest of the Empire's military services would be as well. The Solar Guards would become so powerful in that one stroke, they would take over the Galaxy in a week. Or even less."

Erikk indicated his colleagues around the table. The grand StarLiners did not rely on the Big Generator for power. The same held true for the UPF guys. But even combined, their forces would be minuscule, compared to the SG.

"We certainly couldn't stop them for very long," Erikk admitted. "And there are indications they'd be coming for us first."

Hunter just shook his head. This must be another symptom of his madness, he thought glumly. Another vision.

It was just too insane. . . .

Erikk read Hunter's mind. "Like you, my friend, I needed proof," he said earnestly. "But be warned please, the proof might be even more astounding than what I have just told you."

Hunter knew the Legionnaire had a point. Where did this crazy story come from? How did his friends on this isolated planet, halfway up the Two Arm, thousands of light years from Earth, know these deep dark secrets about the SSG and them manipulating the Big Generator? Where was the proof?

At that moment, there was flash of green light in the room. An instant later, Hunter found himself staring up at a tall, dark person dressed entirely in black. He was wearing a large, floppy hat that hid his face and had a cape thrown dramatically over his left shoulder. There was still an aura of emerald light around him, the sign of a subatomic string transfer, an ability shared only among the very high Specials and their ilk.

In a snap, Hunter's ray gun was out of its holster and pointing into the shadow that was so expertly hiding this person's features.

"Who the *fuck* are *you!"* Hunter roared at him.

"You're very quick," the voice from beneath the large hat replied calmly. "But believe me, offing me now would be a great mistake. Though I know you would have little compunction in killing an Imperial spy."

Imperial spy? Hunter thought. This really wasn't making any sense now. Why would such a person be allowed in the Star Legion's HQ?

He must be in the middle of an illusion. It was the only explanation. Wasn't it?

The spy spoke again. "I know it's hard to believe," he said in his slightly echoing voice. "But I have come to help you, Mr. Hunter. Help *all* of you. And not for the first time."

Erikk gently put his hand on Hunter's arm.

"My friend," the Legionnaire said. "By all that is good in me, and my family, I believe this man speaks the truth. Just hear him out, please . . ."

Hunter reluctantly lowered his weapon. A sigh of relief went through the room.

The spy pulled his hat farther over his face. "What your friends have just told you is accurate," he said to Hunter. "The Special Solar Guards are indeed trying to manipulate the Big Generator, and the consequences will be as dire as they have warned you.

"Now, true, I am part of the Imperial Court. And I have sworn an oath to serve the Emperor and rid the Galaxy of any enemies it might encounter. You, Mr. Hunter, certainly qualify in that respect, as an enemy of the state.

"But at the same time I know that great institutions ebb and flow, and when the tide goes out, innocents are usually the first to suffer. Trillions of them may lose their lives if the SSG succeeds, and if they don't, the Galaxy might become dark again—and that, too, would be catastrophic. A new Dark Age could be upon us, and that adjective would have more meanings than just one. The chaos that would ensue would be unimaginable. Loyalty oath or not, I simply cannot let that happen, not when there's a chance I can do something about it."

Hunter thought a moment, then said, "Let's assume that what you say is so. What can any of us do about it? The regular SG have the One Arm sealed off. I'm sure the Pluto Cloud is an impregnable fortress by now. And Earth itself? The entire Space Forces fleet would probably not be able to fight its way in and somehow rescue the Big Generator from the SSG. And that's even if the SF was working at full power."

He looked around the table. No one argued with him.

"All true," Erikk said. "But there might be another way. Our unusual visitor here came to us with this information, at great risk I might add, thinking that we might have the solution to it. And, as it turns out, we might . . ."

Hunter spread his hands before him, as if to say, *OK, let me hear it.*

Erikk took the cue. "Good friend, Hawk," he began. "Obviously the SSG have their best experts trying to attempt this manipulation of the Big Generator. Their mad scientists, if you will."

Hunter nodded. "Obviously . . ."

Erikk almost smiled. "Well," he said. "We might have a mad scientist of our own."

Hunter laughed. "Really? I didn't think any of us were that smart."

"We're not," Erikk replied. "But we might know the whereabouts of someone who is."

Erikk turned to the ancient Quasar TV. "And the person we seek," he said, "is a friend of *his*. . . . "

The TV's test pattern suddenly disappeared and was replaced by the image of a man dressed in a very old spacesuit, bulky and gray. The spacesuit was adorned with four letters: NASA. This man, Hunter knew, was more than 5,000 years old and was an astronaut. Literally, an Ancient Astronaut.

Like Hunter, he was also an American. And like Hunter, he had been taken out of his time and thrust forward into the future, for a purpose beyond anyone's complete understanding, but apparently to counterbalance the forces of evil that were running rampant throughout the Galaxy no matter what time frame one found themselves in. This man rose to the occasion, creating the very mysterious Third Empire—about which very little was known these days—and restoring justice to the Galaxy after the catastrophic reign of the bloody Second Empire. As a reward for his heroics centuries before, the Astronaut had been given what was apparently an eternal life. At least, so far.

It was to him that Hunter went for help in gathering the forces needed to defeat the rampage of the devilish REF. It was then that Hunter realized this strange man and he were of the same blood, too. His story someday might fill yet another book, if not two. But suffice to say, the Star Legionnaires were his men, and they were brave and loyal and believed in the same things as Hunter: freedom and fairness, not just for some, but for all.

The TV screen got brighter. This transmission in real time was coming from across the Galaxy, from the mysterious Seven Arm. As always, the Ancient Astronaut was in bed, propped up by a dozen or so pillows, being attended by two lovely nurses in short white skirts. And of course, he was drinking a Tang martini through a straw.

The Astronaut spoke: "This individual Erikk has told you about appeared on the scene about the same time I did. We were colleagues, in a way, as we both flew in space back in those early days. And we were both chosen, Hawk, just as you were, to help save the unfortunates of the Galaxy, and thus help save the Galaxy itself. And in that cause, he and I succeeded together. He helped build the Third Empire. He was as committed to it as I was—though I must admit, we didn't always see things eye to eye."

Hunter was listening closely now, but at the same time he couldn't help but be amazed by the talking image. The Third Empire had many technologies that weren't apparent in the current realm, ideas that had been lost over the centuries. The Ancient Astronaut was speaking to them from his house at the end of the Seven Arm on a world called Far Planet. Yet he seemed as if he was right there with them, as close as the bedroom upstairs maybe, so clear and crisp he looked. Very strange . . .

The Astronaut continued: "Then, as you know, came a time when the Third Empire was forced to withdraw. We did this to save billions of lives across the Galaxy. When this happened, this individual chose to stay behind, to remain within the realm. Because he was still a very powerful person, the new rulers of the Galaxy knew they had to reach an agreement with him. He would give them no trouble if they promised to treat the citizens of the Galaxy with respect. Well, that went right out the window as we know, but this man held to his side of the bargain. He wanted only one thing from the new rulers in return."

"And that was?" Hunter asked.

The Astronaut looked over to Erikk. "Can you please explain it to him?" he asked his commander. "I don't think I can do it with a straight face."

This mystified Hunter further.

Erikk looked around at his colleagues and then the spy. The next few words would indeed have to be delivered soberly. It was going to be hard, though.

"This individual asked . . ." he began stammering. "His request was, well . . . he *demanded* in return for him laying low, that they allow him to build . . . what used to be called . . . well, an *amusement* park."

Time to go, Hunter thought. Even if this was reality, it had just become plain silly.

"Did you just say, 'amusement park?' " he asked incredulously.

"Yes, he did," the Astronaut replied. "That was his deal. They would allow him to build a place filled with attractions, thrills, spills—you get the idea?"

"They used to call them *dizzylandos*," the spy interjected. "Places where citizens would climb into various contraptions that would then move them in very strange manners with the intent of scaring the hell out of them, all for their enjoyment. An unusual idea, no?"

The Third Empire guys just shrugged. They had carnivals and fairs back in their little piece of the Galaxy, but a dizzylando was a bit beyond their understanding. The same went for the UPF officers.

Strangely, though, Hunter seemed to recall the concept. Somewhere in the deep recesses of his memory, he pulled up bits and pieces of these places, where people went to laugh at being frightened. Back then, they had a similar name. *Was it Dizzy Lands?*

"If what you say is true," he said now, "this was a strange thing for him to ask for."

"*Very* strange," the Astronaut agreed. "Nevertheless, the early rulers of the Fourth Empire let him build it. It had many so-called amusements, many scary rides and attractions, but it went much beyond that. It was infinitely more sophisticated than a typical dizzylando. It contained many imaginary places. Places built to look like other places. Things of that nature. And all of it absolutely realistic, as it was constructed with the same technology as used in terra-forming."

"Amazing," Hunter heard himself say.

"Even more so," the spy explained. "As far as we can tell, no one ever went to the place—except for its creator."

"He built it for himself?" Hunter asked.

The Astronaut just shrugged. "That's the way it looks," he said. "He became a recluse. An eccentric. He had trouble dealing with this reality. So he created one of his own and then went to live within it."

"Weird . . ."

"Well, he's a weird individual," the Astronaut went on. "And he has a very weird sense of humor."

"And you think he is still there—at this place?"

"We hope so," Erikk said uncertainly. "But truth is, he hasn't been seen in centuries. Not since the very beginning days of the Fourth Empire, am I right, sir?"

Everyone in the room turned back to the TV set. "Well, he's as old as I am, let's put it that way," the Astronaut said. "And he stayed close to Earth when I chose to leave. I can't blame him, I guess. We all had to make tough decisions back then. To each his own.

"But as odd as he might be, he *is* a genius when it comes to power-producing technology. That was definitely his forte. The core sources, the generation. The very *mystery* of Super electricity. . . . If there is one soul in this Galaxy who can help with what might be a catastrophic situation, it is him. He will know what to do with this Big Generator business. He will know how we can attack the problem from our end. Or at least I hope he will."

"So, where is this guy?" Hunter asked now. "And where is this amusement park of his?"

Erikk said, "Well, that, too, is strange, Hawk. . . ."

He waved his hand, and instantly there was a three-dimensional star map hovering above the table. Another wave of his hand, the map became more detailed. But Hunter found himself not looking at some far flung star system, but rather into the heart of the Solar System. The *original* Solar System. More specifically, he was looking at Saturn, its rings and its many, many moons.

Erikk indicated those moons.

"His dizzylando is down there, somewhere," he said. "And so is he."

"Saturn?" Hunter asked, astonished. He'd just assumed the mystery man, while still technically located within the realm, had fled to another part of the Galaxy, just as the Astronaut and his army had withdrawn to the edge of the far-out Seven Arm.

Never did he think he would have stayed inside the Solar System itself.

"As part of his pledge, this man was given a bunch of Saturn's moons and the use of the last of the original Ancient Engineers, or the secrets thereof," Erikk explained. "He was given the ability to change these moons into anything he wanted for his dizzylando. Each moon being a separate attraction. That was his deal."

Hunter studied the moons spinning around the huge ringed planet. Between the real ones and all the artificial ones put up over the centuries, there seemed to be hundreds of them.

"I can confirm his moons have been off limits to even

the highest Specials," the spy told them in his darkly regal way. "Their very existence, and the way they were altered, is one of the Five Secrets held by the Empire. You won't catch any of the Imperial Family out there, just like you won't catch any of them on Luna. The Solar Guards avoid the place religiously, too, even though, as you know, they are all over Saturn itself."

This much was true. All of the Solar System's planets had been puffed—made inhabitable—Saturn included. In fact, many of the SG's administrative sections were located on the pleasantly fair, yellow and blue surface of the gigantic ringed planet. But as for the planet's many moons, Hunter had to admit he hadn't heard much about any of them since finding himself here in the seventy-third century.

"Because of the knowledge this man possesses," Erikk concluded, "he could very well know how to thwart this devious undertaking by the SSG. The trouble might be getting him to do it, because, as we have learned, he is a very unusual person.

"But in any case, we think someone should go down there and try to find him . . ."

All eyes in the room turned to Hunter. He shifted uncomfortably in his seat.

"And I guess," he said, "that would be me?"

The spy was the first to reply. "You're a victim of your own success, Major Hunter," he said simply. "Can you think of anyone else who could save the Galaxy, singlehandedly?"

Hunter imagined he could see the spy smiling beneath his hat. But the man had a point. While any number of the

UPF guys or Star Legionnaires were bold enough, brave enough to go on such a high-risk mission, Hunter had to admit he was the veteran go-to guy for such things. He'd been on hundreds of special missions in his life, or so it seemed. And this time the cause definitely seemed worthy—if this wasn't all just a bad dream, that is.

"Let's say I agree to do this," he finally told them. "Exactly how am I getting where I'm supposed to go?"

It was another good question. Obviously the moons of Saturn were deep within territory controlled by the Solar Guards. And while it might have been possible for him to bust through the SG lines with his fabulous Flying Machine, without it, he really was just an ordinary man.

How could an ordinary man move hundreds of light-years into enemy territory without being detected?

He was about to find out.

The spy turned to Erikk and the others. "With your permission?" he asked.

In the next instant, there was a flash.

A second later, a large wooden box was sitting in the middle of the room. It was green and red, about the size of an ancient phone booth, with wires and hoses running all over it.

It was called a DATT, for deatomizing transfer tube.

Hunter took one look at it—and let out a long groan. Suddenly he wished he was back in the badlands.

"I feel obliged to explain this thing to you," the spy told him.

But Hunter didn't need any explanation of this contraption. He knew what a DATT was. It was an ancient form of transportation that used deatomization as the means of travel. The traveler is broken down into individual sub-atoms and sent, by superstrings' vibrations, to his intended destination. It sounded cool, but Hunter knew it was a very dangerous way to travel the cosmos, even when it was considered a new technology, thousands of years ago.

"God, I'd rather walk than go in this thing," Hunter said.

"I would, too," the spy admitted. "But it's the only way I can figure you can get where you've got to go without the SG knowing about it. Consider this: the SG is scanning any ship, back to front, that even approaches the One Arm. They're even scanning their own ships, that's how paranoid they are. So, travel by space vessel is out. You'd never make it within a hundred light-years of the One Arm. The SG can also detect flash transfers anywhere in the Galaxy. And they can detect beam transport technology, too. But the DATT method is so old, they don't even have it on their list of scanning objectives. Indeed, I would guess many of them don't even know it still exists. Besides, you have to get very deep behind enemy lines and do so very quickly. So there really is no other way."

Not many things concerned Hunter about his well-being. He was too lucky to worry about death. However, the thought of traveling by DATT was unnerving. He just shook his head slowly. If only he had his damn Flying Machine! He'd be able to break through the Pluto Cloud and any other obstacle the SG put in his way simply by going fast. And at least he'd have a better chance of making it in one piece.

"Can I ask something?" he said to all of them now, with some exasperation. "How come our big bad spy here isn't going on this mission?"

It was a good question. Imperial spies had access to just

about anywhere. Why wasn't he going after the creator of the dizzylando?

The spy didn't hesitate a moment to reply. "Do you really think if I found this guy, that he would come with me?" he asked. "An Imperial spy? I'm as much his enemy as I am yours."

There was a round of somber nodding in the room. Even Hunter had to agree with the spy's logic.

"I wish there was another way," he told Hunter directly. "And believe me, I have no desire to be found conspiring with you against the SSG. But time is not a luxury we have right now, because as your friends already know, there is another shoe to drop here."

"And that is?" Hunter asked, not quite sure he wanted to know.

The spy replied, "I'm sorry to say that in addition to their manipulation of the Big Generator, the SSG is planning to attack this very planet with a very unusual secret weapon, as soon as they think the BG is under their control."

Hunter just stared back at him. He thought he detected a bit of quavering in the spy's usually resonant voice.

"*This* planet?" he asked. "Why?"

"Because they *know* . . . " the spy replied after a dramatic pause. "They *know* your friends from the Third Empire are out here. They *know* the UPF fleet is out here, too. And they know neither one has ships run by prop cores. Don't you see? If they get control of the Big Generator, the very first thing they have to do is wipe out all of you. You'll be the only real organized force that could stand in their way, even though, as has been established, not for very long.

"So time *is* very short here. And you certainly can't waste it down there, in the dizzylando. The SSG will eventually muck up the Big Generator to a point where they will either have it doing their bidding, or it will be wrecked forever. That is why haste must now be your friend."

Hunter just slumped further into his seat. There was an air of grim inevitability in the room. *Hawk Hunter Saves the Galaxy?* The spy was right; who else was up to do the job? Who else had the experience? He, on the other hand, was in the hero business. That's why he was here.

He looked at the DATT, then over the at the TV set. "Would you go if you were me?"

The Astronaut nodded slowly. "I would have to. And so do you, I'm afraid."

Hunter thought another few moments, weighing the pros and cons—not that there were many pros. Then he thought about Xara and what she would think of all this. She would not want him to go, but at the same time, he knew that he should. That was enough to convince him.

"OK, I'll do it," he said. "Even if this is a bad dream, it beats trudging through the badlands. I think . . ."

"Then we must move fast," the spy said. "Already I'm sure people are beginning to wonder where I am all this time."

He asked Hunter for his quadtrol. The pilot passed the handheld device over his shoulder. The spy began punching information into it, his fingers moving with lightning-quick speed. He handed the device back to Hunter after just a few seconds.

"Once you get down to your destination, you'll have to locate the ticket booths. This information will help you find them."

"Ticket booths?" Hunter asked. "You've got to be kidding me."

"It will all make sense once you're on the ground, so to speak," the spy said. "Just follow the instructions on your quadtrol."

"Anything else?" Hunter asked him.

The spy reached inside his coat and came out with a small white capsule. It was a Twenty 'n Six, a device that could hold large objects in the twenty-sixth dimension until the owner recalled them for use. Items almost as large as a Starcrasher could be stored via the bizarre little devices. Hunter had carried his precious Flying Machine around in one many times.

"There is no sense in denying this DATT is very old," the spy explained. "It might be good only for a one way trip. Or you might not be able to make it back to it once your mission is complete. If that's the case, then activate this Twenty 'n Six. You'll find a lifeboat of sorts inside. But only use it in an emergency. And there's no guarantee it will work, either."

Hunter numbly took the capsule from him. He was more concerned about his means of getting to the first dizzylando moon than he was about getting back.

"Anything *else?*" he asked the spy again, this time in a mocking tone.

"Just to wish you good luck, Major," he said. "A lot is riding on this. Just please stay smart down there, no matter what the temptation. And, whatever you do, please *hurry.*"

With that, the spy glided to a darkened corner of the room and melded with the shadows.

Hunter looked down at the TV screen to see the Ancient Astronaut looking back at him, a finger pressed to his space mask where his lips would be. Suddenly everything in the room froze. The officers, the spy, the ticking of the grandfather clock. Incredibly, the Astronaut had temporarily stopped time, another trick of the Third Empire. It was the only way he and Hunter could talk privately.

It was fascinating, if just a bit creepy.

"Was this necessary for my last-minute pep talk?" Hunter asked the image.

"If you needed a pep talk, I wouldn't let you go," the Astronaut replied. "Just some last-minute details your friend in black might not be privy to . . . and I don't want our guys to know either, in case they ever get brain scanned."

"Lay them on me," Hunter said, anxious again. The sooner he got going, the sooner this whole episode would be over with.

The Astronaut told him, "Your first destination will be the Alpha Moon. Those are the coordinates he put inside your quadtrol. And like he said, once you're down, you'll have to locate the ticket booth. It's the entrance to the dizzylando. It will bring you to the first attraction. You'll need a password to activate your entry. Use these two words: Sky Ghost."

Hunter stared back at him. *Sky Ghost?* Why did that seem so familiar?

The Astronaut went on, "You'll probably have to ride every attraction until you can find out more about the guy we are seeking. But you should know this will not be like simply visiting a bunch of typical moons with things built on them. These places are very, very strange. Their design came from the mind of a very unusual person. Remember, back in their day, these amusement parks were meant to take people to places beyond their imagination. To scare them. To make them laugh, even if they wanted to cry from fright. That's what's *really* going on down there. . . . Multiplied several million times."

"You mean like a mind ring trip?" Hunter asked.

The old man laughed. "A mind ring trip is like a drop in the ocean compared to what this man created. These places exist in another state of mind. Based on his beliefs, his desires, his dreams. His designs. And because they were built with the same technology as terra-forming, *elaborate* doesn't even scratch the surface of what they are all about. He'll try to get into your head, that is if he is still the same person I remember. And it will be useless to ask for him, or to ask anyone about him, until you get to the end of each ride, so to speak. I mean, there's a reason no one has ventured into this place for more than a thousand years. It's not considered holy like Luna, or off limits, like Mars. It's just too weird, too scary—which of course is the whole point of a dizzylando. Or at least it's what *he* thought one should be like. Just be aware that some surprises may be awaiting you down there."

The Astronaut sipped his Tang martini.

"Just go with the flow. Be discreet. Eventually you'll find him—if he doesn't find you first. But have respect for any people you might meet along the way be they real or not. You're entering into their existence now, whatever that existence might be. It will probably seem crazy to you, but it is very real to them."

"You know a lot about this place," Hunter said. "Almost like you've been there before."

The Astronaut laughed. "I don't have to have been there

to know what it is like. As I said, this particular person had a very weird sense of humor. Although, that was the least of his problems or his attributes, depending on your point of view."

"Please explain," Hunter asked him.

The Astronaut sipped his Tang martini again and thought for a few moments. "Let me put it this way," he said. "The man you are seeking is indeed a bit of an enigma. A riddle. A mystery. He could be your greatest friend or your worst enemy. He's cultured, yet he's also a brute. He loves to drink, but he's God-fearing. He's an intellectual, but he wouldn't hesitate a moment to change history to suit his purposes. Or to fuel his amusement. He could be a cold-blooded killer. But in a way, he's just a big softy, too. He has this thing about him where he wants every story to have a happy ending, every dream to come true. But most of all, he was very jealous of the way we used to live—you and I and the rest of the people back in twentieth-century America, so long ago."

Hunter took it all in and thought he'd arrived at some kind of profile of his quarry.

"So, he's a madman then," he told the Astronaut.

The Ancient Astronaut paused another moment, and then shook his head no.

"A madman? Well, not exactly," he replied. "Actually, he's a Russian."

Two minutes later, Hunter was gone.

The DATT shimmered brightly as soon as he'd stepped in and activated its balky controls. It then began shuddering madly as it seemed to resist fading out as it was supposed to.

When it finally left, it did so with a mighty bang and a brilliant and disturbing flash of light, leaving behind a cloud containing a very nasty stench that smelled a little too much like burned hair and bone.

The dramatic departure stunned even the spy. Suddenly all eyes were on him.

Erikk especially turned back to the Imperial interloper. "If any harm comes to our friend . . ." he said, letting his words trail off.

The spy waved away his concerns. "I'm well aware of the power of the Third Empire," he said seriously. "And I have no desire to have it come down on my head."

Now an awkward silence descended on the room. With Hunter's considerable presence gone, the place seemed empty, barren. The Ancient Astronaut had faded out, too, making the presence of the Imperial spy even odder.

But then another thought came to Erikk. A very worried look washed across his face.

"We told Hawk about the Big Generator," he said. "And the SSG's plans for it. And what can happen if they succeed in their plans or if they screw it up. We told him how he can navigate the dizzylando, and what he should look for once he is down there."

"All true," one of the UPF officers said. "What is your concern then?"

Erikk thought for a long moment and then looked up at them.

"Did we forget to tell him about the blinks?" he asked.

PART TWO

When Russians Dream

Chapter 3

The noise was horrible.

Screaming . . .

Like high winds.

Like endless static.

Like he was back in Purgatory, hearing the cries of the dead again, just this time, at very high speed.

He had to shut them out, but it was so cramped inside the DATT tube, there wasn't enough room for him to raise his hands to put over his ears—if he had hands and ears, that is. That was also very distressing. He had no ears, so really he couldn't hear anything. He had no mouth, so he couldn't cry out. He had no hands, no feet, nothing to feel, nothing to feel with. But the screaming was still there.

It was the darkness that was the worst though. The

DATT tube had just a slit for a window; it was no more than a half inch wide and barely four inches across. But it did him no good because he had no eyes, and so, he could not see.

He didn't know what he'd expected, as his body was taken apart and put back together several trillion times a second—this was how it made its way along the vibration net of the universal superstrings. Had he hoped to see stars flashing by? Or planets? Or some kind of new, uncharted celestial phenomena? Or perhaps a glimpse of the nanoworlds of subatoms and quicks, quacks, and quarks?

He wasn't sure. But in the end, he saw nothing at all during the transfer. Nothing but complete darkness. And it didn't help when halfway through, he imagined, in one trillionth of a trillionth of a second, that the sides of the tube were lined with crushed velvet cloth, not the old wrinkly plastic sheeting that had covered the interior when they first locked him inside this infernal box. And the smell, even though he had no nose, was that of spring lilies, favorite flower of the dead.

He was sure something had gone wrong. DATT transfers were supposed to be instantaneous, at least way back when this piece of crap technology was first built. But now, to Hunter's psyche, it seemed to keep going on and on and on . . .

Just when he was convinced that the DATT had indeed malfunctioned and he was now doomed to stay like this forever—cramped, in the dark, disassembled, with the eternal screaming taunting him—it all stopped.

Just stopped . . .

• • •

Dust . . .

He kicked up a mighty cloud of it on his arrival. A bit of light came through that tiny slit of a window now; that's how he knew he had his eyes back. But for the first few seconds, all Hunter could see was a blizzard of white powder on the other side, thick as snow, swirling past. What to do? He couldn't open the hatch. The dust would come in and smother him. He had no choice but to wait, hoping for it to disperse. Only then would he be able see exactly where he was.

He spent the next few moments checking his person, especially his appendages. It was a big surprise, but everything seemed to have survived the DATT transfer in good shape. He let out a long, slow breath of triumph. When he looked up again, the dust had settled, and his field of vision had cleared.

But he was shocked by what he saw. He'd been expecting to be transferred to an inhabited body. He'd just assumed he'd see a city, a settlement, a Ferris wheel—something that would confirm that he'd landed on the Alpha Moon. But the landscape he saw now through the tiny window was as barren as Earth's moon. Craters, valleys, high mountains, deep ravines, lots of dust—and absolutely no signs of life. Or atmosphere.

Am I in the right place?

He crossed his fingers and kicked opened the DATT's hatch. He'd arrived on the edge of a large impact crater. A quick check by his quadtrol said that yes, he was on some kind of moon, and that there was breathable air down here. In fact, the moon's puff was working at an impressive 89 percent. Still, Hunter hesitated before taking that first deep breath outside. The technology of the Ancient Engineers may have done a great job reviving this tiny place, but that had been thousands of years ago. Were the moon's invisible life support systems still intact? If they weren't, he'd be dead in seconds.

He let the moment of doubt pass. After everything they'd been through together, if he couldn't trust his quadtrol now, what could he trust? So he took that deep breath, then let it out slowly. It felt great going in and going out. There really was air here.

So far, so good.

He climbed out of the tube and stepped onto the surface. His boots sank a few inches into the fine white powder that seemed to be everywhere. It was strange, though, because when he looked up, he could see not the blue skies of a typical puffed body. What he saw instead were the stars in their full glory—and of course the massive presence of Saturn, at the moment hanging off to his right, taking up most of the horizon. Its major rings sliced through the sky right over his head. They made the rings surrounding Doomsday 212 look puny by comparison.

It was all incredibly beautiful. And obviously, he was on one of Saturn's many, many moons. But this place seemed dead. In every direction, he saw nothing but dust and desolation. Saturn had so many moons these days, both real and artificial. Had the DATT's preset controls been wrong? Had he landed on the wrong satellite? Or was he inside another mad vision, a delusion of his own making?

The quadtrol set him straight. It took about three milliseconds before confirming that he was indeed on the right satellite, the natural moon the Astronaut had called Alpha. What's more, he was at the right latitude for his purposes here. He was just a little off on the longitude.

In other words, he'd have to walk a bit.

Reassured by the quadtrol's conclusions, he brushed himself off and readjusted his reliable crash helmet on his head. Then he tapped his breast pocket twice. This was where he always kept his small American flag and the faded photograph of the mysterious Dominique. Two taps meant he was wishing himself luck. He was ready to start hiking.

But then he turned around, intent for some reason on closing the DATT tube's door. He was astonished by what he saw.

The tube was no longer a tube at all. It was a coffin.

Not something that *looked* like a coffin. But a real coffin.

Hunter froze for a moment, his breath caught in his throat. Then, slowly, he ran his hand along its polished wooden frame, its brass handles, its gleaming hinges. The inside was indeed crushed velvet, just like what was used to line the interior of coffins back in his former life. And he could still detect the scent of lilies coming from inside it.

What happened? *Had* he gone through something weird during his transfer? Had the DATT malfunctioned after all?

Was he even still alive?

Panic rising, he pulled out the quadtrol again and quickly asked it to check his vital signs. The device burped a couple times but then came back with all good readings. This did not convince him, though. Something about unexpectedly stepping out of a coffin on a very desolate rock had shaken him. It would have shaken anybody.

He asked the quadtrol once more for his life signs. Again, everything came back green. Then he asked it, "Am I still alive?" feeling foolish as soon as he did so. Its reply: "If you weren't, you would not have been able to ask the question."

He almost laughed. The quadtrol had become a wiseass. *That* was very reassuring.

He took a moment, collected himself, then slammed the coffin door shut. But then a thought came to him. He blinked . . . and when his eyes opened, the coffin had turned back into the DATT.

He froze again, a chill running right through him.

More madness, he thought. *From within . . .*

That's when he made a vow. No matter what happened down here, no matter what dangers he faced, or what success he might find, or even how quickly he had to escape, there was no way he was ever climbing into that thing again.

He started walking.

Heading north, the direction the quadtrol told him to go, he wondered again how the puff on the moon could be so stable, and yet the sky appeared void of any atmosphere at all.

And again, why did this place look so forbidding? It was supposed to be a dizzylando, an amusement park—or at least the entrance to one. But then again, maybe it was all a cover. Maybe the creator, in wanting to keep the whole concept here secret, made this place look as uninviting as possible.

Had someone landed here unintentionally in a spaceship, judging from the surroundings, only a fool would open his canopy, without getting proper readings. Just the sight of the place would send even the most hard-bitten space traveler reaching for the power button on their craft and the quickest way out of here. If indeed this had been the creator's intention, then he'd really hit the mark. Walking alone way out here, Hunter felt like he was the last person left in the Galaxy.

He trooped along for about a half mile, crossing natural bridges over two ravines and scaling one small mountain. It was on the other side of this rise that he finally spotted something.

Something very odd.

Off on the horizon was a sign, designed to look like a huge arrow, made up of hundreds of blinking white lights. It was sitting on top of a small red building and was actually pointing to another lighted sign just above the building's entrance. This sign was written in Cyrillic lettering. Hunter pointed the quadtrol in its general direction and then pushed the query panel. According to the quadtrol, the sign read: Welcome to the Dizzylando.

"Must be the place," Hunter muttered.

It took him another twenty minutes to actually reach the building.

It was smaller than he'd imagined, set in the middle of the vast, barren plain. It appeared to be made out of pine, a rare commodity in the Galaxy over the centuries. A porch made of short planks fronted the rectangular structure. It had many windows, was painted bright red, and had a pair of steel rails running past the porch. It looked similar to something from Earth's ancient past, a place known as a railroad station.

The moon dust had permeated every corner and crevice on the outside of this place. Hunter's flight boots made an odd but vaguely familiar sound as he climbed up onto the porch. He stopped and studied the materials around him and realized this was not real wood after all, but a kind of synthesized material that had been made to look like wood. He believed that the sound of his boots hitting it was actually false as well, as this material was equipped with sensors that would imitate the sound of something hitting wood, just to lend authenticity. Very strange . . .

He stepped through the swinging doors. Just like the outside, the interior had been built as a re-creation of an ancient train station. Ticket windows, yellowed schedules, benches for the weary. But the inside also had many flashing lights of all colors, though mostly white. They were strung around all the windows, above and around the door, and crisscrossing the ceiling.

There was another lighted sign hanging on one wall. It read, *Sledyuschaia ostanovka Zemlya Priklucheniy. Xvatit li tebe myzestva chtobi proderzatsya?* The quadtrol knew most of the Russian words. Roughly translated, the sign said: Next stop: Adventure Land. Are you enough of a hero to take it?

Sitting on a very simple table in the middle of the room Hunter found the most ancient computer imaginable. It had a monitor, with a tiny screen made of glass—not superglass. Just regular glass. There was a keyboard attached to it by a wire, another item rarely seen in the Galaxy these days. A power cord ran the length of the room, disappearing behind the far wall.

Hunter ran his quadtrol over this strange piece of machinery and asked it for a name. The quadtrol blinked back: "PC—personal computer."

He contemplated the machine for a moment. It seemed slightly familiar to him now. But in a million years he would never have believed it would actually still work. It took him several minutes just to locate the power switch. It was a recessed button—a button!—placed in the lower right hand corner of the monitor. Hunter gave it a push, expecting nothing more than a click. But slowly, the screen came to life.

He was more surprised when words actually started forming on the monitor's screen. Some were Cyrillic but others were in English, again welcoming him to the dizzylando. He selected a box which allowed him to continue in English. Two more words appeared: "Enter password . . ." Hunter was stumped, but just for a moment. Then he recalled the two vaguely familiar words the Astronaut had told him before he left: *Sky Ghost.* It took him nearly a minute to hunt and peck out the two words on the keyboard. Finally done, he pushed the Enter button.

The screen blinked, then a small icon of a clock appeared. Its second hand started moving very slowly. Hunter waited patiently, wiping the dust from his uniform's sleeves, studying his boots and thinking maybe it was time to get a new pair, even whistling a tune.

Five minutes crawled by. Finally a new screen appeared. He read the words—and groaned. It said: "Enter password again . . ."

It took him nearly a half hour to type his way through this and three more security walls, always entering the same password as instructed, and brushing off his uniform twice, while waiting for the old PC to keep regurgitating his entries. Finally, the word "Processing . . ." appeared on the screen. This was the longest wait of all. But again, after whistling what seemed to be an entire symphony, the screen changed and said, "Entry authorized . . ."

A device down at the bottom of the computer began churning. It was a printer of some sort. A piece of yellow paper slowly emerged from a slot in its side. The printing on it, again, was in English. It said, "Good for all rides. Get ticket punched after each feature." On the reverse side was a faded, out-of-focus picture of a man, possibly midthirties, clean shaven face, bald head, cracked-tooth smile, and an absolutely insane look in his eyes. He was laughing, with his hands out in front of him, in a sort of greeting gesture. A name below the picture was too faded to read, but Hunter didn't need to see it to know who this was.

It's the Russian, he thought. *The Mad Russian . . .*

He stuffed the ticket into his pocket, and the computer screen changed again. Now it read, "Last Page." Below were two blank fields. He was instructed to fill them in. One wanted his name. He typed in "Hunter, Hawker," his given name. The second field asked, "What is your hobby?" Hunter hit the Enter button, hoping the information wouldn't be required. But the screen would not budge. He tried to override it again. Still no luck.

He returned to the original screen. *What is your hobby?* He wasn't even sure he'd ever had a hobby. He was beginning to feel a time creep now. Whatever he was supposed to do down here, he had to do quickly. But if the PC wouldn't let him proceed, then he would have to fill in this innocuous little field. Hobby? There was only one thing he could think of.

He typed in "Flying."

Then he hit the Enter key . . .

"Can you fly this thing?"

Hunter was standing in the same position as when he hit the Enter key on the computer. Right hand extended, looking almost straight down.

But everything around him had changed. He was no longer inside the Adventure Land station. Instead, he was standing on a cliff hanging above a very deep ravine. High, craggy peaks were all around him. Wisps of smoke were rising from every crevice in these mountains. The air smelled of sulfur and burned oil. The landscape below was forested, but rough and hilly. The sky above was purple and not blue, and filled with streams of electrical sparks instead of stars. The wind was blowing fiercely. There was much noise, confusion in the air. And the massive presence of Saturn was gone.

He was definitely not on the Alpha Moon anymore. But it wasn't Purgatory, either.

There was an elderly gentleman standing in front of him. He had a long, woolly, white beard, yellow teeth, and eyes that looked positively deranged. He was wearing a very tight, unflattering costume of bright red and green material. On his chest was a large letter Z.

Explosions started going off all around them. The guy was suddenly right in Hunter's face.

"Answer me, man!" he was screaming. "Can you fly this thing?"

But Hunter was still stunned by his sudden transformation. He'd been transported many times via flashing, mind rings, and now the DATT. But in those cases there was always some kind of indication—an aura, an electrical jolt—that told you something unusual had happened.

Not this time. This was different. One instant he was there; now he was here.

The old man in the strange clothes was shaking him by his flight suit collar.

"Tarnation, man! Time is running out—can't you see

that?" He was nearly spitting in Hunter's face. "Can you? Can you fly that thing?"

Hunter's synapses finally snapped back together.

"Fly what?" he yelled back.

The old man stepped aside. Behind him, teetering on the edge of the cliff, was . . . well, what was it?

It might have been some kind of spacecraft. But it was certainly not of Empire design. There wasn't anything remotely wedge-shaped about this thing. It was stout, cylindrical, maybe fifteen feet long, curved like a fancy wine goblet turned on its side. It was built of bright silver something—a metal, Hunter assumed. It also featured a lot of unnecessary ornamentation up and down its frame: an elaborate nose that looked like an ancient grease gun, a nonfunctioning single wing poking out of the top of the fuselage, three ridiculously curved fins on the back. An exhaust tube was sticking out of its rear end, wimpy puffs of smoke dribbling out of it.

"Can you?" the old man was beseeching him. "Please— you're our last hope!"

Finally Hunter saw what the old guy was so upset about. Looking down into the ravine, he could see three roads, coming from three different directions, all leading up to where he, the old guy, and the whatzit were at the moment. These roads were filled with soldiers. Very weird soldiers. They were dressed in hideous metal battle suits, dumb-looking helmets, short tunics, and sandals. *Tin men in skirts,* Hunter thought. They were also carrying spears. They were charging up toward them and would be on the cliff in a half minute or even less. It would have almost been comical, if there weren't so many of them.

The old man grabbed Hunter by the collar again.

"We've got to get out of here," he said in desperation.

And this time, Hunter was inclined to agree with him.

"Can you fly it, man?"

"I can try!" Hunter finally yelled back at the guy.

They both bounded into the craft. It was actually made not of metal but some impossibly thin material—maybe cardboard. The door almost came off its hinges as Hunter tried to close it behind them. He was somehow able to lock the flimsy hatch, though; only then did he get a good look at the cabin.

Despite the evident danger—either the rampaging armies would reach them, or the stiff wind would blow them over the cliff—Hunter had to laugh. The interior of the craft was insanely primitive. It looked like a toy. The control panel consisted of six lightbulbs arranged on a piece of corrugated metal, a tiny toggle switch beneath each one. The directional assembly was an automobile steering wheel. The throttle was a gas pedal, with a brake pedal beside it. Hunter looked aft. The craft's tiny power plant appeared unable to produce enough juice to light the lightbulbs, never mind make this thing fly.

The old guy was on his sleeve again. "Can you do it?" he was whimpering. "Please tell me you can. . . ."

Hunter studied the very rudimentary controls. He'd driven everything from Empire Starcrashers, to his own Flying Machine, complex vehicles that took real skill to fly. Now, looking at the six lightbulbs, the gas pedal, and the brakes, it was almost too elementary for him to comprehend. There wasn't even a chair for him to sit down.

What should he do? He came up with a quick strategy.

Gas pedal makes it go. Brake pedal makes it stop. He had no idea what the lightbulbs were for. Therefore, push the gas pedal.

But just as he was about to do this, the old guy began digging his fingernails into Hunter's skin.

Hunter turned to him. "What is it now?"

The old guy said just one word: "Annie!"

Hunter froze. "Who's Annie?"

The guy was suddenly wailing. "She's my daughter." Hunter was confused—make that doubly confused. "Well, where is she?"

The old guy dragged him over to the tiny porthole.

"Out there!" he cried.

He pointed to the cliff just behind the craft. Sure enough, there was a very pretty girl in a very short skirt, for some reason tied to a pole at its summit. At the same moment Hunter saw the three armies were converging nearer the top.

Damn, he swore.

He didn't even think about it. He didn't have time. He ran back through the cabin, out the flimsy door, across the top of the cliff, up the short peak to where the girl was located. It was strange, especially in this reality blur, but even in the danger they faced, the armies just a few hundred feet away, Hunter couldn't help but notice how cute she was. Long brown hair. Enormous blue eyes. Sparkling smile.

"I'm Annie!" she screamed in his ear as he tore away her bindings. They were made of paper and broke easily. He grabbed her around the waist, pulled her close, then dashed back down the hill and into the craft.

He delivered daughter to father, then jumped behind the control panel again. The three streams of soldiers reached the summit a moment later. They were barely fifty feet away from the craft at this point.

Just for the hell of it, Hunter hit the six switches below the six lightbulbs. They all blinked on, but dimly. Then he put his foot on the gas pedal, grabbed the steering wheel, and yelled, "Hang on!"

He pushed the gas pedal all the way to the floor panel. There was a loud crackling noise from the rear of the craft, and suddenly the smell of sulfur was everywhere.

But nothing happened.

They weren't moving.

Hunter tried again. Pedal to the metal, hands on the wheel. But again, nothing. Outside, the soldiers had reached the craft. They were banging on it with their spears. Suddenly a blade came right through the ship's skin. Annie screamed. Her father let out a long moan. Hunter's mind was racing. One moment he was standing on the Alpha Moon, the next he was here—wherever *here* was—trying to prevent himself from being skewered.

Why weren't they moving?

He turned back to the old guy. The man looked back at Hunter in confusion. Then it was as if a lightbulb—another one—went off over his head.

"The strings!" the old guy bellowed, finger pointing straight up.

Hunter ducked another spear that had come through the craft's skin.

"Strings?" he yelled back. "You mean, *super*strings?"

The man screwed up his face a moment, and then said: "No—these strings!"

He pointed to a lever on the ceiling. A sign next to it said, Control Strings—Pull Here to Engage.

The old guy pulled on the lever. The craft shook from one end to the other.

"Try it now!" he yelled up to Hunter. Hunter hit the gas pedal again—and finally they began moving.

But slowly. Very slowly . . .

The soldiers in the tin men outfits were climbing all over the craft at this point, ramming their spears through the cardboard fuselage, and nearly hitting Annie and her father numerous times.

Hunter could barely see out the window in front of him. But he knew the edge of the cliff was right there and at the moment flying was a relative term. He jammed the gas pedal down further, and suddenly the floor fell out from under him. They had gone over the cliff, taking many of the soldiers with them.

Now Hunter was looking straight down into the chasm; its bottom was rushing up at them. He yanked back on the steering column, but to no effect. He tried pushing more power to turn the cardboard beast, but the pedal would not go down any further. They were just seconds away from impacting on the chasm floor, when one last idea hit him. In this crazy world, if you want to stop, what do you do?

He hit the brakes—and sure enough, the craft came to a screeching halt in midair, nose pointed straight down, not one hundred feet away from crashing. It came to such an abrupt stop, those unlucky soldiers still clinging to its sides were shaken loose and kept on going, unable to stop their momentum. Hunter heard a chorus of "Ahhhh!" as a dozen of them went by the cabin window. A grisly way to go.

But he and his new friends were safe—at least for the moment. True, they were suspended in midair. And why gravity wasn't causing them to topple toward the front of the craft, he had no idea. But Hunter's boot was coming apart as he pressed down on the brake pedal with all his might. He was certain if he let up on it, they would continue their plunge downward, and add to the splat already at the bottom of the chasm.

So, now what?

Again, he had to use the same wacky logic of this very wacky place. With the brake pedal still pressed to its limit, he began slowly turning the steering wheel. Annie and her father were somehow holding on behind him, still locked in an anxious embrace. Sure enough, the craft began moving on its axis. Now, instead of staring down at the chasm floor, they were looking at one side of the ravine. Hunter kept spinning the wheel, and soon the nose of the craft was pointed straight up.

He let out a whistle of relief. Then he eased off the brake pedal, at the same time lightly tapping the gas.

Slowly, they started moving vertically again. Sparks flying out of its rear end, they climbed up and out of the chasm and into the expanse of purple sky above. Hunter spun the wheel again and soon got the craft to fly horizontally. Only then did he start breathing normally again. He turned back to Annie and her father. They were beside themselves with joy.

Annie left her father's arms and ran into Hunter's. She hugged him very tightly and not for a short time. Hunter felt her body, warm and soft, fold itself into his. She felt very good, and very real.

"Thank you!" she was saying over and over again. *"Thank you!"*

Finally, her father stepped forward. "I am Dr. Zoloff," he announced dramatically. "I am the head of all scientists of this world. I, too, thank you for saving our lives. Flash Rogers never lets his friends down!"

Flash who? Hunter wondered.

He began to correct the doctor and launch into the reason he was here, when the man cut him off.

His face had suddenly turned very concerned again, almost as if another program had kicked in.

"You must help us!" he told Hunter. "Annie's husband-to-be is being held by the evil Ping the Pontificator. He will die before midnight if we don't save him! Will you help us rescue him, dear sir?"

Before Hunter could say a word, Annie was up against him again, squeezing him. Grinding him. "I know he will, Father!" she was saying excitedly. "I just know it!"

The Astronaut's last few words began passing between Hunter's ears. *Just go along with what is happening there,* he'd said. *Have respect for the people you meet. Their existence might seem crazy to you, but it is their lives.*

Hunter just shrugged. "Sure, I'll help," he finally replied. "If you promise to help me, too."

Annie squeezed him even tighter. Tissue was beginning to move and grow. Several awkward moments went by before Hunter gently tried to ease her away. But it made no difference; she wasn't letting go.

"Then it's a deal!" Zoloff cried.

Annie still tight in her embrace, Hunter eased both of them back over to the control column.

Someone had to fly this thing.

He followed Zoloff's directions and flew to the top of another mountain. It was not much different from the one they'd just left.

There was a white building at its summit though, with an observatory attached. Hunter had noodled out the controls by this time. Using a combination of gas, brake, and steering wheel, he set the craft down with ease. Annie never did stop hugging him. Her father shook his hand.

"I have brandy in my house," Zoloff said. "Please, indulge in one with me."

Before Hunter could reply, they swept him out of the ship and steered him toward the house. He couldn't resist looking back at the craft, though—and was nearly blown away by what he saw. The strings that Zoloff had talked about were actually strings. They were attached to the craft at the nose, along the spine of the fuselage, and all the way back to the tail. Hunter followed them straight up into the deep purple sky, losing sight of them after a mile or so. This was obviously how the small ship really flew, and not by any kind of puny power plant on its rear end. But did that mean some gigantic puppet master was literally pulling the strings way up there?

Just go with the flow, he thought.

Annie and the doctor ushered him into the house. That's when he discovered the house *was* the observatory. It was mostly one big room, with a large but oddly plastic-looking telescope at its center. Strangely, the place seemed a lot bigger on the inside than it did from without. The interior was done in polished wood and chrome, an odd combination. One wall was dedicated to dozens of control panels. All blinking lights and soft buzzing, the switches, buttons, and lightbulb arrangements looked as primitive as those inside the tiny flying craft.

Annie disappeared, only to return wearing another short skirt outfit, this one with a very tight-fitting top. Her hair was now curly, her lips were flaming red. Where she'd been just plain cute before, now she looked gorgeous. The doctor suddenly appeared behind Hunter with two snifters of brandy.

Hunter gratefully accepted his and took a big gulp. It tasted like nothing more than colored water.

"We are so lucky you came along when you did," the doctor said. "Flash *never* lets anyone down . . ."

Hunter began to correct him again—but stopped for a moment. All of this had to have some kind of wacky reason to it, something that would lead to something else. Plus the Astronaut told him he had to play it out, and go with the flow. But was there really any harm in asking?

He took the yellow ticket from his pocket and unfolded it. Turning it to the side with the faded picture, he held it up for the doctor and Annie to see.

"Do you know this man?" he asked them. "Do you know where I can find him?"

It was strange, because not only didn't they reply, they simply seemed to stare right through him. His question did not compute. At least not at the moment.

He tried again. "It's important that I find this man," he said. "Just as important as it is for you to rescue Annie's fiancé."

With that, Zoloff came back to life. "Yes, that's exactly what we must do!" he cried. He dramatically threw his brandy glass into a roaring fireplace. Annie rushed forward to embrace Hunter once again. She pulled him even closer and whispered very seductively in his ear, "Yes, we *must* save him . . ."

Hunter just closed his eyes for a moment. Once again, the Astronaut had been right. This place—this existence—

was more than just a moon that had been puffed. Its reality had been radically altered, too—and was maybe getting a little rough around the edges. It was hard to tell.

And the people *were* strange here, no doubt about that. Nothing had been said about events prior to when Hunter appeared on the scene. Why Zoloff and Annie were up on that mountain, why three armies were climbing up to seize them, how Annie got all tied up. It was like he'd just walked into the middle of a space play, somewhere at the beginning of the second act. What's more, there might not be any explanation, he thought. Not one he could understand, anyway.

Despite this oddity, Zoloff was an immensely sympathetic character. And Annie . . . she seemed to get more attractive with each passing moment. Even now, she was snuggled up against him so tightly, her pert breasts seemed permanently imbedded in his chest. Not a bad feeling.

A very strong emotion was welling up inside him. Suddenly, Hunter really *wanted* to help these people.

So he just gave up on getting any information about the Mad Russian from them, at least at this point. Just as the Astronaut had suggested, he decided to play along.

"OK, so where is he being held?" he finally asked the doctor. "This lucky guy?"

Zoloff seemed surprised. "At Ping's castle, of course!"

Hunter looked around the big room, wondering if there was any chance of a bottle of real booze being in here somewhere.

"And where is that?" he asked absently.

Zoloff's face screwed up in a mask of incomprehension, but then he let out a hearty laugh.

"Flash Rogers—jokester!" he declared in a very loud voice. Annie smiled sweetly—and blocked her ears.

Free again, Zoloff dragged Hunter over to the telescope, cranked a mechanism that lowered it from pointing toward the heavens to pointing horizontally. He practically forced Hunter to look through the eyepiece.

What Hunter could see was a huge palace that appeared to be as close as the next mountain range away. It was gold with many spirals and towers, and was so high up in the mountains, a layer of clouds had apparently taken up permanent residence just below it. Combined, it made the castle look like it was floating on top of the clouds. Almost like . . .

"Can you see them?" Zoloff was screaming in his ear. "The devils? The hedonists?"

Actually, Hunter was seeing neither. What he could see was about a hundred scantily clad dancing girls going through very outlandish gyrations on a concourse of sorts in front of the palace main gate. The choreography was atrocious.

Surrounding the gyrating dancers were hundreds of soldiers, all wearing the same tin man suit of armor as the ones who'd nearly caught them earlier. Some were walking guard duty along the top of the palace walls, others were marching up and down the palace's main street.

"Our friend is there," Zoloff was saying to Hunter. "In the Dungeon of the Doomed, at the bottom of that infernal place. The son I never had. My only daughter's only love!"

That was getting a bit more difficult to believe as Annie was back at Hunter's side, hugging him closely.

"Do you know exactly where your friend is being held?" he asked Zoloff, eye still looking through the telescope.

"As I said—in the Dungeon of the Doomed," he

moaned again. "As deep as one can go in that horrid place."

Hunter studied the palace and the mountain, or as much as he could see of it through the mist. It seemed impenetrable, at least from the bottom up. To him that meant that the only way to gain access to the place was from the air.

He turned back to Zoloff. "Did you say there is a clock ticking here?" he asked.

"Ping has vowed to kill our friend at the stroke of midnight," was Zoloff's breathless, anxious reply.

Hunter thought a moment. "What time is it now?"

No sooner were the words out of his mouth when "the sun" above them slid down to the horizon. Day turned to night, just like that. Annie hugged him tighter. Her father moaned again.

"Night has fallen!" Zoloff cried. "We must hurry!"

Hunter was astonished by the sudden sunset.

"Yes," he said. "I guess we should."

They were quickly back inside the flying craft—their only delay was waiting for Annie to do another costume change. She emerged wearing a stunning micro-miniskirt, tight silver blouse, and very alluring boots. Her long brown hair was now tied up by a piece of golden sash. She was mind-bogglingly beautiful.

She was also holding another set of clothes. Long red leotards, purple shorts, a skintight tunic, and a cape. She handed them to Hunter. "I got some new clothes for you, too," she said sweetly. He would have done just about anything for her at that moment—she was so stunning. But he looked at the outlandish outfit and just shook his head. "Sorry," he told her. "But I ain't climbing into that."

• • •

They lifted off the cliff in good fashion, Hunter expertly manipulating the simple controls of the spacecraft as Zoloff worked the lightbulbs.

Hunter had briefly studied the contraption's strings before climbing aboard, amazed at the long, thin lines disappearing up into the sky. What was going on up there? What would he find on the other end? Did he really want to know? Maybe not . . .

The ship moved ever so slowly now across the divide between the two mountains. The windows at the front of the craft were small, Hunter could barely see what was in front of him, never mind the terrain below. He looked up into the sudden night sky but saw no stars, no other moons, and certainly not the gigantic mass of the planet Saturn or its rings. *How did they do that?* he wondered.

It was more like he was driving a boat than some strange aerial machine. The air seemed thick, the going sluggish, and the rumbling whine coming from the faux power plant was beginning to hurt his ears. But Annie was right beside him, as always. She was radiating both beauty and innocent vulnerability. This had the potential of being a very dangerous endeavor once they reached the castle. Why then was she here? There was no reason. Yet here she was. Just another part of the plot.

They were about halfway across the divide when Zoloff let out a cry.

"The Wingmen!" he bellowed, nose pressed against the ship's tiny porthole. "They are coming to attack us!"

Wingmen?

Hunter looked left to see that, yes indeed, there was a squadron of winged men heading right for them. They looked just about as ridiculous as the tin soldiers they'd battled during their escape from the cliff. It's just that they all had wings.

Now what?

"Use the smoke gun!" Zoloff cried.

Smoke gun?

Annie unclenched from Hunter just long enough to point to a lever on the control panel. He would have sworn it was not there just a moment ago.

"The smoke gun?" he asked her.

She clutched him again. "Yes—the Wingmen hate it!"

Hunter just shrugged and turned the ship to meet the incoming aerial attackers. They were firing some kind of weapons at them, but Hunter could see only tiny pebble-size shrapnel hitting the side of the spacecraft. The tin soldiers' spears had gone right through the craft's skin up on the cliff. That's how thin it was. Yet these BBs were bouncing off.

The attackers were now just one hundred feet off his bow. Hunter pulled the weapon lever. There was a burst of smoke from a muzzle that had suddenly appeared on the ship's nose. Though seemingly in defiance of physical law, the puffy smoke traveled faster than the craft itself and soon covered the dozen or so winged men. That was all it took.

Suddenly their tight formation was in great disarray. The Wingmen began streaking all over the sky, out of control, almost as if they were surprised to see this simple weapon used against them. They quickly regrouped, turned themselves 180 degrees, and beat a very haggard retreat.

"That was easy," Hunter muttered.

That's when the huge flaming arrow went by.

Hunter's highly advanced sixth sense detected the crude missile coming about a second before it would have nailed them. It was just enough time for him to spin the steering wheel and push the strange little craft enough to starboard to avoid getting hit.

Yet no sooner had he saved them from one arrow when another rose out of the palace, trailing smoke and weak flame, but heading right for them. Hunter stood on the brakes and spun the wheel at the same time. The craft fell off to the left; the missile just kept on going.

The palace was now just a few hundred feet below them, but it was obvious their arrival had been detected.

"Fear not!" Zoloff cried. "We can defeat them because justice is on our side!"

The third flaming arrow hit them an instant later.

It came out of nowhere. Like the smoke gun and its muzzle, one moment it wasn't there, the next it was.

The arrow rammed them head-on. The flames and wimpy smoke spurted through the cracked windshield, making almost no noise but causing Annie to scream and her father to groan. By instinct, Hunter looked down at the controls. All six lightbulbs had blinked out.

We're screwed, he thought.

But then he realized that although they had a big flaming arrow stuck in their nose, the ship's flying integrity didn't seem to be affected. He floored the gas pedal and put the ship into a dive.

Their sudden increase in speed served to both put the fire out and dislodge the smoldering arrow from their bow. Trouble was, they were only about twenty feet away from the palace courtyard—and still heading nearly straight down.

Damn . . .

The slatternly dancers scattered as Hunter yanked back on the steering wheel and managed to hit both the gas and the brake at the same time. The corresponding jolt served to bring them to a stop a mere six feet from the surface. They hung here like this for just an instant; then the marionette strings above them finally snapped, and they crashed the last few feet to the ground.

Annie screamed, of course, but Hunter had grabbed her at the last moment and was able to cushion her from the worst of the blow. Zoloff was tossed about, but he, too, was unharmed.

The flimsy door fell off, and the three passengers tumbled out of the strange little craft. When they all looked up again, they were surrounded by tin soldiers.

Hunter got Zoloff and Annie to their feet as the circle of palace guards closed in on them. They were similar in dress to the tin soldiers they'd fought on the cliff, except they wore larger helmets, and the tips of their spears were spouting weak tongues of flame.

Hunter's priority at that moment was protecting Annie. She was stuck to him like glue as always, but he managed to put himself between her and the creaking guards. He didn't have time to think about what they should do next. Zoloff, however, was way ahead of him. The elderly scientist took a roundhouse swing at the nearest soldier, hitting him square in the face. The guy went over like a lead weight, hitting the man next to him, and the man next to *him*, setting off a chain reaction that toppled a dozen of the palace guards in a second's time.

The unexpected bulge sent several of the guards falling right into Hunter. He dispatched each one with a solid punch to the jaw. The most ridiculous aspect of their battle suits was their buckethead-style helmet. It was a wonder that they could see anything out the two tiny slits provided for the eyes. Plus the helmets appeared to be very heavy, making the palace guards needlessly clumsy and slow.

Zoloff kept punching, and so did Hunter. The guards were easy to hit. One punch usually did the trick, flattening them. With heavy armor weighing them down, it was hard for them to get back up. The problem was, they just kept on coming. There seemed to be no end to the ridiculously armored soldiers pouring out of the palace gate. Zoloff was punching them two at a time. Hunter's hands were becoming numb simply because he'd hit so many of them. Yet their slow-motion onslaught was relentless.

This went on for more than fifteen minutes. The pile of incapacitated guards was soon twelve men high. Still the fistfight continued. Zoloff was very winded; Hunter's arms felt like they were going to fall off. It finally dawned on him that this was a fight they could not possibly win. Not when there was an endless supply of the tin men.

So he just stopped swinging, and so did Zoloff. Annie screamed. Two tin men picked her up by the shoulders and carried her away.

Hunter tried to get to her again, but the sheer weight of a dozen guards piling on top of him was too much even for him to handle. Subdued more from exhaustion than anything else, he and Zoloff were bound by the wrists and led through the palace gate to the throne room, prodded all the way by the weakly flaming spears.

No surprise, the throne room was ostentatious to the max. Very high ivory-like ceilings, gleaming golden walls. Shafts of bright light coming from no discernible source.

Hunter couldn't help be impressed by the tacky grandeur of it all—but oddly, it looked a little familiar, too. Almost like . . .

A guard shoved him forward, breaking his thoughts. "You must kneel before Ping!" was his muffled order.

But Hunter just turned around and head-butted the guy. He went over in a heap. Zoloff did the same with his guard. Like Hunter, he was too proud to bend to anyone. More guards rushed forward, but a flash of light from the center of the room froze them in place. Suddenly, where there had been nothing a moment before, a huge throne had appeared, complete with a hundred or so steps leading up to it and an accompanying bank of greenish fog. Behind it was a banner of sufficiently tacky red and yellow colors, boasting a cascade of crests and scrolls and icons, all proclaiming how great the person seated on the throne really must be.

When the last of the mist cleared, indeed a figure was sitting on the jewel-encrusted chair.

He barely looked human. A long snout face, very beady eyes, pencil-thin mustache, heavily greased goatee. He was pale, with very feminine hands and long fingernails. He was wearing a silver lamé robe and womanly sandals.

This was Ping the Pontificator.

He looked down at them with the appropriate disdain, but seemed bored and far away at the same time.

Very weird, Hunter thought. *And very familiar . . .*

Ping weakly clapped his hands twice. A new troop of tin soldiers waddled in. Annie was being led behind them. Though she'd only been out of Hunter's sight for a few minutes, she'd undergone yet another wardrobe change. She was now wearing a very low cut, see-through gown, white high heel boots—and nothing else. Hunter got a rush seeing her like this. She was both gorgeous and sexy.

She also appeared to be hypnotized. Eyes wide and un-blinking. Blank stare on her face. So stiff, she was having trouble walking. At this rate, the same would be soon true for Hunter.

Annie was led to the bottom step of the throne and left there. A light from behind showed all her natural beauty. Hunter was getting very distracted. At least Zoloff's eyes were elsewhere. He was glowering up at Ping, his archen-emy in the endless chapters of this place.

"You have my daughter and her betrothed!" Zoloff thundered up at Ping. But the man on the throne simply waved away his protestations.

"It's your constant meddling that is the cause of all this!" Ping thundered right back at him. "Your noodlings and your science! Once I've eliminated you and your kind, then can I rise to my proper glory!"

Even the tin soldiers seemed to be rolling their eyes at the bad dialogue. Hunter was hardly paying attention though; he still could not drag his attention from Annie. Even in a near-comatose state, she looked very desirable.

Finally he broke out of his own spell and contemplated the situation at hand. He had to rescue not just Annie now but her fiancé as well. But how?

"Is Ping not a man of honor?" Hunter suddenly heard himself bellow.

Everything else happening in the throne room came to a crashing halt. Hunter could still hear his words echoing off the high ceiling.

Ping turned his attention away from Zoloff and leveled his gaze on Hunter.

"It is honor which is in such short supply these days," he said to Hunter in a very singsong voice. "What would a friend of Zoloff know of honor?"

"Enough to know that an honorable man would allow another to fight for the woman he loves!" Hunter yelled back at him, surprised at the mossy words he was tossing out.

Ping sneered at him but then pulled on his tiny goatee in an approximation of deep thought.

"This woman is the one you love?" he asked Hunter, pointing down at Annie.

"She is!" was his dramatic reply.

"And a contest of strength for her freedom—this is what you propose?"

"It is . . ."

Ping thought a few more moments, then lifted his hand and gave a kind of royal wave. "Let it be," he said.

A curtain off to the left opened, and no surprise, there was a small arena located here. A large cage covered it. The bars looked as flimsy as the tin men's armor. Inside was a monstrous figure, at least fifteen feet tall, arms already flailing, roaring loudly, its entire body covered with hair.

Hunter took one look at it and murmured, "What the fuck is this?"

It was too big to be a man, so, he surmised, it must be a robot, one covered in fake hair.

He'd just assumed he'd have to battle it out with some of Ping's tinny guards; he could fight them all day, if they came at him one at a time. This thing, though, might be a bit more difficult.

He was led to the cage by a clutch of soldiers. With little ceremony they opened the gate and threw Hunter in. Zoloff was screaming at him not to do it. He was so animated more tin men had to hold him back. Ping, however, was smiling fang to fang. Annie remained immobile.

Hunter turned to face his opponent. It looked even bigger up close. His first thought, that this might be a mechanical man of sorts, was dashed as soon as he was in the arena. Robots made noise, even in a crazy place like this. Whirring, motor-driven. Robotic. He could detect no sounds like this from the monster. Instead, he heard a lot of heavy breathing, along with a fair amount of grunting and whispering.

Hunter rolled his eyes, walked up to the creature, and just stood there. The creature looked down at him, smoke coming out of its nostrils on cue. He heard a roar—no, two roars, one right after the other—and it was apparent that neither originated from the monster's mouth.

Hunter held up his fists like an ancient boxer, ready to fight. More smoke. Most out-of-sync roars. Hunter believed now he knew what was going on here.

He was deciding exactly where the best place to hit the beast might be, when the beast hit first. Its right arm swung around with such speed and force, it sent Hunter reeling through the air before crashing him to the hard stone floor below.

The crowd in the throne room gasped, then cheered. Zoloff cried out, "Stop this madness! We are men of peace!"

But no one was paying attention to him. Ping meanwhile never lost his detached grin. Annie was still a statue.

Hunter slowly got to his feet. He boldly walked up to

the beast again. The snorting and smoke-blowing was drowned out by the sounds of an angry, whispered, unseen argument going on between two people. The monster had hit him with a lucky shot, but Hunter knew at that moment that the creature had blown its load.

He taunted it to hit him again, pointing to his chin and dancing around a bit. Once more there was a wild swing, but this time Hunter was able to limbo himself out of its path with seconds to spare. More smoke, more snorting, and even more heated unseen arguing.

Hunter stuck his chin out even farther, once again daring the thing to hit him. There was yet another swing, another nimble move by Hunter to avoid it, but this time as the arm went by, Hunter grabbed onto it and yanked it back toward him. Two near identical yelps could be heard, followed by some deep groaning.

Those in the throne room just gasped now. They'd feared the monster since . . . well, since their existence here had begun. No one had ever really hurt it before. Even Ping looked concerned.

The thing swung again, and Hunter repeated his earlier action. He ducked as the punch went by, and then grabbed onto the arm and yanked it back toward him before once again letting go.

This time the pair of screams coming from the beast could be heard by everyone in the throne room. Hunter almost laughed; it was funny. But he was getting tired of this game. The next time the thing took a swing, he grabbed onto its arm, and this time he held on.

The beast began flailing wildly again, trying to get him off, but Hunter hung on tight. He cracked the arm near the elbow, then threw himself at the beast's chest. He heard two successive thuds, and then two short cries of pain.

Time for the revealing act, he thought. He climbed up onto the beast's shoulders even as the thing tried to reach up to grab him, a distinct impossibility. Hunter threw two roundhouse rights into the beast's mug. This stunned the creature long enough for Hunter to reach around the back of its neck, where his hands found just what he knew would be there: a zipper.

He gave it a yank; he heard it start to unclasp. He gave it another pull, and that's when he heard it rip. He jumped over the head of the beast and, still clutching the top of the opened zipper, dove for the floor, taking the creature's hairy overgarment with him.

A louder gasp went up from the royal court. Even Zoloff let out a cry. The hairy overcoat was just that—a prop to make the creature look more menacing and to hide its secret. With this outer garment torn away, what lay beneath was revealed for all to see. This was not some space being or something from one of the really low-rent dimensions. Instead, it was two short royal guards, one with his feet on the other's shoulders, each with a different hand control to operate.

They were still arguing as their two-man contraption fell to the hard floor. The confusion was hilarious.

Hunter just shook his head as the two men scurried away, still arguing with one another. Then he turned back toward those in the court and performed a dramatic bow.

That's when the trapdoor beneath his feet opened up . . .

It seemed like he fell for ages.

He was in a tube, sliding, round and round, pitch black,

the sound of running water filling his ears. Just when he thought he couldn't get any more dizzy, the tube ended, and he was deposited into huge tank of inky black water.

He went all the way to the bottom but was able to quickly push himself back up to the top. No sooner had he surfaced when Dr. Zoloff came flying out of the tube, landing right on Hunter's head and carrying him back to the bottom again.

There was a moment of disentangling themselves and then they both made their way back up for air. Hunter swam over to a point under the tube, hoping against hope that maybe Ping's men would throw Annie—*beautiful* Annie—down as well. Even at this uncertain moment, Hunter found his thoughts flash to an image of her in that see-through gown, soaking wet. He shook off a chill that had nothing to do with the temperature of the water. He hoped Zoloff couldn't read minds.

"They will not send her down here with us," the doctor told Hunter, who nearly snapped his fingers in disappointment. "They will bring her instead to see her true love—before he is executed. That was Ping's dastardly plan all along!"

Hunter had to take his word for it. "That will just make it easier for us to rescue them both!" he yelled back to Zoloff boldly. "We've just got to get out of here first . . ."

At that moment they heard a huge splash on the other side of the thirty-foot tank. Then came another, and another.

What the hell could this be? Hunter wondered. He got his answer a moment later, delivered with a painful punch to his jaw. It was the second such shot he'd taken in the past few minutes.

The haymaker came out of nowhere and knocked him below the surface again. That's when he first saw the guy with the fins on his back.

Even underwater, this guy's uniform looked, well . . . *unmanly*. Tight, green, with fake gills and ridiculous fins, obviously its owner was the cause of one of the splashes they'd just heard. This meant at least three of these aquamen were in here with them.

Hunter stayed down this time, diving deeper and looking for a swirl of legs above. Sure enough, he could see three dark figures heading toward a fourth; the strangely dressed swimmers were converging on Zoloff.

Hunter pushed himself off the bottom of the pool again and, moving swiftly, fists put together, he torpedoed one of the fin men just as he was about to hammer the good doctor. He hit the guy square on the back of the head, and his victim let out a yelp so shrill, Hunter actually heard it underwater. He surfaced an instant later, coming over the top with one fist cocked. One of the swimmers had Zoloff by the throat. Hunter clocked this guy on the way down. He, too, let out a yelp that would have seemed more appropriate for a young girl and not a big bad fin man.

With his two colleagues quickly out of action, the third swimmer splashed around for a few moments, assessed the situation, then turned tail and started swimming away. Zoloff was furious and began pursuing the man, but Hunter caught him at the last moment.

Hunter said to the doctor, "If we let him go, then he will lead us to the way out."

Zoloff thought a moment and then smiled, a rarity.

"You are more brilliant than my son-in-law-to-be!" he declared.

Then they both dove back below the surface and began swimming after the fleeing fin man.

There was one light in the vast tank. It was located next to a metal door, which Hunter could only surmise led to an air hatch.

He and Zoloff held up a moment and watched the swimmer desperately turn the wheel on this door. It took some effort to open it against the water pressure, but finally it did spring free with a great whoosh of air bubbles.

The swimmer tried his best to delicately swim into the hatchway, but Hunter and Zoloff had other ideas. They hit the man with both barrels just as he was closing the door. The fin man was more stunned than hurt. Hunter pushed him out of the way, finished closing the hatch, and then activated the oxygen valve. The water quickly drained from the chamber, and finally he and Zoloff could breathe again.

It was cramped quarters, and awkward now with Hunter, Zoloff, and the fin man fighting for elbow room. Hunter hauled back and was about to fire a punch at the swimmer, but there was no need. The man fainted dead away even before Hunter threw the punch.

"Bravo!" Zoloff yelled. He studied the man soaking and crumpled in the corner. "Should one of us take his costume off, then put it on, in hopes of fooling any guards we meet along the way?"

Hunter looked at Zoloff, then at the unconscious fin man, then back at Zoloff.

"That won't be necessary," he said.

They stole out into the adjacent corridor. It was lit by torches that smelled of wax and oil. The floor was flat in both directions, giving no indication which way was up or down. So they just stopped and listened. To their right, they heard music. Distant, discordant. And with a lot of bass. This told Hunter it was coming from somewhere above them. To their left, they could hear mechanical noises and groaning. The dungeon had to be that way.

They began running. And running. And running . . . Finally, the hallway started to curve downward. The sound of machinery got louder, the air, cooler.

They came to an intersection of hallways; Hunter skidded to a stop just before the two tunnels met. They both peeked around one corner and saw two prison cells, with six guards out in front of each. *Maybe we should have taken the fin man's costume,* Hunter thought.

He needed a moment to dream up a plan here. How were he and the feisty but elderly doctor going to take on a dozen of the walking trash cans?

Zoloff had no such inclination to wait, though. He stepped out from behind the corner, let out a great scream, and started running headlong down the hallway.

"Damn," Hunter said, springing to his feet and quickly finding himself on the doctor's heels. So much for getting a strategy together.

The soldiers saw them coming now; they had about fifty feet separating them. They aligned themselves at twelve abreast, spears up and ready. The doctor never hesitated. He left his feet ten paces in front of them, and with remarkable agility, laid out half the guards with a perfect running block. They went down again like dominos.

. Those not hit by the initial blow were thrown off their feet by those who were. In seconds, the doctor was wrestling with all twelve of them, at the same time yelling to Hunter, "Don't worry about me . . . I've got them covered. Save the others!"

It sounded crazy, but Zoloff was right. He'd bowled over all of the guards, and they were now engaged in a massive slow-motion wrestling match with him. Hunter body-slammed a couple of the soldiers on the periphery of the action and then turned his attention to the first prison cell.

Annie was within. She was lying straight as a board on a small bunk. Hunter called to her, but she could not hear him. She was obviously still under some kind of hypnotic spell. She wasn't going to be much help in her own rescue.

The cell door was locked. Hunter looked back at the mass of sprawled arms and legs on the floor and knew it would be impossible for him to find which guard had the keys. And while Zoloff was still remarkably holding his own, that might change at any moment. But how could he get into the cell to rescue Annie?

His mind went back to when he first landed in this weird place—how the rocket ship's door nearly came off in his hand. And later when the tin men's spears had gone through the fuselage. And how these so-called soldiers were so easy to defeat—when there wasn't an unlimited supply of them, that is.

That's probably when it finally sank in what this place was all about. It wasn't about armies, or prisoners, or observatories, or castles in the sky. It was about weakling soldiers, damsels in distress, and worlds to be saved. It was Adventure Land! A place custom-made for heroes.

So he looked back at the cell's bars and thought, *What the hell?* He put his hands on them and with all his strength began to pull on them. They parted like rubber.

Hunter was soon inside. Annie was still out of it, eyes

wide open, looking into space. Hunter tried to revive her, but no amount of gentle shaking would do the trick.

He tried to lift her off the bunk, but she was literally stiff, so much so he could never have gotten her through the space he'd created in the bent bars. What's worse, outside he heard indications that the tin men might be turning the tide in the battle against the doctor.

Time was running out. He had to get Annie up and moving. So he did what he thought any hero would do: he kissed her, long and hard on the lips. She woke right away, took one look at him, and jumped off the bed. She was quickly glued to his side once again.

He carried her out of the cell just as a few of the wimpy soldiers were getting their footing back. Holding Annie with one arm, Hunter began punching the recovering soldiers with the other. Between these blows and a revived Zoloff, they were able to knock over the lot of them again.

"Time to go!" Zoloff announced. Annie squeezed Hunter, showing her full agreement.

But Hunter stopped them both in their tracks. "Aren't you forgetting someone?" he asked.

Father looked at daughter, and daughter looked back.

"Your boyfriend," Hunter had to remind them. "I thought he was locked up here, too."

They all turned back toward the second cell. Once again, Hunter quickly parted the pliable bars. Lying on a bed inside, stiff as a board, apparently suffering from the same hypnotic spell was a tall, dark, and handsome man, approximately Hunter's age.

"Please, we must revive him!" Zoloff said, suddenly up to speed again.

Hunter laughed. "Don't look at me."

Annie timidly left his side, walked quickly into the cell, and planted a kiss on the sleeping man that lasted no more than a tenth of a second. The man leaped off the bed, hugged Annie, hugged Zoloff, and shook hands heartily with Hunter.

"Buck Gordon, at your service!" he said with a bow.

Then he took a look at the guards who were recovering yet again—and suddenly bounded from the cell. Hunter, Annie, and Zoloff started off after him.

"Maybe he knows the way out!" Hunter cried.

"Or he's running away," Annie replied. *"Again . . ."*

They ran. And ran. And ran . . .

At points along the way they actually lost sight of Annie's husband-in-waiting. The corridors were murky and winding, with only a few odd torches available to light the way. They were also covered with great swatches of torn, dingy silklike material, held together by long pieces of silver twine, remnants, no doubt, of the palace's former glory. Between the dirty silk's ghostly flowing and the darkness in the hallways, it was impossible to determine if they were running up or down. Every so often they would hear the unmistakable clanking of the tin soldiers in pursuit. But with just a little more effort, those sounds were quickly left behind.

Finally they reached a ramp of sorts that went nearly straight down. At the end of it was a huge door built not into the wall but into the floor. They all skidded to halt in front of it.

"I heard them talk about this door," Buck said. "As a way out, in case anything happened up above."

It seemed a little too pat for Hunter. But then again, what didn't in this crazy place?

He studied the handle on the hatch. It looked old and elaborate and immovable. Yet when Annie simply reached down and gave it a twist, it opened easily.

Everyone stepped back and let Hunter actually pull the door open. As soon as he did, he was hit with a great burst of air. It stunned them all. Hunter instinctively moved the others back. Then he took a look at what was beyond the door. The simple answer was: nothing.

They were looking down through a cloud to the rough terrain of the strange little moon about a half mile below.

"Damn," Hunter breathed. "This place does ride on the clouds!"

At that instant, they heard the unmistakable clanking of the palace soldiers coming toward them.

"We're trapped!" Zoloff cried.

Hunter was still looking down through the hatch at the ground below. This was weird. He'd seen just this type of thing at least once before.

"They'll kill us all this time!" Annie cried. But Hunter didn't think so. He figured it was about 2,000 feet to the ground, maybe less. And what was the most heroic thing he could do at the moment?

"Get some of that stuff off the wall!" he yelled to the others. "Some of those cords, too!"

Hunter wasn't really sure how to make a parachute. But how hard could it be? Lots of fabric, lots of cord to serve as the control lines, lots of time before the plodding soldiers finally tracked them down.

They all worked quickly, gathering the silk and attaching the cords. They soon had two huge things that looked like parachutes, sort of.

That's when they heard the soldiers at the top of the

ramp. The clanking was at first loud but quickly became almost deafening. There were hundreds of the metal men coming at them now. Hunter didn't hesitate. He put Zoloff and Buck together under one chute and with little ceremony, pushed them through the opening.

Then he grabbed Annie and stepped into the abyss himself.

The two parachutes worked like a charm, of course. They rode the gentle air currents, expertly spiraling to the ground below. Zoloff and Buck came down in a bit of a heap; luckily, a soft meadow was their landing pad. Hunter and Annie came in standing up. As soon as their feet hit the ground, the silk chute fell down around them, covering them. Annie took the opportunity to plant a passionate, tongue-lashing kiss on Hunter that ended only when the chute finally passed over them and blew away.

Hunter tried to stay cool, but it was not an easy thing to do with such a gorgeous girl in his arms. He looked back up at the aerial palace. Never did he think he'd find a floating city here. They moved down the meadow to a grove of trees. It gave them both cover and shade. They sat down and got their heads together.

The adventure now seemed complete. Buck was rescued, and Annie was safe. Hunter thought it was time to get to the business of his being here. He pulled Zoloff aside and explained how he'd learned about this place and how it was important that he complete his mission. Zoloff could only shake his head though. Such things still did not compute. Hunter retrieved the Mad Russian's image again and once more asked Zoloff if he had ever seen or heard of the man.

Try as he might, the good doctor just could not reply.

The disappointment must have shown on Hunter's face, because Zoloff asked him, "Your visit here has not been a success then?"

Hunter looked over at Annie, who was reluctantly gravitating toward Buck.

Hunter just sighed. "It wasn't a total failure," he said. "I guess . . ."

Zoloff did know where the ticket booth was, though, the place Hunter had to go to get on the next ride. Lucky for him, it was just over the next hill. Hunter shook hands with Buck and Zoloff, then he turned to Annie. Of the entire adventure, she looked the most beautiful at that moment. He gave her a very platonic hug. Still she managed to slip a note in his pocket and give him a peck on his cheek in return.

Then he bid them good-bye. They went one way, and he went the other. It was only after he was sure he was out of sight that he reached into his pocket and took out Annie's note.

It read, "Next time, take me with you."

Chapter 4

Hunter found the ticket booth just where Zoloff said it would be: over the hill and atop a small rise not a half mile away.

He had trudged up the side of the rise to find a lush valley on the other side. It seemed very inviting. Green grass, swaying trees, sparkling rivers flowing through it. On a whim, he blinked his eyes, but the valley was still there when he opened them again.

At the top of the rise he found a small hut, just big enough for him to fit inside. It was built with the same fake wood. It had the same noisy planks. Above the door was a hand-painted sign in Russian: *Dobro pozalovat v Dom Uzasov. Tvoiy strashnii prazdnik cranet pravdoi. Otkroi— esli osmelishsya!* According to the quadtrol, it read: Welcome to the House of Horrors, Where Your Worst Fears Come True. Enter Only If You Dare.

"Sounds promising," Hunter whispered to himself.

Inside the hut he found the same kind of ancient personal computer. He went through the ritual of turning on the PC and getting it to accept his English-language password. A prompt told him to insert his ticket. He did as instructed, the ticket quickly returning to him with a second hole punched in it. The picture on the back was even more faded now. But if anything, the Russian looked even more insane.

He made his way through the security walls, filling in the final fields just as he had done the first time, by typing in his name and stating his hobby was flying.

But before he pushed the Enter button, he turned and looked back into the valley from which he'd just come. This strange place. A moon that was not really a moon, orbiting an enormous planet that really wasn't there. He'd been warned to expect weird things down here, but some things he encountered weren't exactly that weird.

True, this particular moon was a place custom-made for heroes. A world of altered reality, activated, he guessed, after hundreds of years of lying dormant. But there were some startlingly familiar images here as well. A city that floated on clouds. Armies that marched endlessly in its streets. An emperor who in the end didn't have a clue. It was practically a blueprint for the current Fourth Empire, if written by a child.

Was there a connection? Or was it just a coincidence?

Hunter didn't know, and at the moment, he didn't have the time to even think about it. He had to get going.

He returned to the computer and paused for just one more moment. Reaching inside his pocket, he took out Annie's note and read it again.

Maybe next time, he *would* take her with him, he thought. Then he pushed the Enter button.

It was snowing.

Blowing, freezing, with heavy sleet, rain, ice. All in the dead of night.

Hunter was suddenly frozen to the bone. His flight suit soaked through. Icicles hanging from his nose.

Someone ran up to him, appearing like magic out of the blizzard. Hunter could hardly see their face.

"Can you fly this thing?" this person was screaming at him.

Hunter was suddenly aware of more people rushing around him. They all seemed confused, anxious, panicky. He realized he was on an airfield. There were flying machines everywhere he looked. Not rocket ships, or Starcrashers, or spacecraft of any kind. These were airplanes. With jet engines, propellers. Run by aviation fuel and dependent on the movement of air around them to fly. Hunter knew all this because in his former life—or make that in *one* of his former lives—he'd flown vehicles like this. He was a fighter pilot back then. One of the best, maybe the best ever.

They used to call him the Wingman.

Of that, at least, he was sure.

But that was then, and this was now—and he'd been suddenly thrust into this incredibly realistic horror ride. And he was standing on a taxiway, in the frozen wind, watching many of these airplanes scrambling to get into the air. And this person was in his face. He was just a kid, and he was wearing a cold-weather parka that said United States Air Force on it. Sergeant stripes ran down his arm.

"Can you?" he was screaming at Hunter.

"Can I what?" he finally screamed back.

"Fly this!" the kid yelled. He stepped to the side to reveal an aircraft directly in back of him. It was almost lost in the snow, but Hunter didn't have to see it to know what it was. He could *feel* its presence.

It was an F-16 jet fighter.

Some called it the Fighting Falcon. Others, the Viper. Take your pick. By whatever name, it was a kick-ass jet engine with an airplane built around it. It was small, light, could carry a shitload of bombs and missiles and still dogfight with a full rack. Yes, even blindfolded, Hunter would have known what it was. Way back when, a few lifetimes ago, he used to drive one of these babies.

The confusion around him increased threefold in just a matter of seconds. He turned back to the teenage sergeant.

"Yes, I can fly it," he told him. "I can fly the hell out of it!"

"Then, if I might be so bold, sir, I suggest that you strap in and get your ass going!"

"Going? Going where? What's happened?"

The kid seemed furious and on the verge of tears at the same time.

"The Soviets just wiped out half of Europe!" he yelled at Hunter through the torrent. "They launched thousands of Scud missiles with poison gas warheads—on fucking Christmas Eve! Now we've got to stop them before they wipe out the rest of it!"

With that, he ran off into the snow.

Hunter looked down at his hands and realized for the

first time he was holding his crash helmet in one and a map case in the other. A huge airplane crossed in back of him. He recognized it immediately. It was a KC-135 in-flight refueling plane, a flying gas station that other planes could draw precious fuel from, while still in flight. It took off in a great explosion of exhaust and dirty-water spray. Right behind it was another one. Behind that, another one. To his right, on another slippery runway, two F-16s took off in tandem. Behind them, two more. Back on the main runway, a line of big planes with propellers and gun muzzles sticking out of their sides were waiting for their turn to take off. *Gunships,* Hunter thought.

He turned back to see two ground crew members standing beside the lone F-16, frantically beckoning to him. Hunter started running, putting on his crash helmet as he did so. He had to get going! Bounding up the access ladder, he literally jumped into the cockpit. The two drenched airmen strapped him in. He fired up the fighter's engine and felt a jolt of electricity surge through him. His entire body began vibrating. His hands automatically went to the side stick controller and the throttle. His feet to the control pedals.

And suddenly he didn't seem so insane anymore. He blinked—and when his eyes opened, everything was still there. The plane. The snow. The two airmen. No flash. Nothing.

Completing their task, one of the airmen smacked him twice on the top of his helmet and then disappeared down the ladder. The bubble top canopy came down with a thump. Hunter looked at his control panel and saw nothing but green lights. He knew this meant the plane was ready to fly.

Someone was trying to talk to him through the radio headphone in his helmet, but Hunter wasn't in the mood for conversation. He had places to go, things to do.

He looked over his shoulder and saw that the airstrip to his left was unoccupied. He gunned his engine, steered onto the hard tarmac, and a moment later went screaming down the runway.

This was *very* strange. Hunter really did feel like he was part of this machine. His hands seemed to be melded to its controls, his brain to its flight computer. He didn't even have to think about doing what he was doing. The F-16 was essentially the same flying machine he'd built back on Fools 6—from memory. If he didn't know how to drive this one, then he didn't deserve to draw another breath.

A flick of the stick, a push of the throttle, and he was airborne. The electricity rippling through his body turned into a lightning bolt. He hadn't felt this way in a very long time.

The airplane threw itself into the air. Hunter booted full throttle, which engaged the plane's afterburner and shot him forward with bone-crushing acceleration. He pushed back on the tail and was immediately going nearly straight up. In ten seconds he was already a mile high.

At thirty seconds he was passing through 25,000 feet. Only then did he level off and take a breath.

His ship's clock told him it was 0430 hours. There was nothing but darkness all around. He clicked on his cockpit light, unlatched his map case, and found a folder within marked Operations and Orders. He tore open this envelope; inside was a single piece of yellow paper. These were his orders. He was to connect with the large aerial convoy that had just left the airfield. He was to ride escort for it to Rota, Spain, and from there "engage in combat operations against any Soviet units found on continental Europe at the discretion of the local commander."

World War Three . . .

The words suddenly popped into his head. Though he arrived in the seventy-third century suffering from near total amnesia, some of Hunter's memories had returned to him in bits and pieces, some coming hard, but others very easily. First and foremost, he knew he was an American. He knew he was a soldier, a pilot. Some kind of national hero. But he also knew that he'd fought in a great war as a young man, several lifetimes ago.

That conflict was called World War Three. And for some reason, here he was, fighting it again.

He headed east, out over the water, streaking above the snow clouds, the storm in full retreat behind him. A bare hint of the sunrise came off his airplane's nose. The sky above was clear, filled with chilly stars. His first job was to catch up with the hundreds of airplanes belonging to the massive convoy that had taken off before him. He figured he was about five minutes behind them at the most.

His orders gave two radio frequencies, both UHF, that the convoy of refueling tankers, jet fighters, and AC-130 gunships would be using during the long flight across the Atlantic. Getting a communication link going was essential if everyone wanted to make it to Spain in one piece. He punched the first frequency into his radio set, adjusted the volume, but heard nothing. He tried the second frequency, but again could find no chatter between the dozens of airplanes.

This was strange.

While he was sure that the air convoy would be flying under the cloak of radio silence for the majority of the 2,000-plus mile flight, with this many planes in the air, there were always a few last-minute radio calls back and forth. From air traffic control to the departing airplanes. From one plane to another. Or, at the very least, one last weather report. But all Hunter could hear in his helmet headphones was static.

He pushed his throttle ahead. The engine roared in response. He scanned the skies ahead of him. The planes in the air convoy would be flying without their navigation lights, but the sky was quickly getting bright, and he was surprised that he couldn't see at least a few silhouettes of the last few planes to take off. But even though he had tremendous eyesight, the sky in front of him held nothing but scattered clouds and fading stars.

Very strange . . .

He went up to 30,000 feet, a mile above the convoy's assigned altitude. Sometimes it was easier to find something in the air if you were looking down on it. Hunter scanned the huge expanse of sky before him again, still he could not yet see the tail end of the convoy. He read his orders again. They included his heading, altitude, and so on. He compared the numbers on the yellow sheet with what his navigation computer was telling him. Everything checked out. He was where he was supposed to be, at the right speed, going in the right direction. Yet from what he could see, he was the only one in this very big, empty sky.

He tried the radio again. Nothing on the first frequency.

Static on the second. He turned the UHF tuning knob through the entire range of frequencies the radio was able to receive. He heard nothing on any of them.

He checked his flying orders again, double checked them, then triple checked them. He was heading in the same direction as the hundred or so planes in the air convoy; they'd all received the same orders. The sky should at the very least have been filled with contrails, so many planes were supposed to be up here, but for as far as his eyes could see, his was the only aircraft.

This was getting very weird. He booted his throttles, and in an instant, doubled his speed. He felt a double sonic boom as he broke the sound barrier and was soon driving the F-16 at 1,000 mph-plus. He held this speed for exactly thirty seconds, which by his calculations, would have put him right where the air convoy's location should be.

But all this did was use up his extra fuel. The sky around him remained empty.

He was just about to consider turning around and returning to the base when his radio suddenly came alive with voices. It was immediately horrible. Screams of panic and fear were pouring out of his headphones. He could hear the sound of explosions, too, and of jet engines failing, airplanes going down, people dying.

It was obviously the convoy, and obviously it was in big trouble. The entire concept of radio silence was out the window as Hunter could hear dozens of voices in the cacophony. They were screaming altitudes and positions of other aircraft. He had no doubt what was happening: the convoy was under attack.

But where were they?

If nightmares are a conglomeration of a person's most acute fears, then Hunter was suddenly living a nightmare. The most helpless feeling any soldier can have is to hear his comrades dying and know there is nothing he can do about it. That's what was happening to Hunter now. He flew on and on, desperately looking for the convoy, but he still could not see them. He flew for another ten minutes, twenty, then thirty. He flew for more than an hour, and not once did the cries go away. If anything, they grew in intensity and desperation.

It was only when he met the sun that the voices began to fade away. They went out not with a bang but with a whimper. One last pilot, helpless as someone was shooting him down, leaving a message for his wife and kids that was cut off in midsentence. His voice was replaced by static, and then nothing at all.

Hunter found the convoy a few minutes later. It was scattered across the next ten square miles of ocean. Every plane reduced to debris floating on what looked like a sea of red aviation fuel. Or was that blood?

There was no piece of wreckage bigger than a few feet across. The planes in the air convoy had been the victims of an ambush. Hundreds had been killed. But how?

Hunter had his answer a few moments later. Sitting about five miles east of the vast sea of debris was a warship. A very big one.

An aircraft carrier . . .

Hunter didn't even think about it. He armed his weapons, specifically his four antiradiation HARM missiles. He knew they had a warhead powerful enough to blow apart a radar station. He was sure they could do a job on the skin of a boat.

He was furious. Scores of his countrymen were dead, and the people on this ship did it, of that he was sure. He went into a power dive, dropping four miles in a matter of seconds. The ship was now just a few thousand feet in front of him. The sun dawning on the horizon provided him with a perfect silhouette of the target. He went so low he was certain he would not show up on any of the ship's radar screens. He checked his weapons again. They were ready to go.

The ship was dead in his sights now, this as he lowered himself to just twenty feet off the surface of the rough Atlantic. He was intent on putting at least one of the guided bombs into the ship's midsection where he was sure the fuel compartment and the magazines lay. There was a chance he might even crack the hull in two.

He spotted the ship's mast. It was flying only one flag. Big and red with a yellow sickle and hammer on it. Even over thousands of years and several lifetimes, he remembered this flag, too. It was the banner of Soviet Russia, the people who'd just wiped out half of Europe and had killed many American pilots and airmen just minutes ago.

Mad Russian or not, it was now time for some payback.

It struck him suddenly as strange that this aircraft carrier would be out here all alone, with no escorting ships, not even any of its jump jets patrolling its airspace. No matter; that just made his job easier.

He fired the first HARM at about 500 feet out. It shot ahead of his airplane, leaving a long trail of yellow smoke in its wake. Just before it impacted, he let loose a second missile. Both were designed to home in on the signals produced by radar, and the big Soviet carrier was literally crackling with these waves. Again, he knew one HARM missile impacting on the right spot could do serious damage to the ship. If two hit on the money, he could set this murderous boat on fire. If three and four hit good, he might even send it to the bottom and revenge the American souls just lost.

The first missile hit the hull of the ship just where he'd wanted it, directly below the superstructure, about fifteen feet above the waterline. He instinctively knew that something either combustible or explosive was located there. But as he was pulling up over the ship, he saw his missile not bursting through the carrier's hull as he intended, but instead bouncing off of it.

The missile exploded harmlessly in the water. It didn't even chip a piece of paint off the ship's skin. The second missile arrived just a second later, to the same effect. A hit, a bounce off, an explosion, and absolutely no damage.

Everything went into slow motion after that. Not only did Hunter see the two missiles fail, he could see hundreds of Soviet sailors lining the huge flight deck and the catwalks ringing the superstructure. They were pointing and laughing at him as he roared over. He couldn't believe it!

He turned the F-16 sharply and found himself approaching the huge ship at the same low altitude, but now from the opposite direction. Either way, a missile hit here or there would have the same effect. He let both HARMs go, again in tandem, and watched their yellow trails head for the side of the carrier. From this angle with the sun at his back, Hunter saw the ship in a brighter light, and he was amazed how gleaming and special it looked. He couldn't have imagined a ship like this. It seemed to be made of the brightest chrome and shiniest steel. It was spotless, glowing, sparkling in the rising sun.

At the same time, he was beginning to notice that the inside of his jet was actually quite old and run down. His seat was threadbare. The canopy was scratched. Some panel lights were not working. He looked back up at the ship. He saw even more sailors now, massing on the deck, pointing and laughing at him.

The two missiles hit, and the same thing happened . . . which was nothing at all. They bounced off and exploded in the water, doing absolutely no damage to the ship. All this was to the great delight of the sailors on the deck. Hunter pulled up and away again, feeling like he'd done no more than provide a few moments of entertainment for these people who had just killed hundreds of his countrymen.

This only enraged him further. He turned the F-16 over a little too sharply, causing him to collide violently with the right side of his cockpit. He nearly lost control of the plane, regaining flight only through a quick boost of the throttle and a sharp turn to the left. This put him in a position just behind the ship, pointing toward its stern. He opened up with his nose cannon and watched the stream of shells rush toward the vulnerable ass end of the ship. There were sailors on the rail here, too. They weren't making any effort to shoot at him. Instead, they were waving at him, jeering at him, shaking their fists, and even giving him the finger. Making him look foolish.

And the cannon shells?

They bounced off, too.

He arrived over Rota two hours after daybreak.

According to his orders, he was to link up with American warplanes already on the ground at the Spanish NATO base, and then join in a systematic aerial assault on the advancing Soviet forces.

The background section of the orders stated that the Soviet army would take at least forty-eight hours before moving into those areas of Europe they'd poisoned with their Scud attack.

The main thrust of this assault would come, it was believed, through the center of West Germany, with Soviet forces moving in from Poland, Hungary, and, of course, East Germany. There were many bridges along this 300-mile section of the autobahns. By taking out a few of these key bridges and then hitting the Soviet columns in the rear areas, a large air armada, such as what was supposed to be waiting here in Spain, could deal a crushing blow to the invaders, perhaps delaying them long enough for the bulk of U.S. forces to get to the war zone.

But there was a problem. While Hunter could indeed see dozens if not hundreds of warplanes on the ground below him, he could see no activity going on around them. Instead it looked like they were simply left standing where they'd stopped rolling after landing. Many were gathered in haphazard fashion at the end of the main runway. Others looked simply abandoned. Even the clarity of the air around the base told him that nothing had taken off or landed here in hours, perhaps even days.

The final clue: although Hunter was calling the control tower asking for landing clearance, no one was responding. Finally, he just landed on his own, having to reduce his airspeed to the bare minimum so he would use less runway and not wind up colliding with the gaggle of airplanes at the end of the landing strip. It was a close run thing though, as he had to zigzag down the strip, trying to dodge the tails of some planes that had become stuck in the side ditches. He finally slowed down enough to pop his scratched canopy and taxi by the haphazard parking lot of warplanes located at the end of the runway.

He was horrified by what he saw. Some of the planes still had pilots strapped into them. Slumped over their controls, they were all dead, killed by poison gas. And at that moment, Hunter was glad that he hadn't taken off his oxygen mask. He quickly closed the canopy again and kept on taxiing.

He moved to the end of the airplane ramps, past the hangars, the admin buildings, and the living quarters. He taxied right out of the air base itself, steering the F-16 on to the base access highway and rolling for a half mile or so before he finally stopped. He paused a moment, then popped the canopy again.

He was guessing that the air base had been hit by soft gas, a type that dissipated quickly. He was certain the Soviets would want to occupy any allied military bases for their own use eventually and therefore would have been unlikely to lob some hard gas at the place, as it could make the area inaccessible for months. So while the interior of the base was still probably too hot to spend any time in, one deep breath told him the outlying areas were clean.

It was very strange to be driving a fighter jet down the highway as if it were a land vehicle, but that's what he did for about another mile. He eventually reached an off-base housing complex. To his surprise, he found five more jets here: three F-15s, and a pair of A-10s. They were parked in a blacktop lot outside one of the larger buildings.

He knew there was only one reason these planes were

here. Their pilots had landed at the base, and just like Hunter, had determined the situation enough to know that they were best in a closed environment—their aircraft—and wise to put a mile or so between them and the base.

Hunter pulled his F-16 into the parking lot as well. He popped the canopy, shut everything down, and jumped to the ground. He walked into the main building. Here he found the five pilots, huddled in the corner of the lobby, helmets still on, masks attached, sucking on portable oxygen tanks.

"Who's in charge here?" Hunter asked them sternly.

One man took his mask off long enough to say: "You are . . . until you drop dead from the gas."

Hunter took a quick scan of the men's uniforms. Three were lieutenants, two were captains. He, meanwhile, was wearing the uniform of a major. He was the senior man.

"Take those masks off," he told them. "You don't need them. The gas didn't spread this far."

"How the fuck do you know?" one pilot cursed right through his mask.

"Because if it was hard gas, we'd all be dead by now," Hunter shot back at them.

They mulled this over for a few moments, and then gingerly, each man lowered his mask and took a tentative breath.

"Hey, how about that?" one said. "The dude is right. . . ."

Hunter was instantly furious. "Get up off your asses," he roared at them. "That's an order."

The five men reluctantly got to their feet. Hunter looked about the first floor of the building. It was typical off-base housing, more like a college dorm than anything else. It was also clear that whoever lived here had cleared out quickly. Scattered belongings, from clothes to record albums, littered the floor and the stairs leading to the upper rooms. He also detected the scent of liquor in the heavy air.

The men formed a ragged line in front of him, and Hunter proceeded to read them the riot act. He couldn't remember exactly what he said, losing each angry word the instant it came off his tongue. But he reviewed for them the tough situation the U.S. was suddenly facing, the need for America to counterattack, and the need for every able-bodied soldier to pitch in. The men just stared blankly back at him.

He then told them what he'd experienced coming over the Atlantic, and how his orders stated that an aerial assault on the advancing Soviets was critical before the situation got further out of hand.

"We have to fuel up, bomb up, get our asses up over West Germany," Hunter told them. "If we can stop them there, we've got a chance to—"

The five men all burst out laughing at him. Hunter was so mad, he couldn't speak.

"Major," one of the captains finally said. "You're a little behind on this thing. "There *is* no more West Germany. The Soviets took it over last night. The last we heard, they were marching on Paris."

Hunter was stunned to hear this news. But he instantly formulated a new plan. If indeed the Soviets were already as far as France, that meant their lines of communication were stretched even thinner than before. It also meant more targets for American aircraft, more bridges to bomb, more supply columns to attack.

"The farther these guys move west, the more they'll be strung out," Hunter said now. "If we can hit them somewhere in the middle at a choke point, we can have a very big effect. Plus their soldiers are weighed down by all that chem gear. They must be dragging ass for at least a hundred miles by now."

But the pilots just laughed at him again.

"Who the fuck made you the hero?" one asked. "We just want to get the hell back home."

Another pilot spoke up: "I've got a wife and three kids. I want to see them one more time before the world comes to an end."

A third said, "Why should we die trying to save a bunch of assholes in France?"

Hunter was momentarily stumped for a reply. Finally he shot back with the only response he could think of.

"You're going to go," he said. "Because I'm giving you a direct order to go."

They found a large fuel truck on the edge of the base that was filled with JP-8.

Testing his theory that soft gas had been used against the base at Rota, Hunter drove the truck back to where the jets were parked without the aid of oxygen. The pilots reluctantly worked together to fuel their aircraft. While this was going on, Hunter returned to the periphery of the base and canvassed it for ordnance. There was plenty to be found on the outlying edges. Mostly 2,000-pound blockbusters, but also antipersonnel weapons and even some high-explosive bombs.

This time he wore his oxygen mask not for the gas but because there were hundreds of bodies lying about. The air was getting fetid. He loaded up an ordnance truck by himself, using a portable hangar crane to do the heavy lifting. By the time he returned to the others, they had fueled up their aircraft.

Loading the bombs was long and sweaty, and a major pain in the ass. They were pilots, not ground crew guys, so it was trial and error at first. After a few hairy moments, they'd finally bombed up the A-10s. They would carry the heaviest loads.

The F-15s came next. They, too, could carry an awesome amount of munitions, plus they were easier to work than the A-10s. Lastly, Hunter's F-16 was given two 2,000-pound bombs, plus an additional 5,000 pounds of antipersonnel munitions.

By the time they were through, night was falling. Hunter ordered the pilots to get some sleep, which they did right on the first floor of the off-base housing building. Hunter, however, stayed awake all night planning the route they would take tomorrow.

The flight up from Spain to the Franco-German border would burn more than half their fuel, this due to the overloads of bombs they would be carrying and the route they had to take. No matter which way Hunter spun the numbers, there just would not be enough gas for them to return to Rota. That was OK, though. Why would they want to come back here?

But where was their alternative base? If the latest news reports were accurate, most of Western Europe was flooded with deadly gas. Hard or soft, that meant many, many rotting corpses or lots of territory under control of the Soviets.

So there was no way Hunter could find a safe place for them to set down once they'd unloaded the munitions.

Unless some sort of miracle came along then, this was going to be a one-way mission.

Dawn arrived.

The sky was bloodred, always a sign of bad things to come. Hunter woke the five reluctant pilots and lied to them. He told them that he'd identified an air base still in friendly hands just outside Paris. They could fly their missions, land at this base, possibly load up again, and go up again. The five pilots greeted the news with only mild grumbling. They did one last check of their airplanes, and then it was time to go.

By design, the highways leading into the base at Rota were long and straight and wide. Their size allowed them to be used as emergency runways. The six airplanes lined up on the highway heading north. They took off, one by one. Hunter was the last to get airborne.

Per his orders, the three F-15s took the lead, forming a loose chevron about 1,000 feet in front of Hunter. The two bomb-heavy A-10s took up positions in between.

They flew in silence. Hunter's flight plan took them out over Spain to the French Alps. It was a slightly roundabout route, and would use up precious fuel, but there was a method to Hunter's madness. The small strike force had one main enemy: radar. If they were picked up too soon, no doubt the Soviets would send masses of aircraft after them. While the F-15s and Hunter's plane could dogfight with ordnance attached, the A-10s were not aerial combat weapons. They would be sitting ducks.

Hunter knew they could not avoid being picked up on radar forever; the idea was to delay detection as long as possible. Thus the strange flight plan. The Soviets would have many air defense radars attached to the columns advancing into Western Europe. These radars would be activated to protect the nose of their columns, but would they be watching the flanks? Possibly not. Not if the Soviets were trying to make as much headway as possible.

That's why they were taking the long way around. They would hit these guys where they weren't looking.

It was strange because at first the terrain below them appeared fine. Small villages, red roofs, winding roadways, gradually filling with snow. The French Alps seemed positively idyllic, the new sun glistening off the snow.

But everything changed once they got over the mountains. Below them now was complete devastation. Cities, villages, dams, power stations, military bases—all of them utterly destroyed. The horror seemed to get worse every mile they flew north.

About ten minutes into this, the other pilots broke radio silence. They started freaking out. They wanted to turn back. They wanted to give up.

Hunter's blood pressure went through his eyeballs. His first instinct was to tear each one of these guys a new one. But he stopped himself, keyed his microphone, and calmly but firmly ordered the five of them to press on—and to stop talking on the radio.

But Hunter knew what he was seeing below didn't make any sense. Poison gas killed people, but it did not cause widespread destruction.

Why then the devastation below?

They went over a number of French cities, all of which had been leveled. Their rivers seemed to be running black with debris, their streets rainbow-colored by gasoline.

Then off in the distance, Hunter could see storm clouds. They stretched across the entire northern horizon. This was strange. The weather all around them was ironically pleasant and fair. No cloud banks. And certainly no atmospherics that would lead to any major storms. So what was this out on the horizon?

Hunter ordered the five pilots to stay their course, then he zoomed up to the ear-bleeding altitude of 50,000 feet. From here, using his amazing eyesight, he could see the source of the tremendous commotion. This was no storm. Not a typical one, anyway. It was the Red onslaught. No less than ten Soviet armies on the march, pouring out of the lowlands of southern Germany like a long river of blood. Tanks, trucks, APCs, mobile rocket launchers, millions of Soviet soldiers, swallowing up the territory in a massive and ravenous fashion. Hunter felt his stomach do a flip.

This was getting serious now.

It was not the smart thing to do, but Hunter booted in his afterburner and went down to almost ground level. Soon he was zooming right above the advance columns of the Soviet juggernaut. He seemed to be moving in slow motion again. The scene below him was indeed like a nightmare. Soviet soldiers were marching in step in parade formations, insanity in a combat environment. They were all spit and polish, their bayonets gleaming in the early sun. And civilians were lining the roads, greeting the Red Army as heroes. The Soviets just about ignored Hunter as he flew over. As before, those that did acknowledge him, did so with laughter and derision.

It went on like this for miles. Small towns. Villages. Red flags flying everywhere. Then, on the outskirts of one large city, Hunter saw a most horrible sight. Thousands of American soldiers lying on a vast killing field. Among the still bodies, American flags were burning.

This was worse than any nightmare for Hunter. He had to get away. He put the F-16 on its tail and climbed for five miles straight up. Tears were streaming down his cheeks. He was having trouble breathing. He turned over and found his five reluctant pilots in almost the same spot where he left them, as if they'd been standing still all this time.

He put on his best bravado voice and told the five pilots he'd identified the choke-point target he'd been hoping for. It was a bridge spanning the Vogel River, close to the border between France and Germany. It was approximately 300 miles behind the head of the Soviet columns.

Hunter went back down to the deck, the five other planes grudgingly following behind. They soon had the huge span in sight. It was at least two miles long, with large cities on either side. Soviet tanks were rolling over the bridge four across. Troop concentrations were also in evidence on both sides of the riverbank, as were typical rear area components such as fuel dumps, staging areas, and repair stations.

Hunter flew over the bridge at high speed, not dropping any ordnance, simply hoping to draw any antiaircraft fire away from the main attack force. But not a single round was fired in his direction. Even though Hunter could see mobile AA units in the nonstop Red Army parade, none of them seemed to want to bother to stop and shoot at him. He did three passes while the rest of the strike group orbited at low altitude nearby; still no one even looked up at him.

Hunter radioed back to the other five jets. No need for military niceties here. He simply told them to bring it on. He went up to 3,000 feet and began circling over the target area. As they had planned, the A-10s went in first. Just one 2,000-pound bomb could drop the bridge's middle span if it hit right. Each plane was carrying four of the kick-ass bombs.

The Thunderbolts streaked in, again with absolutely no antiaircraft fire being thrown up against them. The A-10s were side by side, and each dropped two of its big bombs in tandem. Hunter's heart leapt from his chest when he saw the four iron bombs heading dead-on for the middle span of the bridge. And all four hit; but just like his attack earlier on the Soviet carrier, incredibly, all four bounced off. Right behind were the three F-15s in a ragged line. They were on the scene even before the A-10s' pulled off. These three pilots saw the A-10s bombs bounce off, but they were already into the delivery runs. Perhaps the A-10s' bombs were duds.

The F-15s roared in and dropped two 2,000-pound bombs apiece, plus a 750-pound high-shrapnel bomb. Each explosive had more than enough firepower to sink the span or at least grease everyone on it. But incredibly, all of their bombs bounced off, too.

Hunter felt he was being sucked further down into this bad dream. He flipped over and bore in on the bridge himself, this time making a lengthwise approach. He intended to drop his entire load right in the middle of the central span. No one fired at him as he turned into his bomb run. Those soldiers below riding on tanks and APCs hardly reacted to his presence at all. He let loose everything he had, coming in hard and fast. . . .

But all his bombs just skidded off the edge and fell harmlessly into the river. Furious, he turned over and strafed the columns. But his bullets had no effect. Just like before, it looked like his cannon rounds were bouncing off anything they hit.

His radio came alive. It was one of the F-15 pilots. "Can we go home now?" he asked.

But before Hunter could answer, he saw the F-15 in front of him suddenly get blown out of the sky. There was no way to tell what happened. It was just gone in a ball of flame.

Screams in his ears now. The other pilots were flipping out again.

"We told you so!" one bellowed—before he, too, was hit by something and destroyed. The two A-10s turned to escape, but they were quickly shot down as well. The remaining F-15 pilot simply drove his plane into the ground.

Then Hunter felt his own plane get hit. Suddenly there were flames all around him.

Instinct alone made him reach for the ejection lever. There was a burst of smoke and flames, and an instant later he was floating in the air. No noise. No motion. Just him floating and the bridge and flames below.

Then came a sudden jerk; his chute had opened, a small miracle. Now he seemed to be dropping even faster. The river passed out of view; he was approaching another killing field, a place where many more thousands of recent American graves had been laid out. American flags were everywhere, smoldering on the ground.

It seemed to take forever for him to make it to the surface. He hit hard, rolled, and came up on his feet. The chute disappeared. He was right in the middle of the field of the dead. American rifles with American helmets stuck on top of them. He heard gunfire. Bullets were suddenly zipping by him. He started to run.

Russian soldiers in perfectly pressed uniforms began chasing him through the graveyard. They were laughing at him even as they were shooting at him. Hunter looked down at his uniform and saw it was threadbare. His boots were suddenly without their soles. His hands were dirty, and his fingernails cracked and sore.

More bullets. More laughing. Tripping over freshly dug graves, he somehow reached the top of a ridge and found another small army of Soviet soldiers coming up the other side right at him. He turned left. More soldiers, bayonets extended, were rushing toward him. He turned right. At least a hundred more Red Army soldiers were advancing on him. He was absolutely surrounded and unarmed. At his feet, in the dust, a discarded American flag.

If only I had wings, he thought, *I could get out of this. . . .*

More than a thousand Red Army soldiers were now converging on him. They'd stopped shooting at him and were advancing slowly, with bayonets out front.

If this was the end, then he wanted to do it right. He reached down and picked up the flag at his feet, intending to literally wrap himself in it, when suddenly it burst into flames. Bright orange fire, that covered his hands, covered his face, but did not hurt him.

And at that moment, it was as if a bolt of lightning hit him right between the eyes. *Get a hold of yourself! You're in an amusement park!* No one had been killed. No one had been shot down. This was all just a grand illusion. It was just so real, so personal, he'd gotten caught up in it to the point of not thinking clearly. *Idiot . . .*

The nearest Russian soldiers were just about ten feet away when Hunter simply held up his hand and started waving the twice-punched yellow ticket. This stopped the soldiers cold in their tracks. They all stared back at him for a moment, but then they all seemed to relax a little, too. The show was over.

He flipped the ticket and pointed to the picture of the Mad Russian.

"Anyone here know where this guy is?" he called out.

"That's Crazy Ivan, I think," one soldier said in broken English. "He's the guy who built this place."

Hunter got a bit excited. What better place for a Mad Russian to be than in a world where the Russians always win?

"So you've seen him around?" Hunter asked them. "Recently?"

But then they all began shaking their heads no.

One called out, "No, not in a long time."

"A very long time," said another.

"Last I heard, he was spotted over on Moon Three," said a third. "Or was it Moon Four?"

"OK, thanks," Hunter called back to them. "Sorry to bother you all. . . ."

Most of the soldiers just nodded or waved and started to walk away. One officer was nearby. Hunter flagged him down and asked him if he knew where the next ticket booth was.

The officer just pointed to a nearby hill. Hunter had to

squint to see it, but sure enough, there was a structure up there surrounded by banks of white carnival lights. He thanked the officer and then they shook hands.

"Das-vee-darn-ya," the officer said to him. "And come back real soon. . . ."

Hunter started his way up the hill.

The answer here? Obviously this *was* a re-creation of what was known back in one of his lives as World War Three. But it was that conflict as seen not through the eyes of an American but of a Russian. Soviets invincible and courageous. The Americans threadbare and cowardly. And it had been done so realistically, and had been so close to an experience he'd had way, way back, Hunter had simply fallen for it hook, line, and sinker.

The Ancient Astronaut had said that the person who put this place together had a strange sense of humor and was also very jealous of the American way of life. In this place at least, he'd been right on both counts.

"Some joke," Hunter muttered now as he trudged to the top of the steep hill.

Two moons down, and many more to go.

Chapter 5

This ticket booth looked just like the last.

Same blinking lights, same cramped structure, same fake wood, same ancient computer.

The hand-painted sign above the door read, *Zaidi v Strany Snov—Zdes vse tvoi Snovideniya stanyt yaviu.* As translated by the quadtrol: Entering Dreamland. Where All Your Dreams Come True.

"Sounds better than the last time," Hunter muttered.

He went through the same routine, entering all his information, getting his admission ticket punched, getting past the security walls.

He typed in "Flying" once again, and then hit the Enter button. . . .

•   •   •

The first thing Hunter noticed this time was a strange object sitting on his head.

He reached up and felt that it was dry and made a crunching sound when he squeezed it. He took it off and saw it was a hat, made of intricately wound straw, with a red band. A straw hat?

Who the hell would wear this? he thought.

He looked down at his feet and saw something even stranger. His flight boots were gone; he was wearing red button shoes with white coverings on them instead. Were those spats?

His wardrobe makeover didn't stop there. His pants were gray with blue pinstripes. His belt was made of cloth. He was wearing a vest, a red tie, a white shirt, and a very stiff white starched collar. Everything felt tight and ill-fitting. He didn't want to know what he was wearing underneath.

He tried to get his bearings. He was on a pier, on the edge of a bustling city. Sparkling clean water was lapping up against the pier's wooden posts. There was a huge crowd around him. All along the pier, along the adjacent sidewalks, even sitting on the roofs of the harbor buildings nearby, large numbers of people were gathered. Thank God, all of them were dressed as silly as he. Many were waving tiny flags of orange and blue, a sort of double cross design, while others were displaying flags of the more familiar red, white, and blue.

Multicolored bunting was in evidence everywhere, along with brightly painted signs that read, Welcome to New York City. Farther down the pier from Hunter, an oom-pah band was playing loudly. A man in a bright military uniform with sergeant's stripes was leading the ensemble. His name, written in stylized scroll across his sleeve, was Pepper.

Now the crowd began to roar. The noise quickly became deafening. Everybody's eyes went left. Flags were waved furiously. Hunter leaned forward a bit, enough to see around the corner of the building next to him. An enormous oceangoing ship was moving slowly toward the dock. It seemed to take up half the sky. Indeed as its shadow passed over the crowd, day turned to night. The ship was that big.

People lining the decks of the huge ocean liner were waving as enthusiastically as those on the dock. Streamers of bright blue and yellow cascaded down from the upper decks. A squadron of fire-fighting boats was escorting the monstrous ship into harbor; they were spraying great streams of water high into the air. The band tried hard to play over the sounds of the crowd and the blaring of the ship's horn, but it was a losing battle.

The air became electric. Hunter caught himself waving his own little flag and shouting, "Hurrah!" The ship finally passed by the pier, and he could see the name on its stern.

It read: HMS *Titanic*.

Suddenly someone was tugging on his arm. Hunter spun around to see a young woman had come up behind him. She was dressed in a frilly blue outfit that contained yards of material and covered her from her neck to her toes. She was wearing a high floppy hat with an enormous flower sticking out of the top. A veil covered her face.

"Come on, will you?" she was yelling at him. "We'll be late!"

With that, she took his hand and started pulling him

through the crowd. Hunter had no choice but to follow. Most people were still enamored by the arrival of the huge ocean liner, so they parted the way easily for them.

They left the pier and reached the street. It was filled with ancient motor cars, wagons, and people pushing carts filled with fruit, mostly apples. One man offered a perfectly golden one to Hunter, but the girl pulled him away before he could accept. Everyone Hunter saw on the street was wearing a broad smile.

The mysterious girl was laughing and obviously in great spirits as she led him through the crowded thoroughfares. Hunter wished he was dressed in more comfortable clothes. He would have been able to move quicker, especially in a better pair of shoes.

They passed a crowd on one street corner. Many of the people were drinking beer from foamy mugs. A man standing on a soapbox was addressing them good-naturedly on the virtues of honesty. Hanging off his soapbox was a sign that identified him as Judge Crater. Two of his associates were handing out free mugs of beer. Hunter managed to grab one before the girl pulled him away once again. They continued their race down the street. They were dodging streetcars, smoky trucks, hundreds of creaking taxicabs. Every time Hunter would try to sip the beer, she would pull on his arm again, and laugh: "There's no time for that!"

She led him over another two blocks, and soon they were in a forest of extremely tall buildings. *Skyscrapers* was the word that popped into Hunter's head. It was an apt description, as the tops of these buildings really did seem to disappear up into the sky.

Out of breath, his feet sore from running, Hunter finally managed to get the girl to stop. He took out his handkerchief and dabbed the sweat from his brow. Then he took a long slug from the beer mug. *Drat!* It was only colored water.

"What are you trying to do?" he scolded her cheerfully. "Kill me?"

"Just the opposite," she cooed back.

With that, she lifted her veil and finally revealed her face. Hunter nearly fell over.

It was Dr. Zoloff's daughter, Annie.

Hunter became so excited, he threw the beer mug clear across the street. It exploded on the side of a brownstone with a tremendous splat! Then he grabbed her and squeezed her in an enormous hug. He was suddenly glued to her just as she was glued to him during his first ride.

But she was not hugging back, not really. He let her go and looked into her eyes. She was even more beautiful than she was after their adventure in Ping's Palace. But there was a look of bewilderment in those big baby blues. It was obvious.

She didn't know who he was.

Maybe that's how it worked here.

But she never lost her smile. "Hey, big boy," she told him. "There'll be plenty of time for that later!"

Then she started dragging him through the streets again.

They moved deeper into the city, crossing avenues, ducking through alleys, running the short blocks.

The farther east they went, the sleeker and more colorful and quieter the motor vehicles became. Soon enough, the cars began to look like some of the small civilian spaceships Hunter had encountered across the Galaxy. The clothing styles worn by people on the street changed radically, too. Suddenly women were wearing very short skirts and plunging necklines; there was less material on their entire outfits than this version of Annie had in her hat.

They crossed five major avenues and finally reached a river. It was busy with tugboats, ferries, and ocean liners, smaller but no less luxurious looking than the *Titanic*. She led him across a great bridge; the view of the city behind them was spectacular. Throughout, Annie's energy seemed to know no bounds. But she wasn't talking to him beyond telling him to hurry up, that they were already late, that they couldn't miss what was going to happen next. Sweaty and still a bit confused, Hunter kept up as best he could.

They made it to the other side of the bridge and continued running through the streets. Every time Annie looked back at him, she seemed even prettier than before. *How does she do that?* Hunter wondered.

They eventually reached an airport. The sign above it read: New York Memorial Field. It was crowded with flying machines that were vaguely familiar to Hunter. Their bodies seemed to be made mostly of wood, with stubby engines on their noses and twin fabric-covered wings over the open-air pilot compartment. *Biplanes* . . .

There was another crowd here, it rivaled in size the one back on the pier. They were dressed in more modern clothes, but not quite as revealing as those back on Fifth, Sixth, and Seventh Avenues. Yet strangely, Annie seemed to fit right in.

She managed to pull him right to the front of the crowd. Again he saw people waving flags and holding banners. A sense of great anticipation was in the air.

Suddenly many in the crowd were pointing to the sky. High above, another ancient flying machine appeared. It was a bit more modern-looking than the twin-wings on the ground. It was silver in color and was dropping quickly in altitude. The closer it came, the more excited the crowd became. This party didn't need any music. The energy in the crowd was enough.

The plane spiraled down, leveling off about 500 feet out. Its engine began smoking crazily, but it was close enough to the ground not to cause much concern. It touched down with a thump, bounced once, and then came down for good. The crowd cheered wildly. Even Hunter was caught up in it, though he really didn't know what the hell was going on.

The plane came to a halt right in front of them. The top hatch opened, and after a few seconds, a rather mannish-looking woman popped her head out. The crowd cheered wildly again.

Finally Hunter could take the suspense no longer.

"Who is that?" he asked the man next to him.

The guy looked back at him as if he was from outer space, which, of course, he was.

"Who is that?" he replied. "Son, that's Amelia Earhart. She just flew around the world!"

Hunter almost replied, *Big freakin' deal,* even though the woman's name was also vaguely familiar to him. But before he could say anything, Annie was pulling him along again.

It was time for him to put his foot down; he didn't like being so uncertain about his circumstances. He finally stopped her in her tracks, spun her around, and held her by the shoulders.

"Who are you?" he asked her. "This time . . ."

She just laughed at him. She was pretty almost beyond words, her crazy outfit only adding to the appeal.

"What difference does it make?" she asked him back. "These days, everything is love and peace and inner light. Names don't mean anything. Not anymore. So, don't be so uptight, man."

He just stared back at her. It was hard to tell how old she was, but she was old enough, Hunter hoped.

"OK then," he said, knowing it was probably better if he just played along. "Can I call you Annie?"

"Sure!" she said, pulling him close to her. She smelled beautiful.

"And so, Annie," he went on. "By any chance do you know someone called the Mad Russian?"

"Like, who doesn't?" she shot back playfully.

Hunter became excited again. "Do you know where he is? How I can find him?"

She thought a moment, then said slowly, "No, but maybe we can find someone who does."

"Really? Are you sure?"

"Well, we can give it a try!" She laughed.

With that, she dragged him even farther away from the crowd to an isolated section of the airfield. Here sat a lone twin-wing airplane.

She spun around with a very devilish look in her eye, pointed to the aircraft, and asked him, "Can you fly this thing?"

They were taxiing toward the runway a few minutes later.

The airplane was an old Curtis Jenny, this according to the name on the side of its fuselage. Annie was sitting in the passenger seat, which was located in the front of the plane. Hunter was squeezed into the pilot's compartment right behind her.

He found the controls of the gangly aircraft to be very simple—maybe even too simple. He was presented with a stick, rudder pedals, and a lever that served as a throttle. No lights. No bells. No whistles. No puppet strings. Even the spacecraft back in Adventure Land was more elaborate than this.

Once he'd finally got the engine going—it was a wooden propeller, of course—it took some finesse to wrangle all the levers and pedals and get the plane to move. Hunter was a quick study, though. He'd grasped the concept in just a few seconds, and now he was ready to go.

Annie let her hat fly as Hunter pushed the air buggy on to the runway and up to its takeoff speed. He pulled back on the stick, and slowly, almost painfully, the aircraft left the ground. A zing of exhilaration ran through him. What a sweet sensation! It was familiar, yet new to him, too. Sometimes he really did feel like he was born to do nothing else but fly.

Annie was enjoying it as well, laughing deliriously as they rose above the field, above the crowd, above the buildings of this strange, out-of-time Gotham City. She was directing him as best she could, using hand signals to turn him left or right. They headed out over the harbor, it being smoky with the exhausts from many boats churning its ways. Ahead she pointed out a large green statue—a woman in robes with a crown, a torch, and a book in her hands. *Statue of Liberty* . . . The words popped into Hunter's head very easily.

Yes, he'd seen her before. More than once, in fact.

Annie had him turn again. Now they were heading toward two enormous buildings located on a spit of land near where the Statue of Liberty was erected. These twin buildings could only be described as super-skyscrapers. They were identical in size and girth, perfectly square, and at least 100 stories high. Hunter suddenly felt a twinge in his chest. His eyes began to water. He began to choke up.

The World Trade Center Towers . . .

They were still here.

They flew on for what seemed like hours.

Hunter had turned west, following Annie's directions, knowing this was the best thing to do. He couldn't think of better company to have, here in Dreamland. He had to wonder though. Did she really know someone who might know where the Mad Russian was? Or was she just up here skylarking? Strangely, Hunter didn't care, not at the moment anyway. He was with her again. And that's all that mattered. By now, she was deep inside him.

They passed over high mountains, lush valleys, emerald forests, wide rivers. No surprise, the terrain reminded Hunter of Planet America, the world located out beyond the Galaxy's fringe that was liberated from the Fourth Empire, with Hunter's help.

A sharp turn north brought them to a particularly immense valley that was surrounded by miles of forest. Seemingly in the middle of nowhere, Hunter spotted a huge crowd of people below. It was hard to estimate just how many, but he guessed there had to be at least 100,000 down there, maybe more. They were lining the valley's hills and were especially crowded into a natural grass bowl that dominated the center. A huge stage was set up at the northern end of this indentation. It was surrounded by scaffolding and tall metal towers holding giant lamps and monstrous public-address speakers.

Annie was extremely animated now, yelling things back to Hunter that he couldn't understand. Strictly by hand signals he got her message that he should fly lower. He turned the Jenny over, and down they went to just 500 feet. Leveling off, he buzzed the length of the crowd, much to the delight of those below. What little glimpses he could get, he saw that most of the people were kids, teenagers, with colorful outfits and long hair. They were singing, dancing, frolicking. A musical group was playing onstage. Hunter could hear snippets of their songs even at 500 feet above. A very sweet scent was in the air, rising up as a curious fog. The action of the propeller served to blow it back into his face. *What is that smell?*

All this delighted Annie to no end. She was singing, too, as if she could hear all the music coming from below. Hunter circled the crowd again; now many were cheering them as they flew over. Annie started gesturing again. Up and over the next hill was a field large enough for them to set down. She turned and smiled and indicated that Hunter should land. He pulled the throttle back and started his descent.

The curious sweet fog got thicker as they went down. The field below opened up nicely, and the landing was picture perfect. They'd set down next to one of the roads leading into the grass bowl; it was filled with more kids. They were fascinated by the old Jenny biplane. Many ran over just as Hunter was killing the engine. They all had very long hair; a few had beards. One kid looked up at Hunter, laughing good-naturedly at his strange clothes, even though he himself was wearing a multicolored shirt and dirty jeans. He started yelling something, but the engine was still turning, and it was impossible for Hunter to hear.

Finally, though, the propeller fluttered to a stop. Hunter yelled down to him, "What did you say?"

To that, the kid yelled back, "I said: 'Hey man, the New York Thruway *is closed!'* "

Hunter secured the plane as best he could. Then he and Annie walked down the road toward the music stage.

The entrance to the grass bowl was crowded with hundreds of kids, all in brightly colored clothes, happily dancing and singing. Suddenly Hunter's long hair was very fashionable, as were his retro Carnaby Street clothes. What's more, Annie had taken off her heavy, long dress. Now her slip was a miniskirt, and her vest was her top. Her hair was let down, cascading into millions of curls. She was barefoot. Hunter's heart started pounding. In a sea of beautiful girls, she stood out.

She seemed to know exactly where she was going, too. Hunter followed her to a gate near the rear of the music stage. There were several huge individuals stationed here who looked to be all business as opposed to peace and love.

Annie called them bouncers. She turned on her considerable charm with them, and soon enough Hunter had a huge yellow badge hanging by a string around his neck. She had one, too. This allowed them into the backstage area.

They found a small army of musicians back here. Some were tuning instruments, some were sleeping, some appeared passed out from drinking alcohol. Hunter smelled that curious sweet fog again. It was far from an unpleasant scent, and anywhere it was thick, everyone seemed extraordinarily happy. The vibe back here was one of was happiness and excitement. There was a musical group onstage churning out some tunes. But from overhearing some of the conversations around him, Hunter learned that the real stars of the show had yet to come on.

He followed Annie through the area reserved for dressing rooms. They passed rings of security people, each one waving them through after checking their yellow passes.

Finally they reached a door that was painted in bright psychedelic colors, with a large green apple in the middle. It was marked Dressing Room—Do Not Enter. A battalion of security people were guarding this door. Annie whispered to Hunter that he should wait here. She then charmed her way past the guards and went through the door. That's when Hunter caught a brief glimpse of the people inside the dressing room. It was an image that would stay with him for a long, long time, though he would never be exactly sure why.

He saw four musicians inside. They were all wearing the same kind of silver collarless suit. Each had perfectly coiffered if longish hair, more styled than the people in the crowd or even his own. Three were holding instruments Hunter recognized as guitars. The other was drumming on a table with drumsticks. Just as the door was closing, one of the guys with the guitars spotted Hunter. They stared at each other for a long moment, then the guy raised his hand and flashed two fingers at Hunter. Hunter was baffled for a moment. "Two? Two what?"

But then the guy just mouthed the word *Peace* . . . and then finally the door closed.

• • •

Hunter waited outside for about a half hour. He was greeted in a friendly manner by just about everyone he met. He finally discovered the source of the curious haze; it was coming from a type of cigarette many people backstage were smoking. Hunter had invitations to take a drag from one of these smokes; in fact, just about everyone who walked by offered him a puff, but he declined. His body had been transported thousands of years in the future. He'd undergone entire lifetimes via mind-ring manipulation. He'd been to Heaven and back. What more could this stuff do for him?

The band onstage finished their encore, and the crowd went crazy with cheering and applause. The band members ran right past Hunter; one commented on his "out-of-sight threads." Now Hunter could feel the crowd's anticipation building. He put two and two together. The headliners were the musicians he'd seen behind the multicolored door. If this dizzylando attraction was a world where dreams come true, who then could they be?

At that moment, Annie reappeared. Here eyes were red; she'd obviously partaken in the happy smoke. She was very excited.

"I've got good news," she told him with a giggle.

"You found the Mad Russian?"

"Not quite," she replied. "But I found a guy who knows a guy who knows another guy who knows everything about everything."

It took Hunter a moment to sort that out. "Could there be such a person?" he finally asked her.

She laughed and gave him a tight hug, just like Annie

from the first adventure. "Remember where you're at, man!" she told him. "Anything can happen here!"

Hunter would come to regret that he never saw the four musicians in the collarless jackets play their concert. The crowd was near fever pitch, waiting for them to take the stage; it was almost as if they were anticipating a religious experience. But Annie told him they had to return to the Jenny biplane and wait there. Hunter followed her lead.

They left the backstage area, went through the fence and up the road, this while hundreds were still walking down into the bowl, heading in the opposite direction. Several of the kids stopped them and said, "Where are you going? You're going to miss *them*."

Hunter could only answer with smiles and shrugs.

For the first time in his life, he felt like he was swimming against the tide.

He and Annie returned to the Jenny and waited as instructed.

The screaming coming from the concert area was so loud, Hunter never heard a note the headliners played. It was very apparent, though, when the concert was drawing to a close as the crescendo reached fever pitch. Not five minutes later, four large automobiles appeared on the road leading out of the concert site. There were police vehicles surrounding each of them. The car fourth in the line—it was a stretch limo—stopped. The rear window came down, and a hand from the back waved for Annie and Hunter to climb in.

They did. There were four people in the back of the limo, including one of the musicians in the collarless suit. He smiled at them, but then put his finger to his lips. Where they were going and what they were going to do when they got there had to remain a secret.

They rode along in near silence, following the three other limos, soon passing the army of cars and vans that dotted the fields turned into parking lots. They drove up into the forested hills, past secluded ponds, and along a cold, swiftly running river. The other people in the limo—three beautiful blond girls—spoke softly among themselves. Music was wafting out of the limo's rear speakers. Another funny cigarette was passed around. Annie took a few puffs, Hunter again politely declined, though he was sure that just his proximity to the secondhand smoke was enough to affect him.

But not much though. Because the scenery was beautiful. And it was a beautiful day. And this Dreamland *was* a place where nothing ever seemed to go wrong.

So he just sat back and enjoyed the world going by his window.

The four limos climbed up out of the hills and into the blue mountains beyond.

Soon Hunter was looking down at the rapidly moving river, which was now wide and looking almost icy, but still refreshing. He caught himself on occasion eavesdropping on the conversation among the others in the back of the limo. They spoke with unusual accents, thick as pudding, and it was hard to follow along. The topic seemed to range from music to the current state of the universe. As before, he just stayed quiet, sometimes musing to himself that it seemed virtually impossible that he wasn't on some distant version of Earth instead of one of the many moons of Saturn.

How strange his life had become. . . .

They drove on for about an hour. In that time the terrain outside changed dramatically. The trees and vegetation suddenly seemed more suited to a jungle environment as opposed to a northern forest. The condition of the roads changed radically, too. They went from wide and paved to dirt and narrow very quickly. And Hunter could tell it was getting very hot outside, this even though he could see snow-covered mountains way off in the distance.

The trek ended at the gate of a camp hidden away atop one of the tall mountains. The camp was adorned with many brightly colored flags and emerald-leafed trees. An ancient wooden sign at the front gate gave the only hint of what this place was. In cracked paint, it read: Spiritual Ashram.

The camp consisted of a dozen or so simple wooden huts, a communal dining table, and a large house in the center. There were a few people wandering around the grounds. They were wearing long, frilly, flowing gowns, both men and women. The place was very rustic, yet those in residence didn't seem a bit fazed when the four very modern limos roared in.

The limos stopped in front of the large house. Annie started to climb out, pulling Hunter with her. The guy in the collarless jacket said to him, "The man in that house has the answers to everything. Tell him you're our mate. He'll help you out."

Hunter shook his hand. "How can I thank you?"

The musician pushed his glasses back up onto his nose. "Just do me one favor. Wherever you go, whoever you talk to, please tell them that peace and love are the only answers."

Hunter hesitated a moment. The guy obviously didn't know who he was talking to. Or then again, maybe he did.

"I'll try," was all Hunter could say.

The musician gave him a kind of mock salute. Hunter stepped out of the limo and closed the door. All four cars roared away, out the gate, and back down the mountain.

Annie was waiting for him on the front steps of the big house. She was still giggling, still beautiful. Two men with bald heads were watching the door. They seemed friendly. When Annie explained how she and Hunter got here, the two men let them enter.

Inside the big house was more elaborate than Hunter would have imagined. Candles lit the place, hundreds of them. Incense filled the air. It was darker within than it should have been, as well. They walked together toward the end of the one big room. Here was a platform of sorts, made of immense pillows at least ten feet high. There was a crowd of several dozen people sitting around it. Legs crossed, eyes closed, they were all in a meditative trance, or at least pretending to be. At the top of the pile of pillows was a little man, dark-skinned with a very long gray and black beard. He, too, was sitting cross-legged, eyes closed, several pots of incense burning around him.

Annie looked up at Hunter, and for the first time since meeting her, she showed a bit of uncertainty by way of a shrug. Cute, but different.

"Excuse me . . ." she called up to the strange little guy in a sweet whisper. "Sir?"

The man didn't move.

"Sir . . . do you have a moment?"

Still, nothing.

Annie shrugged again, and then to Hunter's astonishment, she crawled up the mountain of pillows and pulled on the man's very long beard.

"Hey!" she yelled. "Wake up, man!"

Startled, the little guy finally opened his eyes. The first thing he saw was this beautiful creature, not a few inches from his face, grinning ear to ear at him.

It was as if he'd woken from a beautiful dream.

"Ahhhh," he said in a very high-pitched voice. "An angel has come for me. . . ."

Then he saw Hunter, and this deflated him a bit.

"More visitors?" he squeaked.

This brought most of his audience out of their trances. Suddenly all eyes in the place were on Hunter.

Annie explained to the guru how she and Hunter happened to get here, about the musicians and the limos and the ride up to the mountain. Then she looked back down at Hunter. "Ask him quick!" she said.

Hunter took two giant steps forward. Just as in the other places he'd been, he didn't bother to identify himself. He simply asked the question: "Do you know a man called the Mad Russian?"

The bearded man thought a moment, then let out another "Ahhhhh . . . yes! Such a valuable person. A true spirit in this world."

Hunter felt a glimmer of hope.

"Is he here?" Annie asked him. "Have you seen him lately?"

But then the tiny man shook his head and said, "No . . . in fact, I have never really set eyes on him."

Hunter was immediately bummed out again.

"Do you know where he is?" he asked the guru. "Is he

on this . . . world?" Hunter hesitated using that term. But the little guy got his meaning.

He shook his head again, his beard rolling from side to side.

"From what I know, he is not," he said, in a high-pitched, singsong voice. "And has not been for many, many years. To tell you the truth, there are days, dark days, I agree, when I'm not even sure he exists. Is he a real person or not? How do we really know? Perhaps, as many have claimed, he is just an idea, something your hands cannot grasp, but only that your mind can hold on to."

"But I'm *sure* he exists," Hunter insisted, pulling out his yellow ticket and holding it up so the guru could see the faded photo on the back. "I know people who know him."

The little guy just smiled. "Then I can only tell you that your search does not end here. In fact, I think, it is just beginning."

The congregation all began nodding and bowing, as if the swami had just laid out one of the secrets of the universe for them. The little guy waved his hand, and the congregation dispersed, wandering in twos and threes back outside.

Annie slid down off the pillows. For once she was not smiling. She took Hunter's hands and squeezed them gently.

"I'm sorry, man," she said. "I thought if anyone would know, it would be this guy."

They turned to leave, when suddenly they heard the little man call them back. He indicated Hunter should climb the pillows, which the pilot did, but with awkwardness and great difficulty. Finally reaching the top, the guru motioned him closer. Hunter went right down to ear level. The guru started whispering to him, his voice suddenly much lower than before, his spiritual demeanor gone.

"Try the second next moon over," he told Hunter directly, sounding more like a wise guy bartender than a swami. "My boys have told me the Russian used to hang out there a lot."

Hunter was mystified. "Why didn't you tell me that before?"

The guy just shrugged, reached behind him, and came out with a huge cigar. He lit it and spat a few loose fibers of tobacco from his lips.

"I didn't want to bring it up in front of my fans," he said with a wink. "Can't ruin a sweet thing like this, you know?"

Hunter nodded in agreement, even though he wasn't sure what the guru was talking about.

"OK, then," he said. "Second moon over from here. Thanks."

"One more thing," the little guy said, grabbing him by the sleeve. "You ain't the first mook who's been asking for him lately."

Hunter was very surprised by this. "Really? Who else?"

The little guy blew a few smoke rings, then flicked his ashes all over his silk pillows. "I don't know exactly," he said. "A couple of real freaks . . ."

"You mean, like the long hair kids down at the concert?" Hunter asked.

"No," the little guru replied. "I mean real freaks. Tough guys. In funny uniforms. Scary dudes, in a way. I didn't tell them what I told you, though. I didn't tell them nothin' because I didn't like the way they looked. And they were a little lacking in the respect department. . . ."

He blew a few more smoke rings and flicked his ashes again.

"What do you want to find the Russian for, anyway?" he asked Hunter directly.

Hunter thought a moment, then started crawling down the hill of pillows.

"I'm here to make him an offer," he said over his shoulder. "One he can't refuse."

Hunter and Annie returned to the concert site via a ride on the back of a truck leaving the ashram.

Night was beginning to fall. Music was still being played. The crowd was more mellow now, after all the excitement earlier in the day. Play time was over though. Hunter thought it best to get back to New York City and figure out his next move from there. He wanted to start the flight before the daylight was completely gone.

Luckily, the field was clear enough for him to get the Jenny off the ground. Rushing down the improvised airstrip, he pushed the old biplane into the air and quickly gained altitude. He swung back toward the concert site to give Annie one last look at the happening below. She was disappointed that they were leaving, disappointed that she had not helped him find the Mad Russian. Even bummed out though, she looked pretty.

Hunter flew low over the crowd one more time, intent on making a long, slow turn back east, toward NYC. But then suddenly, something inside him started buzzing. His whole body began vibrating. What was this? Similar to his built-in radar, this sensation came to him when he knew something was wrong. But what could it be? The airplane was flying fine. Annie was strapped in and OK.

Was it something below?

He banked around again, flying even lower over the crowd. The people below reacted with cheers, but Hunter's highly advanced vision spotted two unusual characters in the crowd. And these two were just about the only ones not looking up at the airplane. Instead, they were roughly pushing their way through the knot of concertgoers.

The pair were wearing strange outfits, but not in the same style as most of the kids below. These were uniforms. Black, with red trim.

Solar Guards . . .

Hunter freaked out. He landed back in the field as quickly as he could, scattering some concertgoers and mystifying Annie.

These two must have been the pair the swami had told him about, he thought. Jumping from the cockpit, he ran back down to the concert area as fast as he could. Annie was behind, yelling at him to slow up, but he couldn't. He arrived on the edge of the crowd and scanned it in the growing dusk, looking for the two Solar Guards.

But there were tens of thousands of people in the natural bowl; from ground level it would be impossible to pick out just two. He jumped up onto the stage, now vacant, and studied the crowd intensely. But again, sheer numbers and the growing darkness worked against him.

The two Solar Guards had disappeared.

With their plans changed, they slept under the plane's wing that night, wrapped together in a borrowed blanket, holding each other tight.

Hunter was surprised that he was actually tired; for

some reason he didn't think he would get tired here, in this crazy fantasyland. But after studying the strange night sky for a few minutes, and thinking about the ramifications of spotting the two Solar Guards earlier, he drifted off into a deep slumber. He awoke only once during the night, this to find that Annie had taken off all her clothes and was now pressed against him as tightly as she'd been back in Adventure Land.

Hunter smiled for what seemed to be the first time in eons, then went back to sleep.

When they awoke in the morning, they were surrounded by hundreds of sleeping kids who had also taken advantage of the landing field as a good place to spend the night. Hunter hated to do it, but he woke most of them by starting the very noisy engine on the Jenny. They all politely moved out of his way as he and a very sleepy Annie took off again.

He flew low and slow, scanning the road full of departing concertgoers in hope of spotting the two Solar Guards again. But it was no use. There were just too many people down there. Plus, he couldn't imagine the pair of SG thugs wanting to mix with the young flower children—or they with them.

After a while Hunter just gave up and climbed in altitude. He finally turned east and lay on the throttle. That the Solar Guards were also looking for the Mad Russian was a very disturbing development. It could only mean that they knew the ancient Communist was the only person left in the Galaxy who could actually foil their plans of manipulating the Big Generator.

This only increased the pressure Hunter was already

carrying. There was no alternative: he had to find the Mad Russian before they did.

They returned to the airfield on the edge of New York City.

Annie was full of questions on the ride home, yelling them back to Hunter every half minute or so. But he was reluctant to give her any answers. He certainly didn't want her mixed up in anything having to do with the Solar Guards.

She noticed the change in him, though. As soon as they landed, she told him he looked "permanently bummed." He apologized, trying to explain to her that his carefree trip here had now taken on a more sinister edge. And yes, that was enough to bum him out—permanently.

He had to find the next ticket booth and move on. He didn't want to leave Annie; he'd become very attached to her. But duty called. Where would the ticket booth be? In a city the size of this re-creation of old New York, there could be thousands of places. And his quadtrol wasn't much help.

But Hunter got an idea. He asked Annie to lead him to the biggest museums in the city. The search took most of the day, but they finally found a museum dedicated entirely to modern conveniences. Inside, they found a PC, one that accepted his thrice punched admission ticket. His hunch had been right. It was a ticket booth in disguise.

He typed his way past the security walls and up came the familiar questionnaire. He filled in all the fields, including the one about his hobbies. The old PC churned for what seemed like an hour before finally declaring itself ready. At last, everything was set for him to go. According to the English-language box in the corner of the screen, the next ride was called Land of the Lost.

He turned back to Annie. She was crying. Somehow she knew that none of this was real—not *really* real. And he remembered the message she'd given him at the end of the first attraction. But to take her with him now was out of the question. Even if she could go with him, it was way too dangerous.

Maybe that was the point. . . .

So he took her in his arms, kissed her, and held her tight for a very long time.

Then, without her seeing him do so, he reached down and hit the Enter button.

Chapter 6

He was falling.

Tumbling . . .

Out of control.

Hunter tried to get his wits about him, but it was hard to do. There was darkness all around. All he could see was an inky black sky above and very dark shadows below.

He'd spent so much time inside flying machines, his body could tell just how high he was by the thinness of the air and the sensation of the air pressure around him. Both of these indicators came to one dreadful conclusion now: he was about a mile high and dropping very, very fast.

What went wrong? Had he jumped to a moon that was no longer there? Or had it moved off its orbital plane for some reason? Or had this been a trap all along?

He began falling faster.

What could he do? He was the Wingman, but he didn't have wings. Flapping his arms would be a ridiculous way to spend his last few seconds of life. But he just couldn't go limp, either.

He managed to right himself somehow, which from his point of view, was body horizontal, head down. He was wearing his flight suit again, his boots, his crash helmet. He ripped open the front of his suit, allowing the air to collect underneath. This slowed his velocity, but only by a tiny fraction. So he would impact going thirty-one feet per second per second instead of Nature's well-established thirty-two?

What good was that?

All this fussing and physics took time, and before he knew it, he could see the ground, his splat spot in sight. But then something strange happened. What was below him was not rocks or hard ground or even water. He wasn't sure what the hell it was. But in the last instant before impact, he realized maybe it was actually . . . *soft*.

He hit a moment later. It felt like his spine had come right up out of his skin. But at the same time he knew that if he could think at all, the fall had not killed him. Not immediately anyway.

He hit hard on something soft—hit and kept on going. Down ten feet, fifteen, twenty. Finally he stopped burrowing and shot back up, all this happening in the span of a second or two. Next thing he knew, he was in the air again, fifty feet high and tumbling once more. He came back down, hit the surface hard again, bounced a second time, then finally came down for good.

Now it felt as if his heart was coming out of his throat. How could he have survived such a fall? And what the hell did he fall into?

He lay there for a full minute, waiting for his ticker to start beating normally again. Facedown, he had the taste of old cloth in his mouth. Finally lifting his head, he realized he was lying in a pile of cloth. Hundreds of separate pieces of it. Different colors. Different textures. But all just about the same size.

It was still dark out, but he managed to grab of few of these things and hold them up to his eyes.

Socks?

He grabbed another handful. This time, big ones, small ones, white ones, black ones. But they were indeed socks. Not the artificial pliable plastic type worn by the people in the Galaxy today. Rather these were the simple cloth foot covering used way back in Hunter's previous-previous life, back in the twentieth century.

How crazy was this?

He worked his way to the top of this pile and realized that his landing had not been such a miraculous event; he hadn't landed serendipitously into the only pile of these things on this new, very strange moon.

Instead, the entire moon seemed covered with them. For as far as his eye could see, horizon to horizon, the surface was nothing but socks.

This was nuts, of course, and Hunter knew there was no way the Mad Russian would be found here. He quickly retrieved his quadtrol and asked if it could locate the next ticket booth. It quickly replied, "No." So much for the spy's navigation information. Hunter asked the quad if there were any man-made objects on this moon. The answer came back: everything here is man-made. A stupid question.

Finally he asked if there were any computers close by. The device snorted and burped for a couple moments and came back with a reply that yes, a computer was almost in sight, just about a mile away. Hunter got to his feet and tried to walk as best he could in the direction indicated by the quadtrol, but it was no dice. The mountains of socks were just too loose, too soft to support his weight. It would be impossible for him to hike on top of the piles to get where he had to go.

He would have to crawl.

This was obviously another example of the Mad Russian's sense of humor. But Hunter was not laughing at the moment. His only saving grace was his belief that all the socks around him seemed clean. As if they'd just been washed. Of course, that was part of the joke.

He asked the quadtrol what else was unusual about this crazy place, this as he was crawling along. The reply was: no two socks were the same. They were all socks, but they were all just one half of a pair. Interesting . . . but why?

After a while Hunter was reduced to crawling up and rolling down the mountains of socks, this as the day began, and sunlight appeared, this time out of a totally false, yellow sky. The new glow just confirmed what he already knew: that there was nothing but socks everywhere he looked on the strange little satellite. All of them missing the other mate.

It took him what seemed like hours, but he finally spotted the ticket booth. It was at the peak of an extraordinarily high mound of mismatched socks, standing next to an ancient washing machine–clothes dryer combination. His only clue as to where he was going next was a sign on the booth that read: Next Stop: World of Mirrors.

Hunter climbed up to the booth and booted up the PC. He quickly filled in all the applicable fields, then took another look around.

Thousands, millions, billions? of socks, all without mates? An ancient washer-dryer. Land of the Lost?

Even as he hit the Enter button, he had to admit, he still didn't get the joke.

An explosion . . .

Yellow flames. Red. Orange. Then pure, pure white.

Hunter was tumbling again, but this time across very hard ground. His head was going over his heels and was bouncing viciously off anything that got in his way.

Even worse, whenever he bounced, he seemed to stay in the air way too long—long enough to see that he was bleeding from his hands, his knees, from his head and ears. He burst through a cloud of smoke to see that he was tumbling down a hill in the middle of a massive battlefield. Churned-up sections of ground, water-filled bomb craters, and flames were everywhere.

He finally bounced one last time and landed—hard—on a battered roll of barbed wire. It was coiled like a spring, which, lucky for him, allowed him to spring right off, only to land in a pool of putrid water. Suddenly all his wounds were being stung by numerous filthy liquids. He rolled himself out of this disgusting puddle, and the next thing he knew, he was tumbling down another hill, colliding with many other things, all of them big and sharp. More barbed wire, depleted shell casings, discarded military equipment. Bodies . . .

He came to a stop again, finally, at the bottom of this hill. Only then could he see the top of the slope where he'd started his great fall. An aircraft of some kind was up there, burning furiously. He'd been in a crash; a bad one, but he'd somehow survived.

"I guess that was one aircraft I *couldn't* fly," he muttered painfully.

Startled though he was, he tried to make some sense of his surroundings. For as far as he could see, there was nothing but devastation. Horizon to horizon, the smell, the taste, the feel of death and war. Hunter was familiar with these things. *Too* familiar. But never had he seen anything like this.

He took all this in over just a few heartbeats before a huge explosion went off not fifty feet away from him. He put his face in the mud just in time to allow a small storm of shrapnel to go over his head. No sooner had his eardrums popped when another blast went off, this one to his left. Then another, just north of him. And another, right in front of him.

What the fuck kind of ride is this?

He was breathing in the mud now, and thankful for it. The ground was moving like he was floating on water. He reached up and felt his left ear. Blood was pouring out of it.

This was not good.

He managed to roll over on his back. Eyes looking straight up, he could see a formation of huge airplanes passing overhead. Strings of bombs were falling from their bellies. Quick but fuzzy calculations told him the bombs had already passed over him. They fell a half mile away, but he could still feel the ground rumble as each one hit. He was sure another wave was coming over, though. He could already hear the airplanes, and their bombs whistling through the air, heading right for him.

Damn . . .

He began crawling up the hill, thinking this was the most likely path to safety. But he was surprised to see four men carrying a stretcher coming down the hill toward him. At the same moment, the air was suddenly filled with small arms fire. Bullets zinging back and forth, sizzling as they went by. Then mortar shells began landing all around him. Then artillery shells.

Then the aerial bombs hit.

The ground shook with such ferocity, Hunter swore he could feel his bones breaking simply from the concussion of the bombs hitting so close by. They went on exploding for sixty long seconds, some not one hundred feet away. Somehow they all hit around him, missing him completely. But he couldn't imagine anyone within a quarter mile being able to survive.

Yet when he looked up, he was astonished to see the four men with the stretcher jump up from the smoke and continue racing down the hill toward him, undaunted. Gunfire began again. The stretcher bearers ducked and zigged and zagged their way through the blizzard of lead apparently intent on retrieving Hunter from his very precarious position. And somehow they made it. That's when he saw the large red crosses on their armbands. They were medics. And at that moment, he was damn glad to see them.

They jumped into the crater next to him and without a word began tending his injuries. A bandage was quickly applied to his ear. Two more were applied to his leg wounds.

One of the medics shoved a pill into his mouth; another unloaded a gigantic load of something from a giant syringe into his arm. A second later, Hunter felt his body begin to rise off the bloody, muddy ground.

Morphine . . .

There was nothing else like it.

Everything got different after that. No more pain. No more worries. No more war, battlefield, muck, or yuck. They put him on the stretcher and began lugging him up the hill. The bullets were still flying all over the place, but they sounded like notes on a violin as they went zinging by him now. The four stretcher bearers, tripping and scrambling in their ascent, were showing uncommon bravery in the face of near-certain death.

Somehow they reached the top of the hill and managed to dive for the relative cover of a trench beyond. Hunter's stretcher fell to the mud of the ditch, the four medics fell on top of him, protecting him from the artillery bursts that came in just seconds later. It went on like this for at least five minutes, but even more so now, the explosions sounded like the kettle drums in an orchestra to Hunter, thanks again to sister morphine.

Finally the symphony of fire and steel played itself out, and it became eerily quiet. The medics lifted themselves off Hunter's battered body and tended to his wounds again. His bandages put back in place, they picked up the stretcher and began hoofing it down the trench.

Ten minutes later, they reached a dugout, basically a man-made cave cored out of the mud and rock on one side of the trench. Within was a makeshift field hospital. The medics put Hunter's stretcher down just outside the door.

"You will make it," one of the medics told him. "They will care for you here."

That's when Hunter focused his eyes again. He saw the four medics looking down at him, grim smiles all around. Their uniforms were so dirty he thought they were gray, but now he realized they were actually blue.

Then he noticed something else. Each man had a silver badge over his left breast pocket. Hunter did a double take. The badge was a twisted cross, a vaguely familiar symbol.

A swastika?

He cleared his mind of the painkiller just long enough to make sure he was actually seeing this. But it was true. Their badges were swastikas. And even though his memory was clouded over by his 5,000-year time transportation and all of the interdimensional travel he'd been taking since, this memory stuck with him like super glue from his former, former life.

High as a kite or not, swastikas meant only one thing to him: these soldiers were Nazis.

Again, ever since Hunter had started on this long journey of his, he'd been able to remember bits and pieces of his long-ago past, back in the twentieth century. He knew he was a fighter pilot, that he loved a woman named Dominique. That back then, he'd been called the Wingman. That he was a patriot. That he loved his country. That he had fought for it many times.

But very unpleasant memories had made the jump with him, too. Fragments of the enemies he'd fought, people who'd spewed hate and disorder. People who'd killed close friends of his and who'd tried to take over the beloved land of his birth, the United States of America.

Of all these enemies, and there were many, he might have despised the Nazis the most. Their brand of hatred for people of other races was despicable. Their belief that they were somehow better and therefore entitled was just plain wacky. They were *so* bad, the Russians even hated them, possibly more than Americans. But the Nazis were also very, very dangerous, and back then, Hunter had vowed to stamp out every last one of them. And, he believed, he'd come close to achieving that goal.

But now, they were here in this dizzylando, this very weird place. The question was, why?

He lay on the stretcher for about ten minutes. In that time, he came to realize his wounds were actually superficial and in no way serious. He was still very, very high, though, and even when he saw another wave of huge bombers go overhead, and saw them drop their bombs, and heard those bombs falling, and felt the ground shake when they hit, it didn't faze him. Just another selection from the symphony.

Strangely, though, he believed in his opiate state that his eyes had become telescopic, that he could zoom in on the wings of these bombers, and what he saw were *more* swastikas. But that made no sense.

Few things did on morphine.

He was finally retrieved by two more litter bearers and brought into the dugout. No surprise, the field hospital was well-equipped, well-organized, and spotless—in that Nazi kind of way.

There were several dozen operating tables, several dozen recovery beds. The place looked way too big on the inside, considering what it looked like without, but again, Hunter knew morphine did strange things to a person's perception and that the medic had given him an overly generous charge.

Hanging on the wall above the operating tables were two signs. One read, Merciless and Moral, an old saying of the original Nazis back in his time, on his Earth. The other read, It Is the Curse of Greatness That It Must Step Over Dead Bodies. An odd saying, Hunter thought, especially for a hospital.

The place was hustling and bustling. Many wounded were being attended to. But luckily for them, there were just as many doctors and three times as many nurses charged with their care. Hunter's stretcher was placed next to an operating table. He lay here for a few minutes, staring up at the lights on the ceiling and getting the distinct impression that someone was hiding up there, staring down at him. Finally, a doctor and two nurses came over to him. All three were wearing long white gowns and surgical masks.

One of the nurses gently removed the bandage near his ear, by far his deepest wound, and still it was little more than a minor abrasion. The other nurse checked under the bandages on his knees.

The doctor meanwhile stared right into his eyes.

Suddenly the doctor bellowed, "Who is this man?"

The controlled chaos inside the field hospital came to a halt instantly. Just like that, it was completely silent. All eyes had turned on Hunter and the three people standing over him. Suddenly, he wasn't feeling so high anymore.

The doctor screamed once again, "This man—who is he? What is he doing in here?"

One of the nurses tried to reply, "He is wounded, Doctor. . . ."

She pointed to his numerous minor wounds.

"But he is not a soldier!" the doctor bit back. "This place is for our fighting men, not hangers-on!"

At that, the other nurse reached down and started scraping the mud away from Hunter's clothes.

Indeed, he was not wearing a Nazi uniform—thank God! Instead, he was dressed in a one-piece black survival suit with no place to hang weapons or ammunition. He did have a number of pens in his upper left-hand pocket and a small notebook tucked inside his undershirt.

"He is a spy!" the doctor roared. "Bring him out to be shot!"

Hunter was definitely back down now. Spy? Shot? Him? *Why?*

But then one of the nurses saved his life—such as it was. She scraped away the dirt and mud from his left arm and revealed a patch that ran nearly from his elbow to the top of his shoulder. It featured a series of yellow stripes with one word in the middle: Scribe.

"He is not a spy," the nurse said, pointing to the arm patch. "He is a reporter. A war correspondent."

The doctor hesitated only for a moment. "Bah!" he declared. "That is just as bad."

With that, he took off his rubber gloves, quickly, but one finger at a time, and slammed them down hard on Hunter's face.

Then he stormed away in disgust.

"This place is for our brave soldiers!" he said on leaving. "And not for the impure blood of his ilk."

The two nurses were a bit more sympathetic, though a badly wounded Nazi solider had arrived on a stretcher beside him. They quickly put fresh bandages on his wounds,

stuck a vitamin pill in his mouth, and called for two orderlies to get him out of there.

As he was leaving, one of the nurses drew out a syringe and gave him another gigantic shot of morphine.
Hunter closed his eyes, but instantly, he felt like he was
back on the ceiling. He really wished she hadn't done
that.

She patted him twice on the head. He opened his eyes
just as she was pulling down her mask. Hunter's bleary
pupils could barely make her out.

Is that Annie? he thought.

Before he could cry out, the orderlies carried his
stretcher back outside, setting him down in almost in the
exact spot from where he'd been picked up.

Once again, artillery shells were exploding close by,
and the steady drone of bombers going overhead never really stopped. His mind drifted away again. Now in his most
elevated moment, Hunter thought that he could actually see
the outline of Saturn up there, past the bombers, past the
wispy clouds, past the false blue sky. But at the same time,
he knew, the way things were working here, that was probably impossible.

He lay there for a very long time, floating along in his
own little world and watching this very strange one pass
him by. He saw many, many soldiers being carried in and
out of the field hospital. Many more were moving up and
down the trench. They seemed oblivious, or unconcerned,
about the explosions going off all around them.

Maybe they're all full of morphine, too, Hunter thought.
*How well could an army fight if it was totally doped up?
Not very well,* he concluded.

At some point, he reached into his undershirt and pulled

out the notebook that the nurses had found. It, too, had the word *Scribe* on it. Somehow, though in slow motion, he was able to flip through it. It was filled with not only pages of notes but also rudimentary sketches of the battlefield around him. The writing, of course, was not his own, and the artist was a better illustrator than he could ever be, opium-induced or not.

It took him a while to thumb through the notes, lying on his back, higher than high, with the sounds of war going on all around him. But together the notes and drawings gave him a startling portrait of what was going on here. This world, artificial as it was, was engulfed in a war. A total war. From its equator to its poles and everywhere in between. The notes described the movements of enormous armies of men, numbering in the millions if the owner of the notebook was to be believed, and weapons of unimaginable, if conventional, destructive power. This was a "gun powder war," those were the words of the unknown scribe. A conflict in which the idea of a superbomb was for someone to collect, deliver, and detonate several thousand pounds of gunpowder on the enemy.

Bombers filled with gunpowder intentionally crashed into targets. Massive oceangoing ships, similarly loaded, were used to ram into enemy coastal fortifications. Monstrous artillery pieces lobbing five- and ten-ton shells filled with . . . what else? Gunpowder.

What a strange way to fight a war, Hunter thought.

But who was this war against? And what was its ultimate goal?

The scribe gave no clues on that first question. His writings were such that it was implied the reader knew just who the enemy was.

As to its goal? At least on that he'd been very clear: this

war was being fought over a single piece of land, in fact a mountain, with a castle on top of it. The mountain, referred to many times in the scribblings, was called Valhalla.

And where was it? As it turned out, very, very close to Hunter's present location. He knew this because on the last full page of the notebook there was a magnificent sketch of the mountain and the castle, and if Hunter lowered the notebook at just the right angle, he could see that very mountain and that very castle off in the distance, not twenty miles away.

Just his luck to wind up near ground zero in this very messy conflict.

He finally put the notebook back into his undershirt and laid his head down again.

How was he ever going to find the Mad Russian in this mess?

He drifted off into an opium sleep, waking only when an extra large explosion went off close by.

He rolled off the stretcher, and with the last of the morphine draining out of him, found himself back in pain and sucking mud in the trench again.

Two more explosions came and went, the second one raining down a small storm of rocks and debris that covered him head to toe. When he emerged from the rubble, he discovered a column of Nazi soldiers trooping by him, unaffected by the most recent artillery barrage. They appeared to be fresh legs: new uniforms, shiny helmets, huge hand weapons. A certain élan. And where were they headed? There was only one answer to that: the nose of this column was pointing directly to the mountain of Valhalla.

Hunter knew he could not lie there forever. At the very

least, the bitchy doctor might spot him again, decide that he was indeed a spy of some sort, and carry through his threat to have him executed. And instinct told him his quest might be the same as these Nazi soldiers.

He managed to pull his quadtrol from his leg pocket and bring it up to his mouth. He asked it a simple question this time: "Has the Mad Russian been here lately?"

The answer was yes. (So the guru had been right.)

"When was he here?" was his second question.

The quadtrol replied, "Not enough information."

"OK then, where was he, the last time he *was* here?"

The quadtrol directed him to a point just off his nose. The mountain called Valhalla.

What more proof did he need?

If you found yourself on this House of Mirrors ride, the whole idea was to get to Valhalla.

So Hunter waited until he saw the end of the long column of soldiers. When it finally passed him, he painfully got to his feet and fell in behind them.

They marched for hours.

Down through the nightmarish battlefield, following avenues of trench works that stretched off in all directions. They came under artillery attack several times, and were bombed several more. These attacks were unsuccessful, though, because the column leaders, for reasons unknown, seemed to know minutes before that the assaults were coming and made sure their men were under cover before they arrived.

Good intelligence, Hunter thought.

No one questioned his tagging along. To the contrary, the soldiers kept him down when he had to be down, and got him moving when he had to be moving. They might have even saved his life a few times. But there was no such thing as a good Nazi. Hunter knew these guys were only helping him because they thought he was one of them.

They reached a shallow hill that divided the churned-up battlefield neatly in two. The long column of soldiers, weary now from the march, trudged over its summit. At about the same time, Hunter could hear the booming of large guns again. These were not the reports of the artillery pieces he'd become used to hearing, though. These represented guns of very high caliber, and the resulting explosions again told the tale of the gunpowder fetish that somehow ruled this world.

It took nearly an hour for Hunter and the tail end of the column to reach the top of this hill. What he saw on the other side was another scene right out of a fever dream. For as far as he could see, horizon to horizon, a titanic battle was in progress. Easily hundreds of thousands of soldiers were involved, maybe even a million—it was hard to tell with all the smoke and fire and utter confusion.

Most of the fighting was being done hand-to-hand, in very close quarters, among a crazy patchwork of trenches and dugouts and natural fortifications. The big guns were set up about a mile to the right of Hunter's position. There were six of them, on high stilts and treads, and indeed, their barrels seemed a mile long or more. Each time one of them fired, the muzzle flash was so bright and the shell discharge so violent, Hunter imagined he could actually see the round cut through the fabric of time and space, a tear in this false reality, a very subtle, almost hidden reminder that he still was in a very different place.

Beyond this hellish battlefield, ten miles away at least,

Hunter could see the approaches to the tall mountain, at the top of which sat the castle of Valhalla. It was all too obvious now that the capture of this castle was why this war was being fought. In the meat grinder of the battle below him, he could clearly see half of the troops fiercely defending the roads leading to the castle. The others were trying very hard to overwhelm them.

At the same time, the massive guns were pounding the mountain where the castle was located. With each shell hit, a small piece of Hell would rise up, spilling flames and the strange screech of hundreds being killed instantaneously. The column of soldiers in front of him did not hesitate, though. They double-timed it down the hill, right into the action, disappearing into the chaos, the smoke, and noise.

As the last of them started down the hill, one gave Hunter a hearty pat on the back and said, "You are here to write, aren't you, scribe? Then I suggest you start here."

Hunter waited for the entire column to march into the meat grinder, then he proceeded down the road to doom. It was obvious the fighting had been going on here for quite some time. There were bodies everywhere, but many were already skeletons. Some of these were locked in grotesque positions, a sick testament of the brutality that had been going on here. But then, strangely, Hunter saw something that did not compute. He was staring down at a trench full of skeletons, combat passing them by long ago. Two were locked in an embrace of death, both had plunged a long saber into the other apparently at the exact same moment. They'd died together.

But strangely, both were wearing Nazi badges on their uniforms. The uniforms themselves were different. One was blue like the soldiers in the column he'd followed wore. But the other was jet black. Yet both had Nazi regalia on them.

This didn't make any sense.

Hunter resisted the urge to get right down into the trench with the dead; he was curious, but not morbidly so. He continued down the road instead, heading slowly for the thick of the battle. Exactly what he was going to do once he got close to the action, he didn't have a clue. He noticed, though, there were no soldiers coming back up the road. He'd been in combat before. He'd been on battlefields not unlike this one. Always there were wounded and deserters heading in the opposite direction from the fighting. But not now. The road was empty but for him.

Whoever was fighting down here, it was a fight to the death. He was soon within a half mile of the front line. The stink of cordite was almost overwhelming. He came upon many more examples of two Nazi soldiers locked in a death embrace; each one was more baffling than the next. What was going on here? Were the Nazis in the blue uniforms battling impostors, enemy soldiers who were dressed in black Nazi uniforms? That didn't make sense, either, not with a battle of this gargantuan scale. But what could be another explanation?

Suddenly his ears were pierced right down to the drums. The noise was so intense, and came so quickly, Hunter found his hands on the side of his head, trying to keep the sonic blast out. He dropped to his knees as an enormous shadow went over him an instant later.

It was one of the bombers. The ones he'd seen flying overhead at very high altitude. But this monster was coming in no more than one hundred feet off the ground. It was decorated with many swastikas, and it had bombs attached all along its belly and wings. In a world of disturbing visions, this one was especially so. The soldiers all over the battlefield had turned their weapons up toward it and were firing at it. Suddenly the air itself seemed full of lead.

But something else was wrong here. This huge aircraft—its wingspan had to be at least 500 feet long—was on fire. Its fuselage, its tail section, and more than half its dozen propeller engines were all in flames. It wasn't swooping low to bomb the troops in front of him, though. It was in the process of crashing.

And the reason for this was soon evident. Trailing the plane down was a small squadron of fighter aircraft, weird designs with weird engines propped atop their fuselages and racks of missiles and machine guns taking up the entire underside of their wings. These aircraft were still firing into the bomber, even though the plane was about to impact at any second. But again, despite the impending doom, Hunter could see the insignia on these attacking planes . . . and incredible as it seemed, yes, they, too, were marked with swastikas.

He dove into the nearest trench, knocking the dead away so he might hang on to one more moment of life. The big airplane hit a second later, not 500 feet down the road from him. He saw the tail section break off and cartwheel backward right over his head. A string of crewmen, all of them engulfed in flames, came tumbling out of the resulting hole.

The impact of the airplane shook the ground so much, many of the skeletons around Hunter fell to pieces. But then, a heartbeat later, there was another, even fiercer explosion. This one even more powerful.

Hunter looked up through the bones and saw a sea of

red flame go over the trench. The heat was so intense, it sucked up some of those skeletons that had not turned to dust and took them away with it. It was all Hunter could do to stay down, hug the ground, for to be caught up in that firestorm would have surely been the end of him, fantasy world or not. The noise was almost as horrible. His ears were bleeding again. And it went on for what seemed like forever. It felt like his skin was peeling away, the heat was so intense. His battered eardrums were ready to burst. Where the hell was sister morphine now that he really needed her?

Then, just like that, it was over. No more sound. No more fire. No more skeletons getting one last free ride into the heavens. Hunter stayed down low. One minute. Two minutes. Three.

Finally, he got the gumption to lift his head, to look out over the top of the trench.

But he was met with a cloud of cordite before he was halfway to the edge. He fell back down to the bottom of the trench, near suffocation, the stink was so thick. He held his breath another minute, two, three. Until he could hold it no more. If the next deep breath had been more cordite, he would die on the spot.

But it wasn't cordite—not entirely anyway. It was air, or what passed for air on this crazy place. He finally gathered the strength to pick himself up again and peek over the edge. What he saw would stay with him for the rest of his life.

There was nothing left. Not for a mile on either side of him. The land itself, wiped clean.

The bomber? Now it, too, was dust. How much gunpowder had it been carrying? Tons? Enough to equal an atomic bomb?

Whatever the case, it had left a path two miles wide in which nothing existed anymore. What was left was yellow dust. Bombs, gunpowder, bodies, and wreckage reduced to yellow dust.

And this dust now covered one of the roads that led directly to the mountain they called Valhalla.

It took him an hour to get to the base of the mountain, another hour to climb it.

When he reached the top, he found that the castle wasn't a castle at all. It was a prop, a facade in this fake world. Walls, turrets, even the moat was fake. What's more, he saw no indication that any of the Nazi soldiers from either side had even ever been up here. All that fighting—for nothing?

Why? Why had these mental pukes fought so hard? What was up here that was so valuable? Was there a hall of mirrors inside this place? He had to find out.

He walked through the fake door and entered a hall. This place was so phony, the floor was still covered with unused nails. The wind whistled as it blew through the cracks in the thin veneer of fake wood. The walls were bare. No mirrors here.

In the middle of this hall was a pedestal, on top of it was gold box. Gold paint, that is, flaking off in many places. Hunter studied the pathetic-looking lock holding its flimsy top shut. He blew on it. It snapped open.

He brushed the remains of the lock away, opened the box, looked inside . . . and then laughed. That's when it all came together—the secret of this particular attraction. This Hall of Mirrors. More proof of the creator's strange sense of humor.

This place was not so much another world as it was another kind of hell. A Nazi hell. A place where Nazis went to die. A place where they were doomed forever not to rape and pillage the innocent and defenseless of the world, but to fight and kill each other. Over and over and over again. A world of mirrors—Nazis looking at themselves. Seeing the hate, unable to do anything but battle themselves.

And what were they fighting for? This unattainable thing that was secured with a lock that would have broken off with a sneeze. If any of them ever made it to the top and looked inside the box, this was their prize: a photograph of the original Nazi, the first monster of them all, Adolf Hitler.

In a dress . . .

Hunter walked out the back door of the castle, over a rickety bridge that spanned the empty moat, to the edge of the mountain.

The view from here was spectacular, even if the scenery consisted of little more than miles upon miles of utter devastation. Hunter could look down not just on this local battlefield, but on many other battlefields off in the distance as well. This spot was probably the best vantage point on the entire moon, if one liked watching Nazis kill each other. And that's exactly what the last person up here had been doing.

On a small outcrop of rock located at the far eastern point of the peak, Hunter found an old wooden table and chair. There was a plate on the table holding a few crumbs of what had been a very dark loaf of bread. An empty bar glass beside the plate still contained a few drops of a clear liquid. Hunter put one of the drops to his tongue. This was not water made to look like liquor. This was the real stuff. Vodka. A very strong brand.

Beside the glass was an ancient corncob pipe. Its bowl was filled with tobacco ash. Hunter stuck his finger into the bowl and found it was still warm.

Damn, he thought.

He put it all together and came to the only logical conclusion. The Mad Russian had sat up here and watched what to any Russian would have been considered the ultimate in entertainment: Nazis killing Nazis.

And judging by the warmth of the pipe, Hunter had missed him by only a few minutes.

At last, the quadtrol helped him find the next ticket booth. Whether it was a case of proximity, or design, or both, he located it just a mile away, down the other side of Valhalla mountain, and through a field that had seen some fighting in this crazy war, but judging from the rust of the wreckage, not for some time.

The ticket booth was just like the others: a simple structure made of the fake wood, barely enough room inside for him and the PC. The sign above the door announced the next attraction as: *Chyzol Tainii Mir—Smozesh li ti viderzat eto peklo.* Or, in English: Alien Mystery World—Can You Take the Heat?

Hot or cold, after spending time in this bizarre war heaven, Hunter was ready for anything, just as long as it was far away from here. More important, he was hopeful that he was closing in on the Mad Russian. That he might be right behind his quarry as he moved through his own dizzylando. Riding the rides, just as Hunter was.

Hunter turned on the PC and went through the boot up process that was now routine. Name. Password. Punch the ticket. Get past the security walls. Fill in hobby. He didn't bother to take one last look around this time; he'd seen enough of this Nazi quagmire and was anxious to move on.

He hit the Enter button.

Chapter 7

"Do you have your water, Comrade?"

Hunter looked up into a bright, brutal sun to see five men dressed in full battle gear staring down at him.

Each was wearing a one-piece, sand camo combat suit equipped with built-in radio, belts for carrying ammunition, survival kits and flare guns. Each was also wearing a combat helmet that covered the entire head down to the neck, and featured only a slim red glass visor to look out from, and carrying an enormous assault weapon complete with laser range finder and bayonet.

These five individuals looked like something Hunter might have encountered in just about any corner of the Galaxy these days. Mercs, soldiers of fortune, space pirates. Ready to rock.

But these people were not contemporaries. He knew that much, simply by eyeing the tiny red badge each man had attached over his left breast pocket. It showed a small red star surrounded by a yellow field, and the Cyrillic letters: SPZ.

Hunter didn't need the quadtrol to tell him what these three letters meant. He'd seen them before.

Spetsnaz . . .

Russian Special Forces.

So it was the Russians again.

But then he looked down at what he was wearing and was in for another shock: he was dressed exactly as they.

"Comrade . . . I ask you again. Do you have your water? Or are you already suffering from the heat?"

All Hunter could do was nod, as the reality of the new situation flooded in. Yes, he was most definitely among the Reds again. But this time, instead of fighting them, he was one of them.

"Do not short change yourself or us by bringing too little," the man asking him the questions said in broken English. He was obviously the leader here. "This American desert is much more harsh than any in our country. Even more so than in Africa or Iraq."

Hunter dismissed this man's concerns, at least temporarily, with an impatient wave of his hand. He took a quick scan of his surroundings, trying his best to take in as much as he could.

They were in the deep desert, there was no doubt about that. They were standing next to a motor vehicle that had the word *Caravan* on it. It was dusty and beat up; its rear hatch was festooned with bumper stickers. One read, We Drove the Alien Highway. Another, ET Come Home! Next to the van were six piles of clothing: civilian pants and shirts made of polyester, flip-flops, sandals, and sneakers. Even over 5,000 years, Hunter knew these clothes represented the worst in American tourist wear. The metal tag on the rear of the van contained a collection of numbers. Above them, the word *Nevada.*

Hunter put it all together. The dusty van, the corny bumper stickers, the trashy outer wear. This was an undercover Spetsnaz team that had successfully stolen into the U.S.

But why?

And why was Hunter one of them?

They walked ... and walked ... and walked, across the desert, leaving the Caravan by a ditch and burying their trashy civilian clothes nearby.

It was close to noon and the heat was past unbearable. Hunter was astounded, as he dripped with sweat, how this place—this dizzylando attraction—could seem so real, feel so real, and be so damn hot. He was the last in line, his only saving grace being that for some reason his weapon was not the same size as the huge hand cannons the five men in front of him were carrying. His was a simple AK-47 assault rifle, the standard issue combat weapon for Russian soldiers some 5,000 years before.

On several occasions, the squad leader called them to an abrupt halt, freezing them in place. The leader would then switch on a device he had connected to his weirdo battle helmet. It was a sound amplification gadget. Only once did they take any action as a result of this. He had them all lie flat on the ground as an aircraft of some kind flew overhead nearby. Hunter was in no position to look up and see just what kind of airplane it was, but the sound of its propulsion units sounded very familiar.

Jet engines, he thought.

They walked into the early afternoon. There was absolutely no talking among them, and they remained separated about fifteen feet from each other. Hunter was tempted on more than one occasion to sneak the quadtrol from his pocket and take a quick reading. But instinct told him that to be caught with such a device by these characters might lead to bad things. He knew after the last ride that death was a distinct possibility within the dizzylando. He decided to bide his time and pick his spot.

They reached the bottom of a small mountain range and finally, the leader gave the signal that they could take a break. Hunter began chugging his water as if he was carrying an unlimited supply but quickly stopped himself when he saw the others were simply sipping off their canteens, savoring every drop. Still, there was no conversation between them. Whatever mission these men were on, Hunter got the definite impression that they knew what they were about to do, inside and out, and thus talking about anything was unnecessary, which was good for him. He had no idea what he would say if they had asked him a question or simply wanted to chat.

The break lasted just five minutes. Then it was time to climb the mountain. Up they went, over rocks, through crevices, and across precipices that seemed about a mile wide by the time Hunter got to them. This exercise took nearly two hours, but finally they reached the top. On the other side, a vast desert wasteland stretched out before them for miles. It was not empty, however. Far off in the distance, perhaps a dozen miles away, they could see a collection of innocuous white buildings with a gigantic runway next to them. The brutal heat nearly covered these buildings in an impenetrable haze. Nevertheless, they seemed oddly familiar to Hunter, not just in his present life, but in his former one as well.

This place . . . what is it called again?

They started down the other side of the mountain, and here he found his answer on a sign attached to a ten-foot-high chain-link fence. The sign read: This Is a Restricted Area. Deadly Force Is Authorized . . . Groom Lake Military Reservation.

Groom Lake? Hunter thought. Again, very familiar.

Neither the sign's warning nor the fence itself fazed the Spetsnaz soldiers. They fastened a small boxlike device to the chain-link and attached two wires to a hand-held battery. If the fence was electrified, or more likely, wired with motion detectors, then this doodad would prevent those who might be monitoring it from detecting them.

Once attached, the men simply cut one strand out of the fence next to the device, and one by one, scrambled through.

They walked for another three hours, passing through the most brutal heat of the day.

Reaching the perimeter of the base, they skirted the edge of the massive runway, hitting the deck several times to avoid detection from aircraft flying overhead. Finally they climbed the small mountain west of the hidden base. It was from here that they got their best look at the facilities below.

There were perhaps two dozen buildings. White, square, and unimpressive, all together they made up the equivalent of several very small city blocks. There were also a number of larger buildings that were undoubtedly aircraft hangars. Various fuel tanks and support huts made up the rest of the place. They could see very few people moving around down there. *Only a madman would be out in this heat,* Hunter thought. But these days, he was certain he now qualified.

The squad leader ordered them to take up positions along the top of this mountain. Thank God they were able to stay in one place. The squad leader then pulled out a device that looked like an early version of a GPS locator and overlaid a grid across its readout screen. This overlay was labeled like a map.

Try as he might though, Hunter was unable to catch a glimpse of the overlay's name.

So the mystery of just where he was continued.

They lay up there until night began to fall.

Only once the sun had gone down did the base below them come to life. Lights turned on, ground vehicles spotted. Sounds of machinery and engine noise echoing faintly across the desert. Hunter remained still the entire time, it was the only thing to do. His quadtrol was burning a hole in his pocket, but again he resisted the temptation of taking it out.

What did this long, sweaty trek in the desert have to do with finding the Mad Russian? The man he sought certainly wasn't one of these five guys. Even what little he could see through their face masks, he knew none of them fit the grainy image on the back of his ticket. But did they know him? What would happen if Hunter asked—and they didn't? Bad things might result. Or would they? He tried to stifle all these voices in his head. Tried to stop himself from thinking too much.

Wait for your opportunity, his instincts told him. *You might be close to something here.*

Don't panic.

Bide your time.

See how this scenario plays out.

The noises from below increased as the night arrived in earnest.

They observed strange aircraft being towed out of the hangars and brought into others, test bays where the doors were quickly closed tight behind them. Now the bizarre noises really began, as Hunter imagined these aircraft, which he could see only as shadows, had their propulsion systems run up.

At one point, these noises became so loud, it seemed as if the entire mountain was shaking. Hunter kept his eye on the squad leader this whole time. He was alternately watching his primitive GPS device and another gadget that was sewn into his combat suit but had a small speaker attached by wire to his right ear.

This went on for another hour or so. Finally, the leader held up his hand and got the attention of the rest of the squad. He'd received some sort of information through his earpiece. Suddenly it was time to move.

More hand signals, and the squad was up again. Hunter had no idea what they were about to do. True, he saw no weapons, indeed no guards at all below in the familiar secret base. But he couldn't imagine it being completely undefended—at least in the real world, if there was such a thing anymore.

But they did not begin a long climb down the mountain. Instead, they started moving across it. Up and over more rocks, across more crevices, moving quickly yet quietly, trying not to disturb even the smallest pebble. They were soon at a position northwest of the center of the base and looking right down on the test hangars.

Despite his precarious position, Hunter was amazed at the Spetsnaz team's dexterity and stealth capabilities. While his subconscious was still working overtime trying to bring him back a hint of a memory about this place—he knew he'd seen it, maybe even been here before—he was certain that it was a very high security zone and obviously a strictly classified area. Yet, in the midst of this dizzylando anyway, the Russian special forces team had successfully breached its security boundaries, its biggest one being its insanely remote location, and now sat looking down on the place. Strictly on a military scale, it was impressive.

But Hunter's grudging admiration for these Slavic ghosts was actually premature. Because no sooner had they reached this perch overlooking the base, when a land vehicle roared up right behind them.

It was a small black truck of some sort, huge tires and all kinds of body reenforcements that allowed it to climb mountains. It was on them so quickly, Hunter thought they were dead meat. But no one in the squad panicked. They simply laid down their huge weapons and put their hands in the air. Two men stepped out of the vehicle. One was armed with an M-16 rifle, the other with a video camera. A moment of tension passed, then the leader of the infiltration squad started laughing.

"Well, OK, we buy the beer this time!" he yelled to the men now just ten or so feet away. "You caught us . . . but we got damn close!"

The rest of the squad relaxed. Two guys lit cigarettes. The two men from the vehicle smiled, too, but it was obvious they were still a bit confused. As was Hunter. The squad leader took out a pass and handed it to the two security guards.

"We're Delta Team Six," he said in a very thick drawl. "Testing the security line . . . Call us in, will you? And tell our CO what kind of suds you drink."

Hunter stood up finally, took off his silly helmet, and ran his fingers through his very dirty hair. He knew this had been too easy. For them to sneak into such a classified area undetected until now—there had to be a gag. A punch line. And this was it. The Mad Russian was displaying his odd sense of humor once again. This wasn't a real incursion. These weren't real Russians. It was all a big joke. A test. An exercise.

Right?

Wrong . . . because the moment the man with the M-16 rifle let down his guard, two of the squad members were on him. They forced him to the ground and beat him unconscious. The man with the video camera—he was the one making the call to the team's nonexistent CO—dropped it and began to run. But the two other Spetsnaz guys were on him very quickly, too. Taking him down with their fists and gun butts, he, too, was soon beaten cold.

The Spetsnaz soldiers went through the guards' pockets, taking their wallets, watches, radios, and ID badges. They pushed the truck over the other side of the mountain. It landed, out of sight, into a crevice with a dull, almost noiseless thud.

The team quickly reconstituted itself and began moving down the side of the mountain, but not before the squad leader turned to Hunter. He indicated the two unconscious security guards and drew an imaginary knife across his throat.

"Execute them quickly," he whispered harshly to Hunter. "Then catch up."

With that, the five Spetsnaz men disappeared down the other side of the mountain, leaving Hunter sitting there, mouth agape.

Damn . . . now what?

He knew if he didn't hurry and catch up with the others as ordered, they would certainly come back looking for him. And then his cover would be blown. But would that really make any difference? Could he call a halt to the mayhem here, just as he did earlier on the moon that recreated a bizarro version of World War Three? There was no way of knowing. But something told him these Russians would not play along like the last ones did. They seemed too committed, too serious . . .

On the other hand, there was no way Hunter was going to kill these two security guys, either. Yet he couldn't just leave, as the Spetsnaz might come back and finish the job themselves.

He finally took out his quadtrol and gave it a spin. He asked it the standard questions: Where was the Mad Russian? Where was the next ticket booth? He was surprised that he got a hit. The quadtrol claimed "something of interest" was located almost directly below him. The know-it-all device didn't know quite what; it was processing insufficient data. But it was a ticket booth at the very least—and maybe even the Mad Russian himself.

So now Hunter knew he had to continue this game and indeed join the others.

At this stage, it was probably his only way out of here.

He took off all but the guards' underwear and tossed their clothes over the cliff. Then he ran to catch up with the others.

He practically rolled down the hill, colliding with the squad leader at the bottom. They were now on a sort of plateau, just fifty feet above the northwest edge of the base. The squad leader's ability to mimic the guard's twang came into play when the guard's radio beeped just seconds after Hunter arrived. It was the security HQ calling their men on a routine check. The Spetsnaz officer replied in a near perfect imitation of the man's voice and even ended the conversation with a joke about an upcoming sporting event.

Meanwhile, Hunter did his best in pretending to wipe blood from his hands, hoping to maintain a charade of his own. Then he took up a position next to one of the other special ops soldiers and for the first time saw what was below them. At first it seemed like a road that ended nowhere. It started down by the hangars, ran past the fuel tanks and support buildings, and then . . . just ended.

But closer inspection told an even stranger tale. The road ran right into the side of the mountain. The Spetsnaz team did not have night scope devices, but oddly enough, they did not need them. Hunter just squinted a little and saw what the others saw. There was a huge door in the side of the rock. It was made of steel, painted to blend in, but it was a door nevertheless.

And this is where it got very weird for Hunter—if in fact this whole escapade could get any weirder. Because at that moment, he had a kind of convergence of both his previous lives. This door—he'd seen it before, or at least something very much like it. And this secret place—suddenly he knew what that was all about, too.

Way back when he first discovered himself in the seventy-third century and was brought to Earth to eventually win the prestigious Earth Race, one of his prizes was a tour of a place not unlike this. One big valuable secret, hidden away, under the tightest guard imaginable in a mountain in the western desert of present-day Earth.

But back in the time period he'd originally come from, the twentieth century, there was also a very secret place in the western desert of America.

It was called Area 51.

That's where he was now, or at least the dizzylando version of it. Top Secret air base then.

The home of the Big Generator now.

How freakin' strange is that?

The Spetsnaz squad stole down to the door—it was obviously their first objective—and very quickly attached a strip of plastic explosive to its huge right-side hinges. Incredibly there was an explosion with virtually no flash and absolutely no noise.

The door conveniently blew to one side for them. They

rushed in, weapons up, the squad leader in front, Hunter, as usual, taking up the rear. They were suddenly running inside a very dark tunnel. It smelled of grease and spilled jet fuel. It had a sharp slope, and more than once Hunter almost wound up on his ass, losing his balance on the slippery surface. The deeper they ran, the stranger the sounds they could hear coming from below. They were very eerie. And not entirely mechanical. They almost sounded organic. Pulsating, pounding, there was also the element of human screams mixed in somewhere. With each step, these unnerving sounds became louder and louder, not unlike the sound effects back in Ping's Palace. Just a whole lot creepier.

The Spetsnaz guys knew what they were doing; Hunter caught himself imagining that they had practiced this assault many times before. Perhaps in a mock-up. (But then again, this whole place was a mock-up!) They came to several TV cameras hanging in the tunnel. Without breaking stride one iota, the Spetsnaz soldiers expertly shot them off the wall. Any security detectors they came to suffered the same fate.

This went on for what seemed like a long time, though probably only a few minutes. They were getting deeper and deeper into the base of the mountain. The weird sounds grew louder, as the air grew colder. Hunter kept up with the Spetsnaz soldiers but kept looking over his shoulder every few seconds, wondering when he was going to see someone coming after them.

They eventually reached another huge door. Again, the Spetsnaz guys barely stopped. They threw their explosive charges at it, and it blew off its hinges just as they reached its threshold—a rather fantastic circumstance to Hunter's mind. Running past the blown apart door, they slid into a huge room and finally came to a stop.

This place was better described as a chamber. Its walls seemed covered in silver and gold. It was filled with computers and control panels and lights flashing on and off. A Klaxon began blaring as soon as they arrived, but a fusillade from the team leader's assault weapon silenced it as quickly as it had started. Sitting in the middle of the chamber seemed to be what the Russians had come for.

It was a flying vehicle of some sort. Flat, ovalish, with two very small winglets on its tail, and a very small canopy on its front. Hunter was stunned again. This, too, he recognized, though it took him a moment to realize why. Flat. Silver. Tiny wings, tiny top. Way back . . . during the mind ring trip he took to explore the devious origins of the Fourth Empire, in one version of how it all began, a vehicle just like this had crashed into a place called Kelly's Hollow, the site recognized by most as the birthplace of the First Empire.

But how could this be? Why was its re-creation here? What was the connection? Or was there any connection at all?

He had about two seconds to think about all this when he suddenly realized this was not their prize at all. While he stood gawking at the strange aircraft, his comrades were busy blowing yet another door off its hinges. This time the explosion was loud and violent, but that did not slow the Spetsnaz men one bit. They flowed through the new opening, and Hunter was compelled to follow.

Down they went again, deeper and deeper into the ground, through the long, spiraling tube. More weird noises. More slippery ground. More security cameras blown from their stations. They came to another door. It was gone in another brilliant flash. They stumbled into another chamber, but this one was as different as one could imagine from the one before. There was no silver or gold or any wild flying vehicles here. This place was dark, scary. Full of shadows and ghosts.

And yet, once again, it was a place that Hunter recognized. Indeed, he'd been here before, too. On his tour after winning the Earth Race, they brought him to the sacred place where the Big Generator itself was located. And this was a perfect re-creation of that place. But that time, the Big Generator was here, and it was a large black piece of stone, or something that looked like stone. It was imposing and mysterious and really didn't strike Hunter at the time as being able to generate anything. Yet it was the most holy stone of the entire Galaxy, and it was from it, so the Empirists claimed, that all power and knowledge sprang forth.

Though he was now in almost the exact same room, there was no intimidating obelisk here. No Big Generator. Instead, in the middle of the rather musty, dirty room was a device so small Hunter could have held it in his hands. He couldn't help but go over to it, touch it, and indeed pick it up. And strangely enough—and here it got funny again—the device *was* a generator. An old, disconnected, drained-of-oil *electrical* generator. Something that could provide power to nothing more elaborate than a fork truck or a car, or maybe a small static machine of some sort back on old Earth.

Hunter would have laughed if it hadn't been so absolutely fucking weird.

Another door was blown off, and their descent into

madness continued. This time the tunnel was steeper, darker, slipperier. Four TV cameras were blown from their mountings; another Klaxon was silenced. Again at the end of the pack, Hunter was running with his head turned, expecting at any time to see an army of security guards coming around the corner they'd just turned. At this point, in fact, he wouldn't have been surprised to see a bunch of tin soldiers with buckethead helmets chasing him. That's how crazy things had become.

At last they came to the final door. This one was big and black and looked stronger and thicker than the rest by a factor of ten. The Spetsnaz soldiers unloaded all their explosives and quickly placed them around the huge portal. This would not be a blow and go. They had to take cover for this one. The squad leader touched the trigger terminals, and indeed there was a fantastically huge explosion. The door came off.

Another deeper chamber lay beyond.

And finally, they found what they were looking for. Sitting in the middle of this hall was a perfectly round, gleaming flying saucer.

"Damn . . ." Hunter said out loud.

He'd seen one of these things before, too.

Before he could take another breath, all the Russian soldiers turned to him, and the squad leader said: "You *do* know how to fly this thing, don't you?"

But Hunter never got to answer. Suddenly, a bullet went through his back, hit three of his ribs, and exited through his collarbone, making it impossible for him to speak. An instant later, a second bullet went through his arm and out his stomach. A third punctured his thigh. He was spun around by the force of these bullets to see that the small army of security men he'd feared was on their tail had finally materialized from within the smoke of the blown-away door. Leading the charge were the two security guards he'd left up on the mountain, still in their underwear. They were the ones who'd shot him.

The gunfight that broke out now was ferocious. Bullets were suddenly flying everywhere, bouncing off the walls, the ceiling, even the flying saucer. Hunter was down on the oily floor in a heap, feeling like he had a couple tons of concrete pressing on his chest. *Could* he be killed here, in this fantasy world? The answer, bleeding out of his body right now, seemed to be a very frightening *yes.*

He started crawling away, feeling the heat of bullets zinging by him. He crawled past the Russian soldiers who were firing madly at the security guards. They ignored him as he dragged his near lifeless body by them, leaving a sickening trail of blood in his wake.

He somehow found the strength to reach into his pocket and retrieve his quadtrol. It was his one and only hope. He managed to turn on the device and tried to hang on as it searched desperately for the ticket booth. He actually felt his heart leap as the screen indicated that it lay just "beyond the next door."

He spotted the only other door in the chamber and crawled over to it. Bullets still flying all over, he reached up to its handle, only to find it was locked. This took just about the last of his energy out of him. Never before had he felt so weak.

He didn't have enough strength to breathe, never mind try to get the door open. But then serendipity—or part of the program of this place. A fusillade of bullets went over his head and snapped the door neatly in two. One half of it fell away, the other half fell right on top of Hunter. Now it felt like three tons of concrete were pressing down on him, instead of just two.

He never stopped crawling, though. He made it inside the room and suddenly found himself staring up at a stereotypical ticket booth. Cramped interior. Fake wood. The PC sitting as always right in the middle. Hunter was losing blood and breath. He had no time to admire the strange location of the place. He dragged himself to the PC table, lifted himself up to it, and started the painful process of booting up. It took longer than usual—and all this was happening as the gun battle was drawing closer to the tiny room.

Finally he faced the last field. The one that asked about his hobby. He barely had the strength to type it in.

Then, with the last ounce of life in his body, he pushed the Enter button.

Chapter 8

"Let me take care of that stain, sir. . . ."

Hunter watched in dazed confusion as the girl in the very low-cut dress began wiping the blood from his chest.

There is nothing more exhilarating than getting shot at with no result. Someone famous had once said that. But at the moment Hunter was more stunned than exhilarated. It was dark. He was barely aware of his surroundings. One moment, he was pushing the Enter button on the old PC. The next, he was here—wherever here was.

He tried his best to get his wits about him. He was seated at a wooden table, an old gas lamp burning dimly in front of him. He could hear choppy piano music rising behind him, its song boisterous and off key. But his vision was still blurry, and the oil lamp was doing him no good. He could just make out the pair of partially exposed breasts just inches in front of his face.

Am I dying—or not?

This was the only question on Hunter's mind.

He blinked his eyes, and when he opened them again, his vision began to clear. The woman in the low-cut dress was dressed like a saloon hall girl. She'd stuck the hem of her short black skirt into a glass of water and was wiping Hunter's shirt again.

"California red wine," she was saying. "Good thing it's cheap. It won't stain too much if you catch it in time."

Hunter looked down at the table again and saw a wineglass tipped over and a small pool of red wine in front of him. And some of it had splashed on him. In fact, the red stains coincided exactly with where he'd been shot just seconds earlier: up near his shoulder. On his chest. Down on his thigh.

The bar girl began aggressively attacking the stain on his pants.

"I'm sorry, partner," she was telling him. "I'll get you another glass. . . ."

That's when Hunter finally patted himself down—and much to his surprise, found his body free of bullet holes.

"Can you make it a whiskey?" he asked her with a croak.

"Anything for you, honey."

"How about a double then. . . ."

She departed into the blur. Hunter leaned back and prayed that she would return with something stronger than colored water.

His body was still shaking, his brain felt like it was pounding its way out of his skull. He checked his body again. No blood. No wounds. No perforations anywhere. Just some wine stains.

He finally slumped back in his chair and let out a long, low whistle of relief. That had been too freaking scary.

But where the hell was he now? If there had been a sign at the last ticket booth announcing the next ride, he'd missed it during what he thought were the last few moments of his life. So he had not even a hint of his new reality. But soon enough, he began spotting clues.

He was back in his combat suit, and he had his old flight boots on again. But his crash helmet was hanging off the back of his chair. He felt another kind of hat on his head. He took it off and studied it. It was big and broad with its rim turned up in either side. He'd seen one of these before somewhere. He looked at the inside label. It read, Made in Texas. 10 Gallon—Wide Band. Everyone around him was wearing the same kind of hat.

He was in a saloon. A huge one. His table was just one of 200 or more. The bar itself seemed to stretch off into infinity. It was crowded with rowdy drinkers dressed in dirty pants, muddy boots, and long overcoats he knew were called dusters. Across from the bar was a stage. Several girls not unlike the one who'd just cleaned him up were doing a hideous dance that most closely resembled the odd ballet the girls in front of Ping's Palace had been performing.

The music was coming from an ancient upright piano jammed into the corner of the stage. The man playing it looked drunker than the patrons at the bar. He also had an arrow sticking right through his derby hat. If it was real, then it was probably sticking right through his skull, too. But this didn't seem to have any effect on his playing. It was awful, but earnest. Strangely, right above his piano was a huge red star.

The saloon hall girl returned to Hunter's table. "Sorry sir, but we are out of whiskey," she said. "Would you like a glass of vodka instead?"

She put the drink in front of him before he could even reply. He drank it greedily. It looked like water, but it tasted like gasoline, burning his gullet all the way down. At last! Real booze!

The vodka made him relax. His head cleared enough for him to think a bit more rationally. He'd just made his escape in the nick of time from the Alien Mystery World. He shook off any thoughts of what might have happened if he hadn't made it into the ticket booth when he did. He took another long slug of the vodka, finishing the glass. He signaled the attentive bar girl for another. The music began to rise again. The patrons along the rail were becoming more rowdy. The girls on the stage continued dancing very provocatively. His second drink arrived. Hunter downed it on one gulp. He asked for a third.

What was this place? It was certainly more inviting than the brutally hot desert or a reprise of World War Three. It was definitely an homage of some sort to the ancient American West. Yet Russian influences were everywhere. From the big red star over the piano to another, even larger one hanging over the stage, to the glorious vodka he was pouring down his throat.

The Old West and Mother Russia?

It made for a very strange combination.

The piano player ended one song and immediately went

into another. Starting down in the low notes, he began slowly working his way up the scale, intent on pounding the keys to death. Hunter's third vodka arrived. Again he downed it in one gulp. Before he even put the empty glass down on the table, he was signaling for another.

The whole place had turned its attention to the stage. It had gone dark, a lone dancer appearing in place of the small troupe who'd been previously denting the floorboards. Having walked out from behind a curtain, this dancer was now moving gracefully to center stage. The honky-tonk piano continued its slow buildup. The crowd shuddered with anticipation. The dancer was not in the spotlight, rather she looked like a shadow, standing very still. The music built further, approaching its climax. This woman was going to sing, Hunter thought. And no doubt her voice will sound as bad as the rest of the entertainment in this place.

But just as the piano reached its peak, the woman opened not her mouth, but the front buttons of her dress. The crowd let out a soft "Ooooooh . . ." Hunter heard himself gasp. The dancer let the top of the dress drop from her shoulders. Another gasp went through the crowd. Suddenly, she was nearly topless. In the bare red shadow, Hunter could see her perfectly formed breasts.

"Damn . . ." he whispered.

She began swaying to the music, her skirt suddenly gone, too. She had a lovely form from top to bottom. Not buxom, but just right. Her long hair flung back in curls. Garters. High button shoes. Hunter's fourth drink arrived, and he felt his hand shake as he picked it up. What the hell did they call *this* ride?

A combination of the vodka and testosterone started to

take effect. He began to pant. Then, finally, a spotlight illuminated the dancer's face.

Hunter nearly fell off his chair.

Is that Annie?

The saloon hall girl returned at a very inopportune time, and for once she was not bearing another drink for Hunter. Instead, she bent down and whispered in his ear, "I understand you're looking for the Mad Russian?"

Hunter was so close to being in a frenzy, he didn't hear her. She repeated the question.

Only then did he snap out of it. With one eye trying to keep track of this amazing thing happening onstage, he turned to the bar girl and said, "Yes, definitely."

"Then he'll see you now," she replied.

Suddenly she had Hunter's undivided attention. *"He's here?"*

"In his office out back," she said. "He's waiting for you."

Hunter froze. He wanted oh so much to watch this demonstration onstage. *What is Annie doing here?*

But he couldn't pass up this opportunity to finally meet his quarry.

He went with the waitress.

She led him out of the bar area, through a curtain, and into a dark hallway. They walked for what seemed like forever. The oil lamps in the hall started flickering at one point. Not just a little drunk, Hunter started stumbling, nearly losing sight of the saloon hall girl.

Finally they reached a door with a sign that read simply, Trail Boss.

She turned, smiled, and nodded toward the door.

"He's in there," she said. "Good luck."

Hunter staggered in. The room was dark. A log was burning in the fireplace. Two walls were lined with ornamental swords. Ancient muskets adorned another. Bullwhips, spurs, and several lassos were also on display.

At the far end of the room there was a huge, carved wood desk sitting on an elevated platform about a foot off the floor. There was a man sitting behind this desk, almost totally hidden in shadow. His back was turned to Hunter.

It was strange, because Hunter could still hear the piano music. And he was still imagining what was going on, back on that stage and wondering why Annie had shown up inside this attraction, too. To what purpose was she here? Maybe the guy behind the desk would have the answer to that question—along with a few million more.

He took three giant steps and was soon just a few feet away from the desk. He could see over the back of the chair, and thus the back of the person's head.

"I've been looking all over for you," Hunter began, not knowing what else to say.

No response.

"I was sent to search for you by an old friend of yours," he went on. The piano music in the background was becoming more intense.

Still nothing.

"The entire Galaxy needs your help," Hunter tried.

"I know that all too well," the man behind the desk finally responded.

"Then can we talk about it?" Hunter asked him. "I've come a long way, went through a lot, visited many of your attractions just to find you. You should know exactly why I've come—"

"I know very well why you're here," the voice said.

There was a bit of sadness in its tone. And the voice sounded familiar, too. Just a little bit of an accent. "That's the problem. . . ."

That's when the man in the chair slowly turned around, and Hunter finally saw his face. He was shocked.

It was Dr. Zoloff. Certainly an older, hairier version of the man depicted in the faded photo on the back of the ticket stub. But now, in the light, at this moment, Hunter saw the resemblance. The crazy eyes, the long, thin face. The yellow teeth. Though dressed in Old West gear, this was, unmistakably, the good doctor from Adventure Land.

Hunter laughed out loud. "Well, I guess it makes sense now," he said drunkenly. "You were the only one who evaded my questions when I asked about your whereabouts. No one else had a problem with answering me. Just you. I should have known. I should have figured it out sooner."

Zoloff frowned mightily.

"There are many things we both should have figured out sooner," he said.

With that, Hunter saw two other figures move out from behind the shadows.

They were both holding ray guns.

"*Damn* . . ." Hunter cursed.

They were Solar Guards. SSG . . .

Zoloff just shrugged sadly. "I'm sorry," he said. "They were looking for me, too, and they just did beat you to it."

Minutes later, Hunter and Zoloff were behind bars.

Real bars, this time. In fact, they were electron steel bars, impossible to bend by hand alone.

The two SSG soldiers had hauled them out of the Red Star Saloon via a back door and marched them down a very dusty street to the amusement of the townsfolk who inhabited this very strange place. Hunter got only a brief glimpse of his new surroundings: a couple blocks of old wooden buildings, a general store, a bank, an apothecary, a barber shop. With wooden sidewalks everywhere. There were even tumbleweeds blowing around. The sky above them, oddly enough, was bright orange. There was no sun to be seen.

The sheriff's office was empty when they were brought in. The SSG troopers wordlessly locked them in the jail cell, then strengthened its previously rubber bars with the electron-steel reinforcements. Then the SSG men hung up the keys next to a rifle rack, took their seats behind the sheriff's desk, and promptly went to sleep.

Hunter and Zoloff collapsed to the floor of the six-by-six cell. They were very much bummed out.

"I'm living down here for a few thousand years," Zoloff said wearily. "No one bothers me, and I don't bother anyone. Then, all of a sudden, I'm the most wanted person in the cosmos."

Hunter had his head resting on his knees. He was suddenly very, very tired. "I know the feeling," he moaned.

He quickly told Zoloff who he was and who sent him. "And, if it makes you feel any better," Hunter concluded his introduction, "I was looking for you for the same reason as those two."

"The Big Generator thing," Zoloff said knowingly. "And how they want to alter it . . ."

"They told you?"

"They did," Zoloff replied. "I heard the whole story, in fact. From the Empress to the Great Flash to the blackout and the extent of the damage. And of course, their desire to change around the Big Generator's power flows. They might not look it now, but those two over there are rather verbose."

Hunter studied the man next to him for a moment. He was definitely the same Zoloff he'd met in Adventure Land. But he was more genuine now. Like an actor who was no longer in his role, the veneer had been dropped. Strangely, though, he was still a very sympathetic character.

"They didn't mind telling you all this?" he asked Zoloff. "I mean, all those things about the BG are highly top secret. No more than a few dozen people in the entire Galaxy have a clue that any of this is even going on."

Zoloff shrugged sadly. "It makes no difference to them what I know," he said, indicating the two sleeping guards again. "Because they've got plans for me, you see. By telling me all, they know I won't be able to help myself from thinking about how to counteract their designs for the Big Generator. All they have to do is wait a little bit, let my subconscious cook on it a while. Then they will torture me to get the information they seek, and then give me a brain wipe to get anything they missed. After that, they'll put me to death. And though I've been around longer than Methuselah, I have a feeling they'll find a way to pull it off. I mean, I was told I could live forever, but I'm not so sure that applies if I am somehow torn limb from limb or thrown into a star."

"So, it's true then?" Hunter asked him. "That you could come up with a way to counter whatever they do to the Big Generator?"

Hunter saw the twinkle return to Zoloff's eye. Suddenly

he was just like the good doctor back in Adventure Land.

"Of course!" he said with not an ounce of false modesty. "In fact, as soon as they mentioned it, I had the solution."

"Really? What is it?"

Zoloff checked to see if the two SSG were still asleep. They seemed to be. He smiled—and then started to whistle. One long tone. Very melodic, haunting even, if a little sad.

"And that is?" Hunter asked.

Zoloff smiled again. "C major diminished," he replied, lowering his voice to a near whisper. "And that's the secret."

"You're kidding. . . ."

"At a time like this?" Zoloff scolded him gently. "Hardly."

"But . . . just whistling? That's the secret?"

Zoloff nodded with great authority, then slid over a little closer to Hunter. "Look—no one really knows how the Big Generator works," he said. "But I *do* know it has something to do with vibrations. And sound waves are vibrations. And therefore, a certain musical note is the key to the BG's power. I know this because of my extensive studies in super electricity. I also happen to know that by simply using this key, anyone can readjust whatever the SSG does to the BG."

He whistled it again. "C major diminished . . ."

Hunter just stared back at him. Was this a joke? Could it really be as simple as that?

"So are you saying that if the SSG gets control of the BG, you'd want everyone in the Galaxy to whistle that note?" he asked Zoloff.

"Precisely!" he declared. "Actually, if I understand the situation correctly, you have this one military called the Space Forces. And another—these devils, the Solar Guards?"

"Right . . ."

"And the SF is less despicable than the SG?"

"Right again . . ."

"Then what we can do is provide a simple device to all SF warships, something that will automatically retune the power coming out of the BG and allow them to tap into it, no matter what the Solar Guards do to it.

"Now, that will take care of the military side of the situation. Once that's settled, we let everyone in the Milky Way know the tone. If the BG starts to change, or if there is another blackout, all we have to do is all rise up in song— beautiful song!—and that will send the BG's power everyone's way again and remedy the situation. It's an ironic way to overcome the plans of these dastardly people, don't you think?"

Hunter just shrugged. "Beautiful or not, it's not going to do anyone any good. Once they kill us, no one will ever find out about it."

The smile left Zoloff's face. "Again, all too true." He sighed. There was another silence between them. Hunter finally broke it by saying, "I have to tell you, though, this is one crazy place you built here."

Zoloff shook his head sadly. "I did my best," he said. "Though you really have to experience the whole thing to appreciate it. Like a fine symphony. A fine wine. A fine woman. Of course, I know it's frightening at some points and creaky at others. Some of the thrills and spills are a little heavy-handed, too. But what in life isn't a little scary, when you really think about it? And only someone really committed to it will see it all the way through. That's one reason I didn't reveal myself to you right away. I had no idea who you were. The entry booth hadn't been activated in years. The password was a very tight secret. But I knew when everything suddenly lit up, something must be afoot. And I thought if you made it through, even just halfway, then you were here for a serious purpose, and not just by a mistake."

He looked over at the two SSG men again. "How did I know these mooches would drop in halfway through? They picked a moon and crash-landed on it. The heathens. Just my luck it was Dreamland."

"But how did you ever come up with all this?" Hunter asked him. He was intensely curious, even at this dark hour. "This whole amusement park thing? I mean, did it come to you in a dream or something?"

"Ha," Zoloff said. "It came to me in many, *many* dreams, my friend. But, tell me first. Did you figure out the theme? After all, it is a *theme park*. Or was I perhaps too subtle?"

Hunter had to think a moment. "The theme? How to go crazy, when everything else around is already crazy?"

Zoloff laughed a bit too loud, but he was genuinely amused.

"That would be hard to pull off subtly," he said. He stroked his beard for a moment. "The truth is," he began again, "all I ever wanted was to be like you. To be an American, I mean. Or *like* an American. *That's* the theme. That's what the whole dizzylando is about."

Hunter looked back at him strangely. "Really?"

Zoloff started ticking things off on his fingers. "Adventure Land—my love for your Hollywood space adventures of the 1930s. House of Horrors—what I imagined it would be like if the Soviet Army was as principled and disciplined as the American Army. Dreamland—my vision of America as a place where *all* dreams come true and *stay* true. World of Mirrors—the only common enemy we ever had: the fascists. What a delight to see them fighting each other! Alien Mystery World—I desired your deepest secrets and nothing less!"

Hunter held up his hand, as a gentle interruption. "But what about all those socks?"

Zoloff just smiled. "Very simple," he said. "I wanted one of your washing machines!"

"And all this?"

Zoloff was almost embarrassed now. "Well, everyone wants to be a cowboy," he said. "Right?"

Hunter stared back at him in disbelief. *That's what this is all about? A Russian trying to explain what it's like to be an American?*

"But why?" was all he could ask. "You're a cosmonaut. A hero of the Soviet Union."

"The desire was born from an incident long ago," Zoloff replied. "It happened just before I went into orbit, back in the 1960s. I had a rare opportunity to visit New York City. It was a meeting on the peaceful uses of space at the UN, but I snuck out one night and walked all over that fabulous city. I saw it all. Did it all. Drank it all. Ate it all! When I finally stumbled back to the Soviet mission early the next morning, I realized what a cloud I'd been living under." He paused for a long moment. His eyes got misty. "That's when I realized I wanted everything you had," he went on again. "Your women. Your style. Your optimism. Your music. Your sense of humor. Your bravery. Your deep dark secrets. And yes, those wonderful washing machines! Even if they did eat socks.

"I wanted all those things, but at the same time I knew that I couldn't have them. Not in Russia in the 1960s. But those desires stayed with me, even when I was thrown forward in time. Your NASA friend will verify that. Then, after the collapse of the Third Empire, when I had a chance to do something, to make a grand deal, I decided to do what I considered the next best thing. There were never any amusement parks in Russia. I thought if I could build one for myself and continually ride its rides, forever, so to speak, well, what better way to immerse myself in your culture? To play the different parts. To make some different endings. So yes, it came from a dream. A foolish dream though, now, looking back on it."

"I don't know about that," Hunter said, astounded by the story. "It was a pretty wild trip while it lasted . . . and quite an accomplishment, I'd have to say."

Another bit of silence.

Zoloff went on sadly, "All those years, wasted money and time and fear, our two countries, preparing to go to war with each other. That's about the time I checked out—and was thrown forward, where I met your friend and mine, that very old man in the NASA suit. How he and I argued. How we fought! But we were brothers. And we built a great empire. It's just too bad it wasn't like that back in my day. Before the war between our two countries started. If in fact it did ever start."

Hunter told him, "It definitely started in my reality. But I'm convinced now, after what's happened to me, that the way the universe unfolds, there are probably an infinite number of realities, and we are either from the same one . . . or we are not."

"Very true, but people stay the same, my friend," Zoloff replied. "Events change, but people don't. No matter how many realities there might be, humans are humans. And it is our duty to get ourselves right. To correct our flaws. To treat everyone equally. That's what we fought for with the Third Empire. And we succeeded, your NASA friend and I—for a little while at least.

"But in the end, what good was it? Look at me. I'm still a Russian. A son of Mother Russia way back when there was a Russia, five thousand years ago. I changed the way I looked. The way I talked. The way I thought about things. But no matter what, I couldn't change who I was. A sad last chapter. Park closed. The dizzylando is no more."

Hunter had to pat him on the back. He was almost in tears himself. "I have something very important to tell you," he began. "For what it's worth, there *is* a place where you *can* be both. It exists. It's not an amusement park. It's real. I've been there."

"Both?" Zoloff asked. "Both Russian and American, you mean?"

Hunter nodded slowly. "Russian, American, European, Japanese, Indian. White, black, yellow, brown. Everything. It's a place called the Home Planets. It's a place where the original people from Earth were sent against their will when evil forces took over the empires. A deep dark secret kept from you, no doubt. But the Astronaut found out about it somehow. And like me, he knows it is a place where anyone can be all of those things, simply by being one thing: a person from Earth. An original Earthling."

He leaned over and showed him the flag on his shoulder. It was the American flag.

"This is our flag," he said. "It used to represent all that was good and free and just within my country, but now it represents all of those Home Planets as well."

Zoloff became so emotional listening to this that he began to cry. "If I went to this place," he said. "I could have the best of both worlds?"

"Of all worlds," Hunter told him.

Zoloff got a very determined look on his face. "Well, then, that's what I must do!" he said. "But first, we must get out of this jam. And the ones that come after it." He looked around the cell again. "The question is, *how?*"

At that moment, as if on cue, the door to the sheriff's office opened.

A woman walked in with a tray full of food and two vodka bottles. It was Annie, of course.

Hunter unconsciously pressed himself up against the cage. She looked even more beautiful than before—which he would have thought was an impossibility at this point. But it was true: she was now slinky in her very tight, very revealing saloon hall dress. And her face was full of makeup. She was tarted up, in a way.

But was something wrong here? She ignored both him and Zoloff in the cage and walked over to the pair of SSG men. She gently shook both awake, stopping to massage one's shoulders.

"I thought the sheriff and his deputy might be hungry," she said sweetly.

The SSG man getting the massage reached around and grabbed her by the waist. She cried out playfully. Now the "deputy" wanted some. He pulled her away from his partner, and let her wiggle in his lap for a while.

One of the vodka bottles was opened. Three glasses materialized, too. Drinks were poured out, all three began to imbibe.

Hunter leaned even farther into the bars. The two Solar Guards drained their drinks and poured out two more. Annie was openly flirting with them. Her dress being very low cut, every chance she had, she bent down in front of them, giving them a view of her twin nebulas. One guard put his hand on her back. Another started stroking her hair. Hunter was enraged. He tried to bend the bars, but it was no go. Not this time. This wasn't Ping's Palace. This was real life.

Wasn't it?

Annie extended her arms and pulled both men toward her. Then she looked at Hunter—and winked.

In the next moment, both bottles of vodka came crashing down on top of the SG soldiers' heads. They both hit the floor with a simultaneous *thump!*

Then Annie herself nearly collapsed. "I didn't think I could ever do that!" she cried.

She retrieved the electric key from the wall, and soon the electron cage was open.

Annie fell into Hunter's arms and squeezed him tight. He thought he was going to melt. But then the reality of the situation returned to him.

"Is there another ticket booth close by?" he asked Zoloff urgently.

The doctor only had to think a moment. "Yes! Of course!" he roared. "Follow me!"

They ran out of the sheriff's office, across the street, and into the basement of the brothel. Sure enough, there was a battered PC waiting there. Zoloff overrode all the security functions and quickly hit the Enter button.

An instant later, they were all standing on the grand pile of socks.

Out of breath but safe, they did a group hug. But Zoloff was instantly worried again.

"Our problems do not end here," he said. "In fact, they are just beginning."

Hunter slumped into the soft pile; Annie automatically snuggled up to him. What he would have given just to stay like this with her—for a couple million years.

"Those two mooches were foolish enough to reveal something very disturbing to me," Zoloff said.

"Do I really want to hear this?" Hunter asked with a groan.

"There is an officer in this hideous Solar Guards. He's part of a special unit of theirs."

"Yes, the Special Solar Guards," Hunter said. "The SSG. The real bad characters."

"Exactly," Zoloff went on. "Well, on the strength of what these two found, he is due to come down here very soon. Within hours, even. They were supposed to meet him. He is said to be very well-versed in the ways of torture and extracting information from the reluctant. He, of course, will be looking to work me over. And you, too, I would imagine. His name is simply Commander X."

Hunter wearily took out his quadtrol and asked it for information on Commander X. The reply came back that an officer of that name was known to be one of the top interrogators within the SSG. His methods were known to be so brutal, he was even feared by members of the regular Solar Guards.

"He probably knows a lot of what the SSG is up to," Hunter thought out loud. Then he explained the rumors about Warehouse 066 and the so-called magilla to Zoloff and Annie.

"Well, before we know it," Zoloff said. "This monster will be here, in our midst. And if he doesn't find these two waiting for him, he'll have half the SSG down on our tails."

Hunter tried to think, but it was hard to do. He was tired, hungry. And now, very hungover. Finally, he just looked back up at the Mad Russian.

"So . . . what are we going to do?" he asked.

PART THREE

Grand Finale in C Major Diminished

Chapter 9

Commander X wore his best combat uniform down to Alpha Moon.

It was black, of course, with aluminum insignia on both shoulders, signifying his rank in the SSG. Just 210 years old, he was a small man, both in stature and in his respect for the human race. He was a tough nut to crack, though, a man who'd vowed that should he ever get captured by an enemy, he would take his own life before giving up any information to them. Conversely, he was an expert at wearing down a victim, physically and psychologically, to get them to the point where they would tell him anything, even though they knew their own death would be the result. Officially, his job description was *mortis inquisitorus*.

He'd brought his ion-silver ray gun as a side arm this day. Also, his ceremonial silver dagger, his new super quadtrol, which was the latest in know-it-all technology, his electro-shock wand, and just in case he had occasion to grow bored, a flask of gold slow-ship wine, the best of the best.

CX, as he was also called, knew very little about Alpha Moon, the so-called Mad Russian, or the concept of a dizzylando. He'd been directly involved with the renovations on the Big Generator, lording over the Empire scientists and supervising the beating of any one of them who did not seem to be working hard enough. But when the top echelon of the SSG discovered, through a paid informant, that there was a person somewhere in the Galaxy who actually had the knowledge to thwart what they were trying to do to the big black slab, they ordered CX and his men to track him down. Once found, he was to be tortured, brain wiped, and then executed—three talents that Commander X and his men reveled in.

They'd discovered information about the Mad Russian and his amusement park simply by breaking into the inner sanctuary of O'Nay's palace on the floating city of Special Number One and reading one of the Five Secrets. These sacred mysteries at one time were guarded by entire armies of O'Nay's bodyguards. But since the Emperor fled to a second, top secret floating city—Special Number Two—currently riding the airways up near the Earth's North Pole, it was no trouble at all for the SSG to have the run of his first floating palace. Gaining access to the Five Secrets' vault had been surprisingly easy.

So they read about the Ancient Cosmonaut and the deal he made with the early rulers of the Fourth Empire, and how he'd been given a handful of moons around Saturn and tons of secret technology to essentially create a fantasy world of his own. They also learned how brilliant he was, especially in the area of super electricity, which, was believed by many to be the principle behind the mysterious Big Generator. After reading his dossier, they were convinced, as was anybody who knew him, that the Mad Russian would be able to counter anything they did to the BG, first by passing a cure on to the Space Forces, and then by spreading the same message throughout the Galaxy.

Just what that cure would be, the SSG didn't know, and frankly, they didn't care. Their mission was to find this guy, beat the daylights out of him, drain all the knowledge out of his head, and then grease him.

CX sent his best two men down to the dizzylando first. No sense in him getting his own uniform dirty—or his dagger for that matter—until absolutely necessary. He'd received word just that morning that his men had indeed tracked down the Mad Russian—after a rather unusual pursuit that started out with them crash landing on the wrong moon. The last he'd heard from them, their message insisted that the collection of moons was so crazy it was "best to start at the beginning," which sounded logical to him. It was now time for Commander X, the closer, as they said in the torture business, to make his appearance and bring this mission to its inevitable conclusion.

So now he was here, transported to the Alpha Moon via a superstring transfer—not to be confused with a DATT. His trip was smooth and instantaneous. One moment he was in his barracks back on Earth, at the secret base out in the middle of the western desert—the next he was standing on the faux wood front porch of the first ticket booth, armed with his password and all the instructions he needed to work the ancient PC inside.

He went through the procedure of booting up the old computer and getting through its security procedures. When it came time to fill in his hobby, he laughed and typed, "Watching people squirm."

Highly satisfied with himself, he straightened his uniform, wiped the dust from his sleeves . . . and pushed the Enter button.

"Quick . . . jump on!"

Commander X was immediately confused. A moment before he was inside the railroad station ticket booth, not really knowing what to expect, simply following the instructions given to him by his two advance men, and now, suddenly he was . . . well, where the hell was he?

His vision cleared, and he found himself standing on a cliff. Not in the middle of it, but right on the edge. Below him was a very deep ravine, at least five hundred feet down. Not twenty feet behind him were three armies of soldiers in skirts and carrying spears charging toward him. There were explosions going off all around him. The air smelled awful. And it was dawning on him that he was about to either get skewered by a thousand spears or fall to his death.

He was certainly the one squirming now.

"Quick . . . jump on!"

Finally CX looked right in front of him. Here, he saw the most confusing sight yet. There was an insane-looking spaceship of some kind hovering—sort of—just a few feet off the tip of the cliff. Its hatch was open, its tailpipe was smoking heavily, and damn it if he couldn't see three sets of near invisible strings coming out of the top of it. A man was standing in the hatchway, hand extended, pleading for him to leap to safety.

Commander X didn't really jump as much as he was pushed. Three flaming spears nailed him in the buttocks all at once. This and the screams of the soldiers in skirts gave him the impetus to leap toward the spaceship. It was his only means of escape.

It was about a six-foot leap, but again the flaming spears propelled him forward. Still, he just barely managed to grab on to the bottom of the hatch, very nearly falling into the chasm. He let out a scream in a voice he'd never heard come out of himself before. It was very womanly. The man in the open doorway tried to help him on board, but the spaceship started vibrating madly, and then the bottom of the hatch began tearing away from its body. Commander X couldn't believe it. This damn thing seemed made of cardboard!

He pulled off a chunk of it with his right hand—and here came that scream again—as now he was hanging on by just four fingers of his left hand. The spacecraft was shaking mightily now. The tin soldiers were throwing their flaming spears at him, and he was about two seconds away from plunging to his death.

As it turned out, the only reason he didn't fall at that moment was that the spacecraft did an incredible sideways flip, literally turning on its side ninety degrees. So now Commander X, instead of hanging off of the ship, was suddenly on top of it, looking down. He hung there for a second before dropping through the hatch, smashing his head and shoulder as he fell, then cracking his skull a second time as he hit the cabin's interior far wall.

Dazed, bleeding, and stunned, CX felt the ship right it-self and slowly, very slowly, start moving away from the cliff.

He opened his eyes to see two people looking down at him: an old man with bad teeth and a beard that looked fake, and a young girl, pretty but dumb-looking. They were alter-nately trying to help him up and stepping on him. He was blubbering, trying to speak, trying to assess his wounds, try-ing to keep his bladder from bursting involuntarily.

Finally he was able to shout, "Where the hell am I?"

The reply from the old man was maddeningly simple: "You're with us."

"But *who* the *hell* are *you!*"

"I am Dr. Zoloff. This is my daughter, Annie."

CX struggled to get up, but the ship was gyrating so wildly, it proved impossible.

He began sputtering again. "Do you know who I am?" he screamed at them.

"Yes, of course," the old man said. "You're Flash Rogers! And you've come to help us!"

CX finally got to his feet and was hit with a sudden attack of motion sickness. If this was flying, he had to get his legs back on the ground as quickly as possible. But the flimsy ship was swaying so violently, he was lucky he could stay upright.

He cleared his eyes again and saw the old man was now at the controls of the craft, but they looked too simple to actually control anything. Commander X's first instinct was to shoot the both of them, but then who would fly this claptrap? He did make his way over to the control panel, intent upon at least seeing how this thing was able to stay in the air. By the time he stumbled to the front of the craft, the old man had turned it around by using the huge steering wheel, and they had picked up speed. A little anyway.

"Where are we going? What are you doing?" CX demanded of the old man.

The old man turned and looked at him with scary eyes. "We are going to Ping's Palace, of course!" he bellowed at him. "We must rescue Buck!"

CX's response was predictable. "Who the fuck is Buck?"

But before he could get half of it out, the young girl yelled, "The Wingmen!"

The next thing CX knew, twenty spears were suddenly sticking through the skin of the craft, half of them burning him in the ass again. As he was pulling their tips out, the craft suddenly shook from one end to the other. He fell to this rump again, only to see a huge burning arrow was now sticking out of the front of the spacecraft.

Suddenly the interior of the cabin was filled with smoke. Before CX could get to his feet, the craft severely pitched downward, causing the SSG officer to slam his battered head once again.

The craft crashed into something very hard a moment later. It came apart all around him. Cardboard pieces flying in every direction, it disintegrated into nothingness. CX was thrown to the ground, landing on his bad shoulder. He got to his knees only to see another small army of soldiers in huge buckethead helmets advancing on him.

His first instinct was to reach for his ray gun, but it was already too late for that. A tidal wave of tin soldiers fell on him and began beating him severely. The sheer weight of their armor was cracking his bones. Any time he tried to throw a punch, he hit one of their iron heads, further smashing his fingers, his knuckles. Meanwhile, the girl was led away by a couple of the soldiers, with the old man following close behind.

It went on like this for what seemed like an eternity, the soldiers pummeling CX with their fists and kicking him with their shod feet. There were so many on top of him, the SSG officer thought he would suffocate. Only when he started screaming like a girl again did the tin soldiers back off. One soldier ended the lopsided fray with a powerhouse kick to CX's groin. The SSG officer doubled over, falling on top of his flattened ray gun, and was finally dragged away.

CX went unconscious for a few minutes. When he came to, he found himself inside a very tacky, brightly lit throne room. More tin soldiers were on hand. He was dropped on his head before a staircase that led up to a seat on which a guy who looked suspiciously like the Supreme O'Nay was glaring down at him. Even in his battered state, CX laughed out loud at this man's outfit.

That was a mistake. The man apparently liked his clothes, as girly as they were. CX started into his "Do you know who I am?" routine again, but the guy on the throne would have none of it. He clapped his hands twice, and CX was lifted to his feet. Bleeding, his new uniform ripped, he was dragged to a curtain that opened to reveal a small, caged-in arena.

He was thrown inside, landing facedown. He looked up to see a huge hairy robot standing over him. *What hell is this?* Before the next thought went through his head, this monster picked him up, held him in midair with one arm, and swatted him across the arena with the other. CX landed in a heap again, only to have the monster pick him up a second time and hurl him to the other side of the cage. Stunned, dazed, eyes blurry, CX couldn't prevent the monster from kicking him, punching him, and momentarily sitting on him, before lifting him off the ground a third time and dropping him into a hole that had suddenly opened up in the arena floor.

The next thing CX knew, he was sliding in darkness for a few seconds before he hit a pool of inky black water. Three men in ridiculous fin costumes pounced on him immediately, slapping him, kicking him, splashing him. He screamed again, and that was enough to drive them off. Or so he thought. Actually, they swam away into the darkness, and the next sound he heard was that of water rushing. The water in the pool was suddenly going down very, very quickly. Before CX could even catch his breath, all the water drained out of the pool, and he crashed hard to the concrete bottom below.

Unable to get his feet under him, he tumbled through the hatch that had let the water out and found himself in a very wet tunnel. He was in a full panic now, wondering what would befall him next. He was suffering from a multitude of cuts, gashes, bruises, and fractures, both big and small. His uniform was in tatters. His boots were gone. His right eye was so puffed, he couldn't see anything out of it. His ears were ringing. His lips were cracked and bleeding. And all this had happened in the course of just two minutes!

Hearing frightening noises all around him now, he collapsed to the floor and began to cry.

He lay there for just a few seconds, finally retrieving his super quadtrol. After letting the water drain off it, he asked it just one question: "How do I get out of here?"

The reply: "Get up, turn right, start running."

He did as told.

CX ran and ran and ran. He ran until his lungs ached and his knees felt like they were going to separate from his body. The tunnels were dark, covered with weird silk that blew into ghostly formations as he scrambled by. Just when it seemed he couldn't run anymore, he reached an intersection of two tunnels.

Again he asked the super quadtrol, "What should I do? How do I escape?"

The quad replied, "Take a left." He did so, and found twelve buckethead soldiers waiting halfway down the tunnel for him.

He tried to turn around, but his feet failed him. The soldiers were on him in seconds. They fell atop him, crushing him, pounding him again, dragging him along the floor. It was only that he was still wet and slimy that he was able to squirm away after a few minutes of torturous beating. But the soldiers were soon on him again.

Through bleary eyes, he spotted a jail cell close by. It had bars that might protect him, so he leaped for it, slamming the door behind him. The soldiers mindlessly began banging on the door, but they were simply too clumsy to open it.

CX smiled for a moment, temporarily safe—or so he thought. He turned and that's when he first realized he was not alone in the cell. There was a man standing right in back of him. A man with a very familiar face.

"You?"

Hunter smiled: "Me . . ."

Hunter hit Commander X five times hard, right in the face. That was it. The SSG officer collapsed to the floor, rolled himself up into a ball, and pleaded for Hunter to stop.

Hunter picked him up off the floor. "I hear you like to torture people." He punched him five more times, again, all five right on the nose.

"No more!" CX was begging.

Hunter reared back, ready to deliver the knockout blow, when he said, "Tell me . . ."

CX could hardly speak. "Tell you? Tell you what?"

Hunter let CX drop to the floor.

"Everything . . ." he said. "The BG repair. The 066 Warehouse. The magilla."

CX was confused. "But why did you put me through . . . all this?"

Hunter was right in his face. "Would you have told me what I wanted to know if we hadn't?"

Even CX saw the logic in that. He shook his head numbly. "I would have killed myself first."

Hunter grabbed him again. "That's right, butt head," he hissed. "Now, spill!"

The plan worked. Battered and bruised physically and psychologically, CX told Hunter everything he knew. They were soon joined in the cell by Zoloff and Annie as well.

Although they got a wealth of information from the SSG inquisitor, all of it was troubling. The SSG was very close to manipulating the Big Generator to do their bidding. CX said such domination of its power flow was days if not hours away. Furthermore, the SSG was indeed working on a new weapon down on the surface of Saturn, one of frightening proportions, though the details were such deep secrets that CX, by virtue of his position, would not have had access to them. All he knew was that it might be a craft of some kind that didn't rely on the BG for its power.

As far as the mysterious magilla went, CX had never even heard of it.

Chapter 10

There was no need for parachutes to get down from Ping's Palace this time.

Zoloff had simply waved his hand, and the four of them found themselves on the ground of Adventure Land, standing atop the pastoral hill where the ticket booth was located. Hunter took a long look around as he shook off the mild effects of the sudden transfer. It seemed like he'd stood on this very hill just hours before, looking off into the distance, trying to catch one last glimpse of Annie. Now she was here with him, glued to his side, holding on so tight it seemed like she'd never let go.

Strange how things turn out, he thought.

Getting rid of Commander X was their first priority. Both Hunter and Zoloff agreed blasting him with a death ray was too good for him. Instead, with another wave of his hand, Zoloff had magically dressed the battered little man in the uniform of a Nazi private. Then, by quick manipulation of the Adventure Land PC, the Mad Russian sent the sadistic SSG officer to the Land of Mirrors, where he'd be exiled forever, caught in the endless war between the fascists. Annie slapped him hard across the face just as he was fading away. After what he'd been through with these three, CX almost looked happy to go.

But even with his inglorious departure, Hunter and friends still had a major problem on their hands: what to do about the mystery inside Warehouse 066. They agreed it was probably a more immediate threat than what would eventually happen with the Big Generator. And if what CX said was true, it was something that could prove devastating for Doomsday 212 and many other planets of the mid–Two Arm. Hunter felt it was his duty to investigate. Zoloff felt obliged to look into it, too.

They'd confiscated CX's super-quadtrol before he was sent on his way. It pinpointed the location of Warehouse 066. It was in Saturn's eastern hemisphere, about halfway between the equator and the north pole. Like much of the surface of the big ringed planet, this area was crowded with the bureaucratic offices of the SG, some so big, they literally ran for miles in all directions. In the middle of this sprawl was the building in question.

The question was: How could they get down there to check it out?

No surprise, the Mad Russian had the answer.

Zoloff took some time punching more information into the creaking PC. Finally he hit the Enter button, and suddenly Hunter found himself standing on hard, dusty ground, with no grass to be seen or trees in sight. At first Hunter thought they'd beamed right down to Saturn's surface itself. But he wasn't that lucky.

He looked around and saw he was actually standing on the edge of an extremely long asphalt runway. In front of him was a large aircraft hangar, one of several in a row. He was suddenly very hot; he began to sweat. He sniffed the air and then felt a shiver go through him. That's when he realized where he was: back on the Alien Mystery World, the place where he'd almost been killed. This hangar was just one of many at the re-creation of the secret base known as Area 51.

Annie was right at his side again. She felt him tense up. Patting him gently on his arm, she said sweetly, "It's OK. It's all just make-believe."

Hunter could only shrug. "I hope so," he said.

Zoloff waved his hands again, and on cue the doors to the hangar in front of them opened. A very strange craft began rolling out as if under remote control. It was huge. It took about a minute, but finally, this vehicle stopped in front of them. Hunter stared up at it in awe. Zoloff seemed to delight in the amount of time it took for him take it in.

Strangely, it was a design Hunter recognized. Not for any kind of extraterrestrial vehicle, but as a jet fighter from way back on old Earth. It was painted green all over, with the requisite red star emblem on its wings and fuselage. It had a huge opening for a nose, a bubble-top canopy, a pair of extremely swept-back wings, and a high tail with smaller wings on top. It was a design that screamed 1940s Russia; it looked like it was going fast, even though it was standing still.

Hunter tried very hard to dredge up from his long lost memory just what this thing might be.

Then it hit him.

"It's a MiG," he said triumphantly. "A Soviet MiG-17."

Zoloff smacked him hard on the back. "Precisely!" he cried. "The best airplane in the world at one time. Fast, could climb very high. And stay up high, which gave it an advantage over American planes."

But this was no usual MiG fighter. Again, it was gigantic. The original MiG-17 was a one-seat, nimble jet airplane, thirty-five feet, nose to tail. This craft was ten times that size, nearly as big as an Empire culverin, a sort of patrol cruiser. Hunter had to admit the scaled-up fighter design made for a magnificent spacecraft. But it also looked very, very old.

"Where did this thing come from?" he asked Zoloff as the three of them began to walk around it, Annie right at Hunter's side. Obviously, he hadn't seen this contraption during his first visit to this place.

"I built it," Zoloff replied proudly. "Practically from scratch. I used to fly a seventeen when I was in our space program. It was a trainer craft by then, but speedy and great to drive."

"You *built* this? From memory?" Hunter asked with astonishment. That's how he'd put together his own Flying Machine when he first arrived in the seventy-third century. This was another link he had to the Ancient Cosmonaut.

"Yes, from my own brain cells," Zoloff revealed. "I knew nothing about how aircraft were built. I only knew how to fly them. But you have to remember, I've had a few thousand years down here by myself. I needed things other than the dizzylando to occupy my time. So when I created this desert world and this base, I started building this creature as well. I always thought if I ever wanted to leave my precious moons, if just for a short flight to Saturn or Mars, this is what I'd do it in."

Hunter knew Zoloff was not exaggerating. The huge MiG was easily 2,000 years old. And while its design looked spectacular from one hundred feet away, up close, Hunter could see its fuselage was covered with hundreds of irregular ion-steel patches, thousands of uneven aluminum rivets, and more than a few dents and scrapes.

"Has it ever taken off?" Hunter asked Zoloff. "Has it ever left the ground?"

Zoloff just shook his head. *"Nyet,"* he replied. "And it will not unless you tell me what I want to hear."

"And that is?"

Zoloff smiled and said to him, "Can you fly this thing?"

Hunter smiled, too, then just shrugged as he stepped over a small ocean of ion steering fluid dripping out of the right wing.

Zoloff added, "I mean, it's one way I know for us to get down to where we have to go . . . and we are rather pressed for time, wouldn't you say?"

Annie pulled Hunter to a stop and hugged him tightly.

"Can you do it, Hawk?" she asked him dramatically. "Can you?"

Hunter looked over the giant spacecraft again. One of its landing gear tires was nearly flat, and many of its cockpit windows were cracked or broken. And who knew what it looked like on the inside.

"Can I fly it?" he asked the question again. "I guess I can give it a try. . . ."

•   •   •

There were more than a half billion SG troops on the surface of Saturn.

They were spread out all over the terra-formed planet, but most of them were armed with nothing more than an electric pen or a string bubbler. Saturn was the center of the Solar Guards' bureaucratic universe. All personnel changes, logistics files, and supply requests for the fifteen-billion strong Solar Guards emanated from here.

Just as much of Saturn's surface was covered with office buildings and warehouses, some more than ten miles long. Orbit around the huge planet was usually a very busy place as well. But most of the SG ships coming and going were cargo humpers, transition ships, or liaison vessels. It was a rare occasion that an SG warship came anywhere near Saturn. There was never any need.

So it was an extreme rarity that the planet's space traffic control station would get a report of a ship in trouble. Empire starships rarely crashed; they rarely even broke down. The only problem they could have was if something happened to the prop core; starved of the proper amount of power, the mysterious star engine could begin to fail, which would lead to a series of nuclear reactions, whereupon everything involved first blew up, then collapsed into nothingness. Never a pretty sight.

But at this moment the STC station was contemplating a report that a huge, unidentified ship had entered Saturn's atmosphere above the eastern hemisphere, that it was "nearly totally involved in flame" and coming down fast.

The control station put out an immediate string comm asking all ships in orbit around the huge planet to report their status. Within seconds, the space traffic controllers knew that none of the 50,000-plus SG ships circling the planet were having any problems.

Whose ship was crashing then?

Traffic control dispatched spacefighters to the area, this as a large unidentifiable object was picked up on its long-range scan arrays. It was no secret that SG spacefighters on Saturn were flown by second-echelon pilots: retirees, pilots who'd been injured, or men who were no longer fit for combat. Not exactly the cream of the SG's aerial crop.

A squadron of six of these needle-nosed fighters proceeded to the trouble zone, but at a leisurely pace. They knew if this was an Empire ship in trouble, its crew would simply eject in their safety capsules, and the ship would be directed to blow itself up. With Saturn's artificial atmosphere being more than 10,000 miles thick, just as long as the ship in trouble wasn't flying in Supertime, it would take a while for it to fall through that soup. So why hurry?

That attitude changed quickly, though, when the spacefighters arrived at their vector point. They immediately spotted the ship in question, and it was indeed in the process of crashing—or so it seemed. But it was not an Empire ship. What was it then? It was big and green and had wings. It was at least 350 feet long and had a wingspan of at least 200 feet. There was a full size flight deck under its bubble canopy and hatchways down near its nose that allowed the crew to climb in. There were gigantic red stars on its wings and its fuselage. None of the spacefighter pilots had ever seen anything like it.

Their reports both startled and mystified the officers back at space traffic control. Red stars? Big, green, and with wings?

Not knowing what else to do, they ordered the space-fighters to blow it out of the sky.

The spacefighters hastily realigned into two attack formations, a pair of chevrons containing three planes each. The fighters were armed with nose-mounted single-blaster X guns, powerful weapons that lost some of their effectiveness at high altitude but were very deadly nevertheless.

The first flight approached the big green craft from about ten o'clock. The intruder was now about 7,000 miles above the surface of Saturn and still dropping fast. The first three fighters opened up about a mile off the green spaceship's gigantic tail. X beams traveled at several times the speed of light. This meant, to the human eye, a discharge and a strike on target looked instantaneous..But amazingly, the huge mystery craft banked hard left just before the first barrage of beams arrived, causing them to dissipate to no effect. As the SG pilots were contemplating this, they were astonished to see a stream of return fire heading back in their direction. It had come from weapons that had suddenly poked out of the side of the strange green spacecraft's wings. Before the three pilots could react, their spacefighters were hit by this return fire and evaporated in an instant.

Meanwhile, the second trio of SG spacefighters had swooped in from the west. They didn't even get a chance to fire their weapons. Hesitating just a second in the realization that their comrades were so suddenly gone, they, too, met the same fate: three instant beams, fired once again from the wings of the ship; three more spacefighters vaporized.

The big green spacecraft continued its plunge.

• • •

The SG officers inside space traffic control began to panic. They ordered every armed ship within 10,000 miles of the trouble zone into the area. Moving at crank speed—that being the fastest a prop-core ship could fly within the gravitational field of a planet—no less than 300 ships of all types and sizes were soon on the scene.

They set up an aerial gauntlet, stationing themselves at ten-mile intervals all the way down to the surface. These were mostly interplanet ships, not starships, cargo carriers packing a couple nose blasters at best. Still, 300 ships, firing two weapons each, represented a huge wall of destructo-rays that would be near impossible to avoid or survive.

Yet the big green spacecraft was doing just that. Its tail end was on fire, but it was clear now that was simply due to its extreme angle of entry into Saturn's atmosphere. The flames were doing nothing to affect the maneuvering of the strange ship. Indeed, its pilot seemed to know just when and where a beam blast was going to arrive a few seconds before it hit, giving him just the right amount of time to turn this way or that and avoid certain destruction. And while many of the attacking craft were following the intruder down, it was firing back at them wildly, vaporizing dozens of them with well-placed mystery ray weapons of its own.

It went on like this for nearly a half hour. It took that long for the huge craft to make its way through the atmosphere. Only when it was about five miles from the ground did those SG ships still tailing it see three figures exit the craft and glide toward the ground using an ancient escape technology known as a parachute.

The big green spacecraft crashed seconds later into a logistics staging area known as 054. It caused a huge amount of damage.

The three parachutes were seen landing in the vicinity of Warehouse 066.

Hunter was the first to reach the ground.

He'd been the last to bail out of the MiG, but by maneuvering his chute and shifting his weight forward, he was able to speed by Annie and Zoloff and land on an empty concourse in front of a huge rectangular warehouse that he hoped was 066.

He was waiting for Annie when she came down, catching her before she hit the ground. She was wearing a combat suit not unlike his own now, but still she looked gorgeous. She stayed in his arms as he made his way to the spot where Zoloff eventually came down. The Mad Russian landed just like a pro. Just like that, the three of them were on the ground.

They rushed to the front door of the warehouse, Hunter giving the hatch a pass with his quadtrol. Not only were there no security devices in place, the door itself wasn't even locked. Taking advantage of this huge break, the three of them hurried inside.

The warehouse was indeed a monster. It was impossible to see the far end; it looked to be at least a half mile away. The ceiling, too, seemed to be so far above them, Hunter wouldn't have been surprised to see clouds forming somewhere overhead.

But there was something very strange about this place. All of them got it right away.

"It's empty," Hunter said.

A huge building like this, in an area on Saturn where

space was premium, and there were no bubblers containing information bits for personnel files, no storage of weapons or ion nails. Just one big open building that seemed to stretch on forever.

"This is weird," Hunter said. They'd heard some very nasty stuff was going on in here, and yet the place was barren.

"And why did no one follow us in here?" Zoloff asked.

Another good question. Certainly any local SG troops, though mostly electric pencil pushers, would have no problem corralling them in here. And all those many SG ships that had shot at them all the way down. Why did they cut off their pursuit and not shoot at them once they were on the ground? What was wrong with this place? It was almost as if the SG themselves didn't want to come near it.

Suspicious, Hunter did an interior quadtrol check. The environmental controls at the moment were OK. However, there were what the device called "unacceptable residues" lingering in chambers deep underneath the warehouse. "Do not go anywhere near them," the quadtrol warned.

Alarmed now, Hunter asked the quadtrol to define these residues and why they were so unacceptable.

It took the device a long time to answer—always a bad sign. Finally it replied, "The residues are from a super-toxin previously unknown in the Galaxy."

Hunter was stunned by the reply. So were Zoloff and Annie, looking over his shoulder.

But there was more: "This toxin in large quantities can only be labeled an XWMD."

"XWMD?" Hunter repeated the term. "I've never heard of it."

Zoloff shrugged. "Nor have I."

Hunter asked the quadtrol to explain. The reply this time was chilling. "XWMD is an abbreviation for extreme weapon of mass destruction."

Hunter looked at Zoloff, and Zoloff looked at Hunter. They both grabbed Annie.

"This is not good," Hunter whispered. "And it also means we can't stay in here very long."

"Five minutes is an acceptable limit," the quadtrol replied with an unsolicited piece of advice. "After that, exposure levels will slowly rise to critical."

They began walking quickly. Now that they were here, they at least had to see if anything was afoot. After about a minute, they spotted several large piles of litter scattered around center of the huge floor. Neutron wires, electron torches, ion bolts—construction materials. There were also many sections of disengaged staging lying about.

Zoloff the scientist came to the fore. "What were they building here?" he asked.

"It had to be a ship of some kind," Hunter replied. "Judging from all this stuff, maybe even two."

He swept his quadtrol around the area. "It wasn't a prop-core ship," he said. "There's absolutely no leftover subatomics in here. There's a lot of other weird stuff, but no subatomics. Anywhere."

He looked around, trying to conjure up a vision of what might have been built here. *Whatever they were, they're gone now,* he thought. *But when?*

He leaned down, felt the floor, and got his answer. It was still warm. "Gone—but not that long ago," he said.

He also noted that it appeared the builders had simply dropped their tools after they'd finished. Same with the staging involved. "And it was a big craft, whatever it was," he added.

Again, Zoloff could only agree. There were literally hundreds of electron torches and other hand tools and robotic-tools scattered about.

"But look at how the tools are dispersed," Hunter went on.

Zoloff didn't know what he meant at first. To him, it just looked like a mad scramble of workers had ensued after whatever they were working on was finally finished—with no need to clean up after themselves.

But Hunter saw something else.

He told Zoloff and Annie to join him in the middle of the huge floor. Then he faced Annie in one direction and Zoloff in another and told them to walk backward until they encountered a piece of staging or a pile of discarded tools. Hunter meanwhile walked backward in a third direction. Counting off their steps as they went, all three stopped at nearly the same moment, this after walking one hundred paces. Then they held their hands out from their sides and pointed to the person on either side of them.

The three of them stood there like this for a long moment. If they had truly walked to the limits of where the vessel had been built, thereby getting a rough outline of its shape, then what was constructed here had not been a typical wedge-shaped Empire design.

Rather, it had been built as a circle. Or a saucer.

Zoloff eyes went wide as this finally sank in. "They built a craft that didn't need the Big Generator to fly fast," he said, repeating CX's words. "Something to deliver a devastating blow to Doomsday 212 and the mid–Two Arm. But obviously, they wouldn't waste their time building an ion ballast engine. They must have been building something else."

Hunter looked back at him grimly. "Or someone was building it for them."

He hurried over to Zoloff. "In the desert world attraction," he said, "I came into a room where there was a flying saucer–shaped vehicle. Those Spetsnaz soldiers wanted me to fly it, before the big gunfight broke out, that is."

Zoloff just laughed. "That was just a figment of my own imagination," he replied. "We were always hearing rumors from America that you had a real UFO hidden away in your Area 51. We, the great Soviet Union, did not have such a thing! But like all things American, we wanted one, too. We did not want to be left behind in the flying saucer gap. But again, it was just a fancy on my part. Our brave soldiers go in and try to steal the Americans' most treasured and secret possession. Thrills and spills result. . . ."

Hunter had to laugh darkly at that last part. Those thrills and spills brought him to within an inch of losing his life, or so it seemed.

"But Doctor, here's the strange thing," he explained to Zoloff. "I've *seen* these saucers. Not just back from where I came from, but here, in this time period."

Zoloff was shocked, and it showed on his face. His eyes went wide, his mouth dropped open.

"Flying saucers? They exist? *For real?*" he gasped.

"I saw them during a battle for a tiny moon called Qez," Hunter revealed. "It was while I was looking for the Last Americans. This little moon way out on the end of the Five Arm, a place where you'd would fall off if you went any farther. The people there were at war with a very mysterious enemy. This enemy had weapons that went way beyond the scope of what the Empire has now. Huge moving forts. Frightening destructo-rays. And at least one flying saucer."

"Incredible!" Zoloff declared. Annie hugged Hunter tighter.

"I even found myself inside one of them," Hunter went on. "Just as it was trying to make its escape. It was a vile place within, as well as a place out of time. But I can tell you the technology employed by whoever owned it was frightening. And very, very advanced."

"But who were they?" Zoloff wanted to know.

Hunter hesitated, his mind bringing him back to that day and to a similar experience he'd lived through during a mind ring trip back to when the Empires first began. It was a concept so horrible, he really didn't like to dwell on it or even talk about it. But Zoloff deserved an answer.

"Frankly," he said, "it wasn't a question of who built these saucers—but *what* built them."

Now Zoloff's eyebrows shot up so fast, they nearly touched his hairpiece.

"You mean . . . ?"

But these were the only words that came out before they heard a very loud bang from the far end of the warehouse. A small army of SG troops had needlessly blown the door off and were rushing toward them, dressed in biohazard suits.

"How are we going to get out of this?" Zoloff cried.

Hunter was stumped; strangely, they hadn't planned for this—and he really didn't know why. But it *was* quite a fix. They were stuck here, on a very hostile planet, surrounded by the enemy, who had finally decided to move in on them. And even if they were able by some miracle to get out of the huge building, they were still deep inside enemy territory, with millions of SG troops and thousands of armed ships all around them, and a long way from the dizzylando or any other safe harbor.

So how indeed were they going to get out of this?

That's when Hunter's hand went to his pocket, where he kept his flag, his picture of Dominique, and now Annie's note—and found something else: the Twenty 'n Six the Imperial spy had given him, a long time ago, in the living room of Star Legion's cottage.

"Stand back," he said. "I don't know what's in here, but it better be good."

He pushed the capsule's activation button, and suddenly a cloud of yellow smoke appeared in front of them. There was another bright flash, and when it died down, a spacecraft was sitting in front of them.

But not just an ordinary spacecraft.

It was about three times the size of Hunter's long-lost Flying Machine, and just a little smaller than a typical Imperial spacefighter. It was shaped like a wedge as most Empire ships were, but it had a very exaggerated tail, and its fuselage was segmented in highly stylized patterns. It was held together by proton bolts, a technology that had not been used for at least a millennia. A mild sizzling noise was coming from somewhere underneath its hood, the telltale sign of a prop core. No doubt about it, though, this vessel was very, very old.

Hunter was astounded. He could only imagine that this was the same spacecraft that had brought the Imperial spy to Doomsday 212—a vessel he then gave to Hunter as a lifeboat of sorts. But it was a very strange-looking contraption. "Have you ever seen anything like this?" he asked Zoloff.

The doctor got very excited. "Seen it?" he roared. "I built it! Many years ago."

The craft's canopy suddenly opened. Underneath its flared lip they saw the spacecraft's name: *KosmoVox.*

"See!" Zoloff cried. "A fine Russian name!"

Hunter just stared back at him—but then they heard another loud boom come from the other end of the warehouse. The doors had opened down there, and they could see, though just barely, another small army of SG troops flooding in. They, too, were wearing protective bio suits and carrying huge hand weapons.

"I'll have to get the history lesson later," Hunter told Zoloff. "At the moment, I think it's time we got going."

They hastily climbed inside the *KosmoVox.* Hunter plunked himself down into the pilot's seat, Annie went to the floor beside him. The cockpit was as stylized as the exterior, yet one glance at the ship's controls told Hunter he could fly the thing. When it came to prop-core rigs, steering and throttles were the most important components a pilot had to pay attention to.

His eye was drawn to one gauge he knew was the vessel's velocity indicator. He was astonished to see it ran up to three light-years a minute—half again as fast as the speed attained by typical prop-core ships. Could this be possible? Could this ancient vessel be capable of outrunning other Empire craft?

"It sure can," came Zoloff's reply. "If it still works as it did, we can outrun anything the SG sends after us—with the right person behind the controls, that is."

Hunter scanned the controls one more time, then said, "I guess I'll have to do."

Hunter started the ship's prop core. It sizzled to life immediately (the mysterious star engines never really shut down). He looked out the cockpit window and saw the two hordes of SG getting even closer.

"Hang on," he said. "Time to go . . ."

He hit the throttle, and with a great wash of g-forces, crashed the roof of the warehouse, rocketed up into the Saturn's sky, through its atmosphere, and quickly out beyond its rings.

This all happened in less than two seconds and at less than one-millionth of the little craft's top speed.

"Wow," Hunter breathed, as Annie hugged him and Zoloff did a little jig of glee.

Next to his Flying Machine, he'd never flown anything so fast.

Chapter 11

SSG Commander Finn-Cool McLyx wished he'd brought a bottle of slow-ship wine with him.

Make that two bottles. Or maybe three.

What had he gotten himself into? He was sitting in a very cramped captain's chair, a seat made of materials unknown, slipping and sliding as he tried his best to stay in place. At the same time, he was holding his nose in an attempt to keep out the rank smell that was all around him. And then there was the lighting. It was flickering so much, his head was beginning to hurt.

He was looking out on a flight deck that faintly resembled one that might be found on an Empire warship. Not as big as the control room on a Starcrasher certainly, but similar in size to something aboard a culverin, as the Empire's smaller, sleeker space cruisers were called. All the essential controls for steering, communications, scanning, and propulsion were in the same places. And there was a deck crew of two dozen men watching over everything, just as on a culverin.

But this was no culverin they were riding in.

If only that was so, McLyx had thought more than once.

No one really knew what the smell in here was or where it was coming from, but it was enough to make some of the crew gag. The floor was slippery, too, covered with some unidentifiable slime, making it hard for McLyx's men to move around.

Most troubling, though, the flight deck was not neatly squared off as it would be on a regular SG ship.

Instead, it was round.

McLyx was a tall, heavy, blustery man, easily recognizable by the scar that went from his right ear to center of his neck. Although he had been commanding their starships for nearly 300 years, McLyx was known among the regular Solar Guards as a very dangerous, almost psychotic individual. His last ship, the *StratoVox*, had been involved in a brutal battle against the Space Forces just after the beginning of the interservice war. Hundreds of Empire ships and millions of crew on both sides had been lost that day. McLyx was relieved of duty by SG Space Command shortly after the clash, charged with disobeying orders and recklessness. But soon after, he joined the SSG, where he was welcomed with open arms. His fanatical hatred for the Space Forces, and anyone else who would dare stand up to the SG, made him a natural for the quasi-secret organization. His undeniable skills as a top starship commander were also a big plus.

When the very top secret and very unauthorized Warehouse 066 mission came about, McLyx was the SSG's one and only choice to fly it.

McLyx didn't know who had built this circular ship exactly, or how. But he had a good idea its creators weren't human beings at all, but rather creatures who'd been floating around the periphery of the Fourth Empire, both in myth and in reality, for centuries. Their saucerlike ships had been spotted near many major battles over the years, and their presence felt or seen during the seamiest nights of the realm. Big heads, big eyes, small bodies. Disgusting to look at, or so McLyx had heard, they were also powerful and superintelligent and frightening. And now, after this, most likely ingrained forever in the workings of the SSG. Like unseen puppet masters dancing their marionettes, they seemed to be pulling the strings these days.

(Technically, it was impossible for such beings to exist. The sacred laws of the Fourth Empire stated that human beings were the only life forms in the Galaxy. These laws also decreed that no life could exist outside the Galaxy. Therefore, no other life forms except humans could exist anywhere. This was a dictate taken very seriously across the realm. In fact, it was against Empire law to even say the word *alien*.)

Though in denial about their existence, at the same time McLyx knew dark deals had been made by people much higher up than him, and that it was not his place to question his superiors. The only thing important to him was that this craft could fly faster than anything in Supertime, and that it would be able to deliver a massively lethal weapon to the planet of Doomsday 212, a place the SSG was convinced

housed an army of anti-Empire rebels, bandits, and criminals who were in league with the hated Space Forces.

What's more, this ship could do so without being detected by the SF, the regular SG, or anyone else in the Imperial armed forces.

For the bold raid to succeed, this was the only way.

The problem was, McLyx and his hand-picked SSG crew
were having all kinds of trouble flying the strange circular
craft.

They had been told it would be easy. There were no
moving parts. They wouldn't have to worry about the
craft's power plant, as it wasn't even on board the ship. It
was somewhere else, in another time and reality—an idea
much too complex for McLyx to understand.

The round ship was supposed to fly in another dimension;
that was supposed to be its real magic. And not the seventh
dimension, either, which was where Empire ships flew in
Supertime. The saucers traveled upon another, completely
different plane, in a four-digit dimension, also known as the
Lost Dimension. The real saucers had used this fantastic
highway for billions of years, or so the rumors said.

But something was wrong with this particular flying
saucer. Since leaving Warehouse 066, the circular ship had
refused to stay in the Lost Dimension for very long. Instead, it was bouncing back and forth between what
McLyx and his crew considered their reality and that of the
Lost Dimension. These jumps came with no warning and
lasted unpredictable lengths of time, from just a few seconds to several minutes or more. The side effects were
highly disturbing. A kind of ultra–motion sickness was the

most prevalent. Extreme anxiety and almost near-fatal nausea were two others.

The saucer did, in fact, go very, *very* fast, but it proved for scary riding whenever it chose to remain inside the Lost Dimension. This place was a complete void: no stars, no planets, no celestial phenomena at all. Just unceasing blackness. With no frame of reference, no feeling of direction or speed or up or down, it was very disorienting to those on board, so much so, it drove two of McLyx's flight crew right over the edge. It happened the fifth time the ship unexpectedly jumped into the Lost Dimension. The pair began vomiting heavily and writhing around on the deck. They recovered temporarily when the ship slipped back to their reality. But when it crossed back over once again, the two crewmen simply went berserk. Alternately retching and convulsing, they screamed so loud and so long, they had to be stunned by McLyx's sergeant at arms, using a low-power setting on his ray gun. The two crewmen finally fell comatose, stiff and bleeding from the ears. Both had swallowed their tongues.

This incident had a very demoralizing effect on the remaining flight crew, most of them feeling poorly in the first place with the smell and the slime on the deck. Whenever the ship would break back into the real dimension, crew members could be seen praying that it would remain there.

But then they would start to freak out whenever it was knocked back into the absolute darkness again.

And the troubles didn't end there.

Even worse, the circle ship was leaving a wake behind it, an unintentional contrail in space. It was made up of unidentifiable substrata debris, things more bizarre than quarks and quacks. Whatever it was, the trail was wide, white, almost phosphorescent—and visible from thousands of miles away. This was not something you wanted while trying to complete a very top secret, unauthorized mission.

The trail of debris at its brightest appeared just as the saucer was approaching the edge of the Star Trench. The plan had been to simply fly over the confluence of Empire ships, as at the time the saucer was thought to be invisible, at least to the standard Empire scanners. Plus this route was the most direct to their eventual target of Doomsday 212 farther up the Two Arm.

But just as the long, dual line of Empire warships appeared on the McLyx's long-range viz screen, the damn saucer popped back into reality and soared nearly the entire length of the Star Trench, exposing itself for all to see. McLyx watched in horror as his defensive weapons suite lit up with thousands of indications of both SG and SF ships turning on their X beams in anticipation of taking a shot at what, from their point of view, actually *was* an unidentified flying object. He knew speed alone could not save them, as some X beams could travel faster than a Starcrasher in Supertime. It was only by dumb luck that just as they'd made this great display in front of billions of witnesses on both sides, the balky saucer popped back into the Lost Dimension, disappearing in an instant.

That's when McLyx just put his head in his hands and moaned, "I should have known this was a bad idea."

Things were just as troubling down at the bottom of the saucer, the area that served as its bomb bay.

Located almost dead center on the underside of the bizarre craft, it was a large, boxy space enveloped in a triple force field. This was necessary, considering what was being carried down there.

It was a flying bomb. Twenty-five feet long, black, teardrop-shaped, it had four winglike fins on its back. Its warhead contained more than five tons of XWMD, the mega-toxin developed by the same beings who designed the saucer. The weapon was actually a gigantic spray bomb designed to ride through the high atmosphere, dispensing its poisons. It was so hazardous, three level-10 force fields were needed to prevent it from leaking.

The plan? To soak the planet of Doomsday 212 with the XWMD, effectively killing everything and everyone on it. Collateral damage? There would much of it. For as the polluted planet orbited its sun, it would leave a trail of the mega-toxin in its wake, and that would serve to eventually spread the alien poison over a large part of the heavily populated mid–Two Arm. Thousands of light-years of space would be uninhabitable for millions of years. This was how the SSG chose to send a message to anyone who would try to oppose them in their nascent, if less-than-secret, bid to take over the Empire. With this bomb, the course of the Milky Way would be changed forever.

But again, things were getting strange down in the bomb bay, too. Two crewmen were designated as the bomb security team. Their job was to watch over the big weapon and make sure that the three-layered force field's integrity stayed at 100 percent at all times. Should even one of the fields break down, it could spell disaster for the crew and the mission.

The two crewmen were stationed on a balcony twenty-five feet above the bomb bay, which looked down on the weapon itself. An opaque ion-lead shield had been placed in a hover over the bomb, this to help insure the top layer of the force field. In order to look at the bomb, then, the men had to move this shield out of the way, which they were under orders to do every five minutes. From their perspective, once the shield was moved, it was like looking down into a pool of slightly agitated water. While a single force field tended to distort all the light waves around it, giving whatever was being held in place a sort of shimmering look, three force fields stacked together gave the impression that the object they locked in appeared to be under water.

Or at least that's how it was supposed to look. Trouble was, sometimes when the crewmen looked down at their charge, they saw something other than the big black spray bomb. And what they saw instead made little sense.

One time they moved the shield, they saw not what looked like a pool of clear water but rather a pool of bilge. Another time they saw water but with human remains floating in it. Most disturbing, though, was when they moved the shield and saw not the spray bomb but a black-and-white image of twenty smaller explosive bombs, stacked in two racks. Below them was another colorless image, this of an ancient bombed-out city. Cement buildings in flames. Blocks upon blocks of devastation. Huge bomb craters. Bodies.

On seeing these things, the two crewmen, both astounded and frightened, would immediately close the shield, convinced they were losing their minds simultaneously. They would sweat out another five minutes before daring to open the ion door again. When they did, and the waterlike image with the spray bomb below it had returned, they would both breathe a sigh of relief.

"Damn blinks," one of them said, after seeing the horrific black-and-white vision. "They're going to drive me crazy before this is over."

"Where the hell are we?" McLyx heard himself bellowing.

It was impossible to tell. The windows in the circular flight deck seemed to be changing perspectives with each passing second. Popping back and forth between dimensions was the cause of the flickering look. This only added to the severe motion sickness that had now affected just about everyone on the bridge.

But the constant interdimensional shifting also made navigation nearly impossible. After the fiasco over the Star Trench, the saucer had apparently lost its way entirely. Worse, it was refusing to stay in the real dimension long enough for the navigators to get any true bearings. More than once, McLyx felt as if they were simply tumbling out of control.

The saucer finally shifted back the real world and held itself there. The navigation team went to work quickly, trying to get them a good spot before they were popped back into the black void of the Lost Dimension. It took more than a minute, but finally, the navigators got a fix on their position. They were about 500 light-years beyond the Star Trench and 350 beyond what was considered the SF's rear areas. This meant they were only about 200 light-years away from their target, Doomsday 212.

This report brought McLyx his first relief from gloom since they'd left Warehouse 066. He was even starting to fit into the commander's seat.

But then the string-comm panels came alive. Suddenly a stream of messages were flowing into the saucer. Messages that only McLyx, as commander of the mission, could reply to. But this made no sense. Not even the top men in the SSG knew this mission was happening. Its dump-off time had been kept a secret, even from them. And certainly no one in the Solar Guards High Command knew they were out here.

So who was calling them? And why?

McLyx slipped out of his seat, nearly fell climbing down from his commander's perch, and then almost slipped a third time making his way over to the communications panel. The comm officers looked worried, distraught even. They'd heard the messages through their comm helmets, and there was no doubt they'd unnerved them. Both men had turned very pale.

McLyx finally arrived and took command of the message flows. All he heard was static at first. Static, and a strange pulsating type of music. But then, slowly, gradually, the messages started coming through. They were orders for them to turn back.

But McLyx knew right away something was wrong with this. First of all, there was no one who had the authority to call them back. But even more frightening, the voice on the other end ordering him to return to base was that of a child.

McLyx was convinced at that point he, too, had gone round the bend. The voices in his ear—and there were suddenly more than one—were saying the right words, even using standard SSG codes, but they were children, first ordering him, then pleading, then *begging* him to turn around and return to Saturn.

McLyx ripped off his comm helmet and hurled it across the room. He looked at the two communications officers. Now they were almost in tears.

He said to them, "This is not a mission we can turn back

from. We have to keep going. We have see it through. There's no other choice."

An instant later, they popped back into the void of the Lost Dimension. A chorus of moans came up from those on the flight deck. More vomiting could be heard. The lights within dimmed even further. Outside the windows there were no stars, no planets, nothing. Just blackness.

That's when the scanning officers called out. Something else was going wrong.

McLyx slid his way over to Scan Control. This station had a large screen with a multitude of dials, half of which had been skewed by all the interdimensional jumping. But the screen itself was working, and the image it was beginning to show was both troubling and fantastic.

"Someone is following us," one of the scanning officers told McLyx.

McLyx studied the big screen. One moment it was empty. The next, five objects had suddenly popped onto it. They were moving as fast as the saucer. In fact, they were coming up alongside it.

This was impossible, though. Wasn't it?

McLyx was simply stunned. Other officers were now looking at the long-range scan screen as well. Panic started to seep in. McLyx knew it was crazy, but he had to keep order on his bridge, to keep events from going out of control.

"It's just a blink!" he yelled to the flight crew. "Get back to your stations. These things will go away!"

But they didn't go away.

Just a few seconds later, the five strange craft had pulled even with the saucer. They could be seen very clearly out the starboard side windows. The craft were bulky, gray green, big enough to carry a few people, with a huge metal spinning thing on their noses. The words "U.S. Navy" were emblazoned on their fuselages, along with a big white and a striped red and blue emblem. People in goggles were looking back at them.

"They are not real!" McLyx screamed again. "It's the blinks! Don't look at them!"

But suddenly the comm set in the control deck came to life again. And this time, everyone could hear it. "This is Flight 19," an eerie voice said. "We are lost. Can you give us a compass check?"

Still shaken by the previous haunting message, the comm officers lording over the communications gear were too stunned to reply. And what would they say if they could?

"This is Flight 19 . . . we are not sure of our position . . . can you help us?"

McLyx just stared at the comm officers, and the men stared back, unable to move.

"I'm sure I'm over the Keys," the voice said. "I just don't know how far down . . ."

With that, the five airplanes banked left and were suddenly gone.

No sooner had they disappeared when another object was detected coming up on the other side of the saucer.

It was another kind of spacecraft, but just as strange as the five objects that had just ridden alongside them.

This vessel was big and white with a black bottom and a high tail. On the nose was the word *Columbia*, but all other writing on the side of the vessel looked to be burned away. This craft had a slightly delta shape, not quite a wedge, but possibly, to some eyes, the beginnings of that omnipresent Empire design could be seen here. Three huge engine nozzles were sticking out of its aft section, but no flames or exhaust could be seen coming out of them. The craft was keeping pace with the saucer, but it did not seem to be moving under its own power.

McLyx was staring at this ghost machine now, unable to take his eyes off of it, mesmerized by its sudden fantastic presence. What was it? What was it doing here, in the Lost Dimension with them? How could it be moving so fast without the power to do so?

He ordered it scanned front to back, top to bottom. The scans came back almost instantly. There were no life-forms aboard the vessel. Yet, no sooner had he heard this report when he saw a person at the craft's small window looking over at him. This person waved to him; McLyx had to stop himself from waving back. Then, suddenly, flames started pouring out of the vessel's left wing. They quickly spread up and over its body and soon engulfed the tail. Just seconds later, the entire craft was close to being totally involved in flames.

Yet throughout all this, the man in the cabin continued waving to him.

"It's just another blink!" McLyx roared again. "Stop looking at it! That's an order!"

No sooner were these words out of his mouth when the flames engulfed the craft completely. But it did not explode nor did it melt away. It just simply banked smoothly to the right and soon disappeared into the void. A moment later, the saucer dumped back into real time.

McLyx closed his eyes and tried his best to keep his emotions under control. It was hard to do. He had a distinct feeling that he was slipping . . . just slipping away to a place that was not good, that had no light, that actually might be very,

very hot, yet dark at the same time. He tried to shake away these thoughts, tried to shake away everything but what he had to concentrate on regarding the mission at hand.

When he opened his eyes again, he realized everyone on the bridge was looking at him.

He was about to scream at them to get back to their stations, when the scan officer called out another alarm.

Something else was chasing them now. An Empire vessel. But going very, very fast.

McLyx ordered its image up on the screen. Again, he was astounded by what he saw.

It was indeed an Empire ship. Just a bit smaller than an Empire spacefighter, it was wedge-shaped. But it had a very high tail, a sort of blunted nose, and open-ended nacelles on either side of the cockpit. It looked very, very old.

"It's another blink!" McLyx roared again.

But this time, he really wasn't so sure.

It was the *KosmoVox*, of course, hot on the trail of the flying saucer, intent on stopping it before it was able to launch its XWMD weapon at Doomsday 212.

Hunter was still at the controls of the ancient spacecraft, had the throttle buried, and was moving faster than he thought possible in an Empire ship.

Following the saucer had been easy—almost too easy. It was leaving a contrail thousands of miles long and nearly as wide and had flown a straight line from Saturn to the Two Arm. True, it was blinking in and out, appearing then disappearing at infrequent intervals. But it was doing this so rapidly, it actually made it even easier for Hunter to keep up with it.

It was a chase then. A fantastic, exciting, exhilarating chase. And Hunter was nearly delirious from the pursuit.

Absolutely nothing had gone wrong since the *Kosmo*'s dramatic departure from Saturn. Just how the SSG-controlled saucer got beyond the Pluto Cloud, they didn't know. But he simply blew past every SG frontier post he came to, following the saucer's phosphorescent contrail in the sky. There were some SG pursuits, especially once they'd busted out beyond the Solar System and headed in the direction of the Star Trench. Hundreds of regular SG ships were moving back and forth through this corridor. Some were spacefighters, others Starcrashers, still others just hump ships with weapons on them. It didn't make any difference. Anyone who tried to chase the *KosmoVox* simply got lost in their cosmic dust.

And strangely, Hunter knew—he just *knew*—what was happening aboard the saucer. He knew about the stink and the slime and the strange calls from ghostly children. He knew about the spray bomb and the popping back and forth between dimensions. He even knew it was the infamous Finn-Cool McLyx at the helm.

He knew these things as clearly as if he was riding aboard the saucer himself.

But he had no idea *how* he knew these things.

And that was starting to bother him.

Annie was at his side during the entire adventure, of course, kneeling next to him, looking gorgeous, her arm hugging his leg. Zoloff was hanging over his shoulder the whole way, too. They had rooted him on continuously during the chase, praising his flying skills and being very vocal in how heroic he was, taking on the SSG practically single-handedly.

For many reasons, though, it shouldn't have been this easy. The *KosmoVox* was so old it didn't have any of the ultrasophisticated long-range scanning equipment that more contemporary Empire ships employed. Nor did it have anything more than a simple navigation suite. But they always knew where they were going and what was around them simply because Zoloff had this fantastic ability to just look out one of the tiny ship's small windows and tell them exactly where they were at any given moment.

And at this moment they were just minutes from Doomsday 212, and they had apparently caught up with the saucer just in time. The SSG ship was flying very irregularly, almost convulsing its way through space. Hunter had the *KosmoVox* flying at nearly full speed, its velocity indicator had long ago disappeared into the red. And even though it seemed like the saucer would have the ability to go much, much faster, Hunter had had no problems at all keeping up with it.

And that bothered him, too.

"Now that we have it in sight, we have to do something!" Hunter yelled up to Zoloff now. Their prop core was sizzling badly, and it was not quiet inside the old ship. It almost seemed like they had left a door open or something, and the wind was roaring in—impossible, of course.

Zoloff yelled back, "What are your suggestions?"

Hunter was stumped. He scanned the control panel but did not find what he was looking for.

"Does this rig have any weapons?" he yelled. He couldn't believe he hadn't checked for such a thing before.

There was just a moment's pause, then Zoloff yelled back, "No! There was never any need!"

"Why not?" Annie wanted to know, asking a rare question.

"We built it to move our spies around," Zoloff replied. "We always flew too quick to shoot at anything or to have anything shoot at us."

Just great, Hunter thought. *Now what?*

"How can we stop it then?" he yelled back to Zoloff. The saucer was getting bigger in their field of vision.

"We'll have to ram it," was Zoloff's surprising answer.

Hunter looked back at him. *"Ram it?"*

Zoloff got that crazy smile again. "It's an old Russian tactic," he said. "Keep hitting it until it goes down!"

Hunter hesitated, but only for a moment. As desperate as Zoloff's suggestion sounded, they really didn't have any other choice. They had to stop the saucer. A planet full of his friends was in grave danger, and the fate of a large section of space was at stake.

If only I had the Flying Machine, he thought again. His six X blasters would have vaporized the saucer in seconds, as it was unarmed, too, at least with defensive weapons. But he was stuck out here, with his prey before him, and no way to take it down.

Unless he rammed it.

"Brave Russian pilots," Zoloff was telling him. "During the Great Patriotic War. They would get up behind German bombers and use their propellers to saw off their tails. A Heinkel cannot fly without a tail. And that monster in front of us cannot fly with half its body missing."

Hunter couldn't argue that. Plus time was running out. They were just minutes from reaching Doomsday 212 now.

So he would have to ram the SSG ship in order to destroy it, its bomb, and everyone on board.

But he knew by doing so, it would be the end of them, too.

Zoloff patted him once on the shoulder. Annie hugged his leg.

"Fear not, my friend," the Ancient Cosmonaut said. "We are what we are, and we do what we can do."

Hunter tapped his left breast pocket twice, then pushed the throttle just a little bit farther into the control panel.

The *KosmoVox* shot ahead, slamming into the rear end of the saucer a moment later. The collision was fantastic and violent. Sparks everywhere, fire coming right up to Hunter's eyes, metal crashed and bent. A thunderous booming noise that shouldn't have been.

So this is how it ends, he thought.

"What better way?" another voice asked.

He looked down and saw Annie smiling up at him. *At least she will be with me,* he thought.

The saucer increased its speed slightly and managed to pull away from the *KosmoVox*. Hunter stayed right behind it, though. He could see the puncture wound he'd caused in its skin. Air and other unidentifiable gases were spewing out of it. He saw a flicker of flame, too.

"Again!" Zoloff cried.

But Hunter was already jamming the throttle forward. They hit the saucer a second time. Again there was a huge explosion of sparks. Again a surprising, thundering *boom!* Again, flames that seemed so close to him, they went right around him without burning his face at all.

Again, the saucer managed to pull itself ahead.

Hunter didn't wait for any encouragement this time. He zoomed up, over, and then straight down, this time hitting the saucer square on its circular flight deck. This was the hardest impact of all; this time he knew he'd caused a mortal wound. He'd penetrated the saucer so deeply, he could see the startled, frightened faces of the SSG deck crew. He was almost eyeball to eyeball with McLyx and his comm officers. McLyx saw him, and in a sort of audio slow motion, screamed at him, "You?"

Hunter blinked—and suddenly they were back out in space again. The saucer, heavily damaged, smoking fiercely, was somehow still staggering on its way.

Another push of the throttle. Another collision. This time right into the belly of the ship. Hunter was astonished to see the two bomb security men up on the balcony, staring down at him. Their faces said it all: *Is this real?* Then they quickly fled the bomb bay. Hunter didn't blame them. The nose of the *KosmoVox* had not only pierced the shimmering pool of water, it came within inches of the big spray bomb itself.

But how could this be? Ramming his way into the saucer's thin skin was one thing. But busting through a trio of Level 10 force fields?

That was almost impossible.

"You're doing it!" Annie cried, this as Hunter laid off the throttle, and the saucer began spinning away from them again. There was no doubt though, it was in serious trouble. "You're doing it!"

But this time, the collision had taken off a huge piece of the *KosmoVox's* nose cone. There was also a giant tear on its starboard fuselage.

"Don't let them get away!" Zoloff cried.

Hunter hit the saucer a fifth time, and then a sixth, both

times on the flight deck again. With each collision, he saw even more damage to the interior of the SSG ship. Just glimpses, quick visions of a nightmare in progress. Control stations covered in bile. Dead SSG crew members sprawled about. McLyx with a ray gun up against his own head, ready to blow his brains out. But at the same time in all this, the *KosmoVox* was literally coming apart at the seams. There were holes opening up all along its fuselage. The glass in the canopy was gone. Its two huge tail wings had broken away. But the wounds Hunter was delivering to the saucer were even more gaping. He was easily able to tear away long sections of the thinly constructed alien craft. And every time he made contact, there was a huge crack of lightning, a massive discharge of electricity, and a deafening sound not unlike a sonic boom. Hunter's eardrums felt like they were going to burst, this noise was so loud. But of course, he knew this, too, was impossible. Sound waves were carried on air. And there was no air in space.

Something was wrong. All these things that were happening to him couldn't possibly be real.

The evidence mounted. There were so many holes in the *KosmoVox* now, all of the air should have escaped long ago. Yet the lack of oxygen wasn't having any effect on him. In fact, he felt great. And there was fire all around him too, yet he wasn't getting burned, and neither were Annie and Zoloff. And the ship's artifical-grav dampeners had to be zonked by now, yet Hunter was still sitting firmly in his seat.

He rammed the saucer once more, a massive body blow right on top of the flight deck again. But this time the *Kosmo-Vox* stayed in place. Driven too far into the circular ship, there was no way it was going to back its way out now. Stuck for good, the two ships were now one, with flames and smoke and sparks and air gushing out everywhere.

I should be dead, Hunter thought. *We all should be. But we're not . . .*

He finally turned to Zoloff amid the chaos and said, "It's not real, is it?"

Zoloff just smiled and then shook his head. "Not all of it, no," he said.

Hunter began to panic. He screamed back at Zoloff, "Am I insane? Just like I've thought all along? Or are we still inside the dizzylando, and this is just another ride? More thrills and spills? Are we in Chase the Saucer Land?"

Zoloff just shrugged. "All of the above maybe? Or maybe it's something else . . ."

Hunter looked at Annie, this as he found himself involuntarily rising out of his seat.

"And her?" he asked Zoloff.

Zoloff just nodded sadly. "The same . . ." he said.

Annie was trying to grab Hunter now as he was being sucked out the hole in the top of the *KosmoVox's* fuselage. But she couldn't quite reach him.

She started crying. "No . . . *don't go!"*

Hunter freaked out. This was happening way too fast.

"Please!" he shouted at Zoloff. "Please just tell me she was real at least!"

But it was too late. He went through the hole in the roof an instant later.

Then the two ships, melded by the last collision, both on fire, both smoking heavily, tumbled away from him, quickly fading from view.

"Annie!" he cried. But it was no use.
She was gone.
And Zoloff was gone.
Leaving him alone, floating in space.

Chapter 12

The StarLiner had been patrolling above the badlands for several days now.

Recent comm interceptions indicated SG ships might
have been in the area of Doomsday 212 lately, possibly
even showing up in low orbit, if just for a few seconds at a
time. These reports had prompted the Star Legion to go on
high alert all around their adopted planet.

This particular Starliner was not just a warship though.
Atop three of its golden masts were ultra–long range scanning devices that could pick up indications of hostile craft
approaching from as far as 10,000 light-years away. They
also had devices on board that could detect body heat,
movement, even DNA samples blowing in the wind. These
things were most helpful when searching for someone on
the ground.

It was one of these gadgets that lit up the ship's center mast. This was where two crewmen in gold suits were monitoring the magnificent starship's primary scanning devices. And even though they were out here more to look for any Empire spacecraft that might be lurking either close to the planet or possibly hidden somewhere on the forbidding terrain below, they took notice when their DNA sniffer began blinking.

There was a body down there somewhere. Badly injured, hidden among the putrid smoke, barely breathing.

The scanning crew immediately reported this to the bridge. The giant galleon-like starship did a quick turnabout and headed down to where the body had been spotted. Once they were within sight of it, a landing party was sent down to the surface to investigate.

Two Legionnaires located the body atop a high ridge close to a vent spewing hideous gases. Close by were several large pieces of burning wreckage. They could have been from some kind of Empire ship, though it was hard to say, the damage was so extensive. Farther across the ridge line, there was another pile of wreckage, also burning fiercely, also unidentifiable, though in the short study given to it by the men on the ground, they thought it might have been more of an oval design than the wedge shape that prevailed among Empire ships.

Oddly, their life support equipment told them not to approach these piles of wreckage as they contained aerial agents so intense, they might permeate their battle suits. Such things were not so unusual down here in the badlands. Still, they were wise enough then to stay away.

They concentrated on the body instead. They found it lying faceup on a bed of sharp rocks, a strange red smoke surrounding it. The two Legionnaires approached cautiously, ray guns drawn. They had no clue as to who this might be.

That's why they were so shocked when they drew close enough to see the face—and discovered it was Hawk Hunter.

The first thing they did was check for a pulse; there was none. They immediately contacted their ship, and a rescue beam was sent down to their position in seconds. But still Hunter was showing no vital signs when they boosted him up to the waiting StarLiner.

Immediately flashed to the ship's ultramodern hospital ward, the Legion doctors were finally able to raise a pulse. It was weak, but at least it was there. Hunter was then put inside a ion-barometric chamber, which served to raise his vital signs slightly. Despite this, he was very close to death.

He was rushed back to the more habitable parts of Doomsday 212 and beamed down to a field hospital located close to the cottage that served as the Star Legion headquarters. Erikk and the rest of the commanders of the Legion rushed to Hunter's side. The top UPF officers were also there. They gathered around Hunter's floating bed, horrified at his wounds and utterly astonished that he was among them again.

What had happened? Nothing had been heard from Hunter since he'd left on his mission to the moons of Saturn. In fact, from their point of view, the last they'd seen or heard from him was when the DATT tube disappeared from the cottage dining room not that long ago. Seconds after he vanished, there came a series of very intense blinks, which caused more crazy things to happen not just on Doomsday 212 but throughout the Two Arm and all across the Galaxy. Moreover, a scan of the dining room after Hunter's departure left them with indications that the DATT had malfunctioned somehow soon after he'd left, but they were uncertain if this was due to the blinks or was evidence of a real problem with the DATT.

In any case, more blinks followed. The Legion's long range scanners indicated that strange things were indeed happening all over, especially in the sector down near the Star Trench. Weird spaceships seen cruising the star roads, SG spacefighters chasing phantoms. Radio calls from somewhere in the distant past suddenly coming alive again on comm sets within SF Starcrashers.

All of these things—very, very strange.

And now, suddenly, Hunter was back.

But he was fading fast. And everyone around him knew it. They tried to talk to him, but he was unresponsive. His uniform had been partially burned away, but the Legion doctors told them his condition was so serious, they were afraid to even cut it off him. One said that he looked like he'd fallen from a great height, this after riding for a long time in space. Yet another said he thought Hunter hadn't left the planet at all. Both agreed, though, that he was fading fast.

Within thirty minutes of Hunter's arrival at the Legion hospital, what had begun as a sickbed vigil soon became a deathwatch.

The hours passed.

Hunter's condition stayed the same. Meanwhile, long-range comm receivers being used by both the Star Legion and the United Planets Forces reported hearing hundreds of messages down by the Star Trench telling of massive waves of blinks bedeviling Starcrashers on both sides. Incomprehensible visions, mass hallucinations, weird music being heard, and again, weapons turning to salt. With each hour, the reports got crazier, more bizarre, more unexplainable. After more than a month of this, many people in the Galaxy were turning religious, believing the blinks were more signs from the Creator than the Big Generator short-circuiting itself. *If God is playing with us*, people seemed to be saying, *then maybe we should start to listen.*

At Hunter's bedside, the situation remained grave. Every friend who came to pay their respects knew their colleague had been to the brink before but had always been pulled back at the last instant, as if his time had not yet passed. As if he was still needed to carry on his fight against injustice across the Galaxy. But this time it seemed as if it had gone too far. He'd given too much. Done too much.

Everything changed around dawn the following day. Erikk and his men were watching over Hunter. An honor guard from the UPF was on hand, too. Just before the first rays of light hit the hospital window, there was a bright flash of green light. It came so suddenly, some of the UPF troopers pulled out their side arms. The Star Legion guys thought it was yet another blink.

In fact, it was the Imperial spy, making his first appearance since leaving shortly after Hunter's troubled departure in the DATT.

The UPF guys kept their guns out, though. There was some belief that the spy was actually responsible for all this, providing Hunter with the balky DATT as his means of travel, and having him wind up like this, knocking on death's door.

But Hunter's serious condition actually overwhelmed any bad feelings for the Imperial interloper now. The man in the floppy black hat and long, flowing black cape glided over to the floating bed. He studied Hunter for a moment. Battered body, burn marks on his face and hands, singed hair. He put his hand over Hunter's face, as if he was feeling for something, breathing possibly, but moved his hand almost as quickly.

"This man has things to tell us," he declared, stunning those gathered around the bed. "And important things at that."

His pronouncement didn't seem possible for one reason: shortly after being brought to the intensive care section, Hunter had been given a noninvasive brain scan. It had displayed nearly every action he'd gone through in the past twenty-four hours. Those that had seen the results had been shocked. It had not been a linear, connect-the-dots sort of readout as most NI scans were. Instead, it contained bits and pieces of strange places and people. Castles. Battles. Devastated landscapes. A huge music concert. Beautiful women. Wild rides in space. None of it made any sense. The conclusion of the Legion's medical people: "These are most likely places he *thought* he went—in his imagination," simply because that was the part of the brain the impulses were coming from.

But now the Imperial spy disagreed.

"Those things were real," he told those assembled now. "Or at least some of them were."

"Are you saying he actually went someplace?" Erikk

challenged the spy. "That he hasn't been lying out in the badlands all this time?"

"Yes, I am," was the reply.

With that, the spy raised both his hands over Hunter's body. Those on hand saw a bright white light suddenly envelop the fallen pilot. It lasted but a few seconds. But when it went away, everyone in the room was shocked to see Hunter start to move. They looked at their fallen friend for a few long moments, then up at the spy.

Who the hell is this guy? they all thought.

Incredibly, Hunter's eyes opened. They seemed stung by the lights. He started to say something, but couldn't. Instead, with great effort, he put his lips together, and to the astonishment of all, he started to whistle. One long tone, sweet, but sad at the same time.

"C major diminished," the spy said. "That's the key. That's what we've been looking for."

The Legionnaires didn't understand, neither did the UPF guys. But the spy understood. He whistled it once himself. Then he bowed—and then he vanished.

When those gathered around his bed looked back down at Hunter again, his eyes were closed.

But he was smiling.

Chapter 13

Things hadn't been the same at the Empire's secret desert base since the Empress damaged the Big Generator.

This sacred place, once guarded by entire armies of elite Earth Guards, was now under complete domination of the Special Solar Guards. Their troops were everywhere. In the mountains, scattered across the desert, and lined three deep along the perimeter, standing as immobile as statues in the climate-controlled but nevertheless uncomfortable desert heat.

Most of the heavy security was concentrated on the facility that housed the Big Generator itself. Located deep inside a nearby mountain, the inside of this chamber closely resembled a church. Candles provided most of the light. Shadows played up and down its black walls. Heavily armed SSG troops, hundreds of them, were hidden in those shadows.

Now that both Commander X and McLyx were officially missing in action, a third commander was running the SSG operations here. His name was Viktorx. In fact, his people were the ones supervising the SSG's "repair" of the Big Generator, which had continued apace.

Viktorx was considered a sudden up-and-comer in the ranks of the SSG. Few people in the organization even knew him; he'd just seemed to arrive on the scene and was in the right place at the right time to take over the SSG's operations within the deep-secret desert compound that in ancient times was known as Area 51. There was even a rumor floating around that he'd been the one who shot the Empress after her attack on the big black slab. But this could never be confirmed, because everyone else who'd been in the BG chamber that day was dead.

All except him.

Viktorx's first official duty this day was to preside over a very unusual award ceremony. Four SSG special operations troops were being given a medal, the First Order of the Fourth Empire. This was a special SSG commendation passed out only to those soldiers who showed outstanding bravery and cunning beyond the call of duty. It was a rare occasion when the SSG even bothered to recognize actions of anyone below the rank of captain. But these four men, lieutenants all, had indeed shown uncommon valor in a top secret mission they'd successfully undertaken several weeks before, one, some would say, that was actually run while other SSG activities were providing a diversion. In any case, all four officers had nearly paid with their lives as a result of this mission. As it turned out, all four might have been better off dying.

Viktorx was met at the mountain chamber gate by an escort of SSG ceremonial guards. It was early morning; the sun was looking rather dim today. He and his small entourage were led down through the chamber's many tunnels, eventually reaching the sacred hall where the Big Generator itself was located. Here they briefly observed the SSG engineers noodling around with the omnipotent power slab. Taking radiation readings where the Empress had shot it with her ray gun, charting the electrical and subatomic fields surrounding the mysterious black slab, and indeed pounding on the side of the obelisk with electron hammers, all in a crude effort to get the big black rock to do their bidding.

Throughout, a low, moaning single note was echoing off the walls of the sacred chamber, the magic tone of sorts that the SSG believed would ultimately lead to the successful manipulation of the Galaxy's omnipresent power source—just as long as a countertone did not interfere with it.

But again, watching the work on the BG was not Viktorx's purpose for coming down here. The unusual medal ceremony held precedence today. That's why he and his entourage and escort guards lingered at the Big Generator's altar for only a minute or so before passing through a side portal and continuing their descent into the mysterious legendary mountain.

They walked for nearly ten minutes, so deep into the mountain that it was actually getting not colder, but warmer. Finally they came to yet another chamber. Its door was extremely thick ion-metal, held tight by several uranium-decay locks, the strongest in the Galaxy. It took the escort guards ten minutes to finally get this huge door open. Viktorx and his men then glided inside.

There was a small army of SSG medical personal waiting for them in here, this very secret place below a very secret place. The four medal recipients were on hand, too. But there was no indication that they knew what was about to take place or even if they knew where they were exactly. Each man was sitting up on a floating bed, each held in place by two medical staff. Though wearing their brightly colored SSG dress uniforms, each man was obviously out of it, head back, eyes rolled up into his head, unable to control his hands or feet. Two of the men were drooling uncontrollably.

They had gone mad, all four of them, during their last mission. They had been secretly sent to a place that drove all who entered it insane to some degree, many irreversibly so. This place was the area of the planet Doomsday 212 just above its equator, which had refused to be terraformed. The place that just about everyone these days called the Badlands.

The four SSG men had been sent there just hours after the disastrous defeat of the regular SG's Rapid Engagement Fleet, that hapless gang of ships that had been somehow sucked into Hell and then unleashed again upon the Galaxy to cause rack and ruin—that is, until the rebel group led by Hawk Hunter and his allies defeated them at the mysterious and still unexplainable Battle at Zero Point.

These four officers had been experts in tracking down missing persons, such as escaped prisoners or enemies of the state. This time, though, Viktorx had sent them into the badlands to look for something else. And by great luck, they had found it, after seventy-two perilous hours on the ground. But they'd also lost their minds in the process, for the things they'd seen and heard and felt and tasted down there were enough to drive even the most stable of men absolutely crazy. Still, it was a job well done from the SSG's point of view, at the cost of four fairly dispensable minds.

Commander Viktorx pinned a gleaming medal on each man, uttering no words of comfort or encouragement, simply going through the motions and doing it as quickly as possible. After each man was honored, he was laid back down on his floating bed and then put inside a so-called maintenance drawer in the side of the chamber wall, a place where they would stay for however long they remained alive, be it days or years or even centuries.

This bit of unpleasantness dispensed with, Viktorx and his entourage proceeded to one last door, the very last portal in this secret underground chamber. He was a man of huge appetites, power being the most voracious, but he also loved to revel in his accomplishments. And that's why he wanted to go through this final door and gaze once again on what lay beyond. For this was the trophy the four SSG special ops soldiers had brought back with them at the price of their own sanity.

The door was open, but only Viktorx was allowed in. The big door shut behind him, and now he was alone in the room. Before him was the prize—alas, the *ultimate* prize in this whole crazy adventure. It was something he considered more valuable than any flying saucer or XWMD bomb.

And yes, he believed it was even more valuable than the Big Generator, even after the SSG finally altered it to do only their bidding. *A crazy thought?* He wondered now. *Perhaps.*

But from his point of view, it didn't get any better than this.

Standing before him was what had been code-named the magilla. It was here, in all its gleam and glory, a little battered, slightly dented, but on the whole very usable.

It was the spacecraft that everyone across the Galaxy knew as Hawk Hunter's fabulous Flying Machine.

And now, it was his.

CPSIA information can be obtained
at www.ICGtesting.com
Printed in the USA
LVOW11s2306250417
532191LV00001B/11/P